The Diary of Allie Katz

Beth Mitchum

UltraVioletLove Publishing

Silverdale

Cover and interior design by Beth Mitchum
Cover photo by Beth Mitchum

Published by:
UltraVioletLove Publishing
PO Box 1634
Silverdale, WA 98383
UVLPublishing@gmail.com

UltraVioletLove Publishing chose CreateSpace.com to be a conduit for publishing because of its print on demand technology. Only small quantities of this title will be printed as needed in order to cut back on the tremendous amount of waste generated by the book publishing industry. As an author-centered publishing house, all profits generated from the sale of our books go directly to the authors. UltraVioletLove Publishing is paid only for services rendered for editing and preparation of a book and its cover. For more information, check our website at UltraVioletLove.com.

Printed and bound in the United States of America

ISBN-10:1463567537
ISBN-13:9781463567538

Dedicated to

Dr. Allan Combs,
Dr. Peg Downes,
and
Dr. Charlotte Goedsche

Thank you for all your feedback
and suggestions while I was working
on this book as my masters project
at UNC-Asheville.

The Diary of Allie Katz

Beth Mitchum

Part One:
Allie's Diary

Tuesday, April 26, 1983

Dear Diary,

I turned fifteen today. That seems kind of old to me. I hope I won't end up being "sweet sixteen and never been kissed." Ugh. Surely I will have my first kiss by then. It will have to be someone special though. I'm not going to kiss just anyone. This diary is one of my birthday presents. Mom says that every woman should have a diary. I'm not sure I'm a woman yet. Sure, fifteen is getting close, but I haven't had sex yet. For that matter, I haven't even held hands with a guy. There are a lot of cute guys at school, but they all seem so immature. All they talk about is sports and cars, cars and sports. Either that or they talk about girls. Please! I don't think they know the first thing about girls. Of course, I don't know much about guys either. All I know is that I don't mind being friends with them, but I haven't found anyone who is right for me yet.

Wednesday, April 27, 1983

I think I'm going to like writing in this diary. My English teacher, Mrs. Haze, says that keeping a journal is good writing practice. She's going to give us extra credit if we write for the rest of the school year. The only problem is that I don't really know what to write about. Frankly I don't think my life is all that exciting. Sometimes interesting things happen at school, but not very often. Maybe I could just make up things to write. Mrs. Haze never said that our journals had to be true to life. She just told us to write whatever pops into our heads. That could prove to be interesting.

It's not as though I'm living through a war or anything, like Anne Frank for instance. That was such a sad book. We had to read it in our history class this year. What she wrote about her life was fascinating, but it's terrible to think about how her life ended. Perhaps I'm better off just writing about the little things that happen in the life of a teenage girl living in the mountains of North Carolina. It may never become a bestseller, but at least I'm not living in a hell on earth. Living a quiet life is way better than hiding from Nazis or becoming a victim of genocide.

Friday, April 29, 1983

We celebrated my birthday tonight so Dad could be here. He's been working late all week. Mom made a Chocolate Cherry Delight cake. She blended in some crushed cherries to make the icing pink. It was gooey and rich. Yum! Not good for my complexion though I bet. Oh well. It's not like I eat that kind of stuff all the time.

Some of my relatives sent me birthday cards with money in them. Including what I got in the mail today, I received a total of twenty-seven dollars. I think I'll use the money for new tapes or maybe books. Or maybe both. Whatever! I can figure that out once I get to the mall and look around. Sometimes the anticipation of buying something new is just as exciting as actually doing it.

Mom and Dad were so nice for my birthday. Of course, they usually are nice. I guess I'm lucky that way. I actually get along with my parents. Most of my friends' parents aren't around very often, and when they are, they don't talk to each other a whole lot. Except for the Mackeys. They're pretty cool. They like talking to their daughters and their daughters' friends. I think they wish they were still teenagers. Sherri told me that they were pretty wild when they were young. I guess that's where Sherri got her wild streak.

I enjoy going to Sherri's house because her parents play their old rock records for us. I really like Elton John's old stuff. Some of his newer stuff is good too, but I like his older albums better. He has a strange way of making songs upbeat, even if the subject matter isn't. Sometimes it's like the words and the music are in direct contrast with one another. Other times depressing topics are made even more so by his choice of music. It's kind of hard to explain unless you listen to his music a lot.

Saturday, April 30, 1983

I can't think of anything to write this morning. Probably because I just wrote last night. I haven't done anything yet today besides eating breakfast and cleaning my room. That's hardly the kind of thing you want to write about in your diary. I guess I'll read. I have a book report due next week. I'd rather go biking, but I have a flat tire right now. Oh well. I guess I'd better stop procrastinating and get my homework done. I love to read books, but I don't particularly like writing about them. Bye!

Monday, May 2, 1983

Gosh, I can't believe I forgot to write yesterday. Sundays are usually boring. Not yesterday though. I went over to Sherri's house to work on our biology project. We got a lot of work done until Steve and Mark Palencio showed up. Sherri is dating Mark, so I ended up spending a couple hours with Steve. He's really sweet and cute. Of course, Mark's cute too, but that's pretty obvious since they're identical twins. You can tell them apart though, if you hang around them a lot.

Anyway, Steve and I talked a lot. He likes old rock music too. He said that he plays his parents' cassette tapes all the time. It's funny because there is a little group of us who don't like 80's rock as much as the 60's and 70's stuff. It's really weird. Sherri's parents heard us talking about music, so they came in and asked if we wanted to listen to Jim Croce.

I had a great time. Steve is interesting to talk to. There's more to him than just cars, sports, and sex. He wants to be a lawyer when he gets older. But he says that he doesn't want to be the kind that rips people off. He wants to be a public defender, so he can help people who can't afford to help themselves legally. I think that's pretty decent of him.

Tuesday, May 3, 1983

Mom is going to take me to the Asheville Mall this evening so I can spend my birthday money. I won't have to buy clothes though, since I got some from my parents already. They have such good taste for people their age. Ha, ha! Seriously though, I can't wait to wear my new French blue button-down Oxford shirt. It makes my blue eyes stand out.

Speaking of blue eyes, some girl at school today (I don't even know who she was) told me I should bleach my hair blonde, because then I'd be perfect—blonde hair and blue eyes. What on earth does hair and eye color have to do with being perfect? At first I thought it was a joke, but she kept going on and on about it, so I know she was serious. I don't know why people think that combination is better than any other. I like my blue eyes, but then I like anything that's blue. But I don't understand why blondes are supposed to be better than brunettes or red heads. Some people are so strange! I happen to like my brown hair, thank you very much. I guess I should just forget about her, but she gave me the creeps.

We've been watching these films in school about the Nazi prison camps and stuff. Maybe that's where that girl got the idea about blonde hair and blue eyes. Perhaps she wishes she could be a Nazi. Ugh! Well, whatever her problem is, I hope I don't run into her again. She was in the bathroom at school when I went in there, and she made a point of staying there talking to me until I left. I think I interrupted her cigarette smoking because it smelled like smoke when I walked in. I'm not even sure she had been smoking a regular cigarette. She seemed rather out of it. Sometimes it just doesn't pay to go to the bathroom at school. That's all I need is to get busted because someone else is smoking pot in the bathroom when all I need to do is pee.

Wednesday, May 4, 1983

Woohoo! I got an A minus on my history test. I thought for sure I had blown it. I forgot to study for it until just before class. That means I should have all A's again this year, so that's good. I'll be glad when school's out though. Baseball season has started, but I can go only to the weekend games because of homework and getting up for school the next day. During the summer Dad and I usually go to all the home games. The Asheville Tourists are really good.

I got a new tube for my bike yesterday when Mom and I went shopping. I offered to pay for it, but she said that I should spend my birthday money on other things. So I did. I got a book Mrs. Haze mentioned in class recently. It sounded kind of interesting. The name of it is *Jane Eyre*. Mom said that she read it in high school. I also got a tape of Jim Croce's *Greatest Hits*. He's so good! He has this deep, rich voice that sounds as though he's smoked too many cigars and drunk a bit too much whiskey over the years.

Saturday, May 7, 1983

I'm glad it's Saturday. I've had so much homework this week. I haven't even had time to fix my bike. Not until this morning, that is. TA DA! My front tire is no longer a pancake. We must have pumped that stupid thing for a half hour. We had to take turns. Personally I think we should have taken it to the gas station and filled it up with one of those air hoses. I didn't say anything though. I figured Dad knew what he was doing.

I've really missed my bike. I ran over a piece of broken bottle a couple weeks ago and punctured the tube with a splinter of glass. Anyway, I'm back on the road again. I think I'll ride over to Sherri's tomorrow instead of walking. I've been wearing out the soles of my Nikes. We need to finish our biology project, even if I have to tie her down to make her pay attention. She's so crazy when she's in love. I hope the Palencio twins don't come over. We really need to finish this stupid thing.

Sunday, May 8, 1983

Sherri and I are almost done with our project. I have to draw two illustrations, and that's it. I should be able to get those done tonight. Sherri can't draw very well, so I've had to do all the artwork. Actually I've done most of the other work too, come to think of it. Sherri isn't the greatest partner to have when you're working on a project. But we're best friends so I could hardly have picked someone else. At least I know Sherri won't interfere with the project even if she doesn't help a whole lot.

Monday, May 9, 1983

We turned in our biology project today. We were actually the first ones to finish. I'm glad it's over. I wasn't sure it would be possible to keep Sherri's mind on genes and chromosomes. All she can think of is jeans and hormones-- Mark's, that is. Ha, ha!

Yesterday she told me that things are getting pretty serious with him. He went over to her house Saturday night, while her parents were at the movies. He wasn't supposed to be there, but her older sister was the only one home. She doesn't care what Sherri does. She's even wilder than Sherri is. Anyway, Sherri and Mark didn't have sex exactly, but they did just about everything else. I don't think Sherri will be a virgin much longer.

Thursday, May 12, 1983

I went for a long bike ride this afternoon. I hadn't been very far since I got the tire fixed. I figured I would pass out if I didn't build up gradually. Some of the hills around here are killers. I have really missed biking. I wish Dad could ride with me, but his job has been keeping him really busy lately. Mom isn't interested in sports. She says that her favorite exercise is to curl up with a good book. I like that too, but I have too much energy to do that all the time.

Saturday, May 14, 1983

Hi! What's new with you? Me, I'm just freaking out. Nothing major. Sherri spent the night with me last night. We had an interesting time to say the least. The evening started out pretty normal. First we watched the videos we had rented (and ate three tons of popcorn). Then we went to bed and talked all night. Well, we didn't talk exactly. Not all night anyway.

Sherri told me more about what she and Mark did last week. I told her that I could not see how she could stand to do that stuff with him. She said that she had been kind of scared at first, but that it felt good. She told me that he unbuttoned her shirt and removed her bra. Then he squeezed and kissed her breasts, and sucked on them.

I must have turned forty shades of red when she said that because she laughed and said, "It felt really good."

I said, "Sure it did."

So do you know what she did? Who am I asking anyway? You can't answer me. You're just a book. God, I hope no one ever finds my diary and reads this!

I was wearing what I usually wear to bed, a long T-shirt and underwear. So all of the sudden, Sherri pulled up my shirt and started kissing my breasts. I could've died! I didn't obviously, or I wouldn't be writing this. Instead I just kind of melted inside. I was tingling all over. She told me to lie down on the bed so she could show me how good sex felt.

I said, "Sherri, I've never even kissed anyone before."

She said, "I know, and it's about time someone showed you what you're missing."

Then she kissed me. I could not believe how soft her mouth was. I mean, I had noticed before how full her lips were. I had even wondered what it would be like to kiss her. I never dreamed I'd ever actually do it!

It was really late when all this happened, so we didn't have to worry about my parents. Besides their bedroom is on the other side of the house. I'm really glad of that.

Anyway, she took all her clothes off and made me take mine off too. Okay, so she didn't make me. I wanted to, but it was kind of scary and exciting all at the same time. I had seen Sherri naked before because we practically grew up in the same house. But last night it was different. I couldn't stop looking at her body. I mean really looking at it. Like I'd never seen it before. It was so beautiful. I hadn't noticed before how round and big her breasts were getting.

So there we both were, lying there naked. Then she lay down on top of me. Her breasts felt soft on my skin. That was nice. It wasn't scary any more. It was just nice and soft and warm. Then she started touching my breasts again, first with her hands then with her lips and tongue. I felt warm all over and tingly. Then she started kissing me all over my body. She even kissed my "place" (I feel tingly just writing about that). She kept kissing it too. I thought I was going to explode. It felt so good.

Finally I sat up and said, "You and Mark did all this?"

Then she actually blushed. God, I have never seen Sherri blush before, and I've known her for eleven years!

"What exactly did you and Mark do?"

"He didn't get any further than my breasts. I was afraid my parents would come home, so we stopped. We didn't even take all our clothes off. We kissed a lot though."

"And here I thought you had done nearly everything! That's the way you talked the other day."

"It seemed like a lot to me at the time. Until now."

Then it was my turn to blush. Here I had been thinking that Sherri knew everything about sex, and now I probably know as much as she does. I can hardly believe it! We didn't do anything else after that. We just put our clothes back on, and went to sleep. I was so tired I actually went to sleep, even though my body was still tingling, and my mind was racing in high gear. I still feel sort of weird inside.

Monday, May 16, 1983

Sherri is acting strange. She wouldn't look me in the eye today at school. I don't know what is going on, but I don't like it. She hasn't talked to me since the night she stayed at my house. I don't know if she's mad at me or what. I wasn't the one who started all that stuff, so she shouldn't be mad at me for anything.

Saturday, May 21, 1983

Hi. Remember me? I'm your long lost journal writer. I haven't felt much like writing this week. I've been afraid to write. If I write I have to think, and I don't want to think right now. My head aches from crying so much. I can't help it though. I'm so confused and depressed. Sherri is acting like nothing happened between us. She's even still dating Mark. I don't understand how she can be with him after the other night. After all she did to me. After all the things we felt.

Yesterday she told me that I was silly to think about all that stuff as anything but a lesson in sex. A lesson in sex? Sex is something guys do to girls. That wasn't sex. I don't know what it was, but it's not what I think of, when I think of sex. What happened between us was some kind of strange fire. Well, I guess I got burned, and she just got singed a little.

Tuesday, May 24, 1983

I've been biking a lot lately. It helps me to think more clearly, especially if I ride way up into the mountains. There's this special place I go when I really need to think. It's very peaceful there. I call it my "quiet spot," because it's where I like to go when the world gets too noisy for me. It's just a little clearing in the midst of a bunch of tall Fraser fir trees. I've been there nearly every day for the past week. I like it so much because the scent of the Frasers reminds me of the Christmas trees we get every year. I really love the way they smell. It clears my head of confusion.

I don't understand Sherri, and I don't understand what happened. But I don't know what to do about any of it. So I guess I might as well forget about it, if I can. My bike can be my best friend from now on. I know it won't ever confuse me. I can just go to my quiet spot after school instead of going over to Sherri's. The trees can listen to my troubles. Sherri never was very good at listening anyway. She always did most of the talking.

Thursday, May 26, 1983

I passed Steve Palencio when I was riding my bike today. He was up on Register Mountain. That's where my quiet spot is. He was on a really nice bike. I didn't know he liked to bike. Not many of my friends are bikers. Biking here is difficult because of the mountains, but it's a lot more fun than riding on flat ground. Sometimes I rent a bike when we go to the beach, but it's not much of a challenge to ride there unless you try to ride on the sand dunes. I've wiped out doing that more than once.

Friday, May 27, 1983

I passed Steve again today. I think if I see him again, I will say something to him. Though it's hard to have a conversation when you're flying down a mountain slope. I can just see it now. I'm flying down a steep hill, when I spot a biker that looks like Steve coming up the hill.
"Hey, Steeeeeveee!"
Some conversation, huh? Oh well. Maybe I'll see him at school long enough to say something to him.

Monday, May 30, 1983

I saw Steve again this afternoon. Only this time, he was the one flying down the hill. So instead of me yelling "Steeeeeveee," he shouted "Allie!" He didn't drag out the last syllable either. Mostly all I heard was a barking noise that sounded like it was saying "Al!" I guess the "lie" part went flying down the hill with him. Anyway, when I realized it was Steve I stopped and went back down to talk to him. It would have been mean to make him ride back up the hill.
He said that he had thought it was me he kept passing, but he wasn't sure. He just got a brand new bike. His brother

wrecked his old BMX doing stunts, so their parents made Mark buy him a new one. Only he didn't get another BMX. Instead he got a mountain bike. It's really cool. It has twelve speeds! My road bike has only ten. Anyway, Steve and I are planning to go biking together some time this summer. I gave him my phone number.

Wednesday, June 1, 1983

Yes! School is out! I'm glad we didn't have to make up any snow days. I don't think I could've stayed in school any longer. I like school, but you can get too much of a good thing sometimes. Dad and I are going to a baseball game tonight. What a way to start summer vacation. I can't wait! I'll probably scream my lungs out and get hoarse.

Thursday, June 2, 1983

Sherri called today to tell me that she and Mark broke up. I'm glad I guess. I'm not sure what to think about it really. She's been acting so strange around me ever since that one night. Personally I think that whole situation got to her too. She'd never admit it though. It still hurts, but I can't make her feel things she refuses to feel.

Sometimes I wish I had someone to talk to about this. They always make a big deal about reminding us that the school counselors are there for us, if we need to talk. Somehow I can't imagine telling them about this. They'd probably accuse me of being a lesbian or something. I really don't think that is true.

Before Sherri and I did all that, I never really thought much about girls that way. Well, except for thinking about what it would be like to kiss Sherri, and that was just curiosity. I mean, I've also wondered what it would be like to kiss guys. It's not my fault I haven't had any experiences with them. There just aren't any decent guys in my school. Maybe if I lived in a bigger town, like Asheville or Charlotte, I would meet someone interesting.

Saturday, June 4, 1983

Steve Palencio called me today. He wanted to know if we could go biking together next week. We decided to go Monday. I'm not doing anything else that day. I'm glad it's summer. I have a lot of free time now. I think I'll go swimming. Mom's home, so I don't have to worry about swimming alone. My parents are really strict about not letting me swim when no one else is around. That can be a real pain when you're an only child.

Monday, June 6, 1983

I went biking today with Steve. We rode up in the mountains for a couple hours. We must have biked at least twenty miles. It was a lot of fun. He's coming over tomorrow to go swimming. It's nice to have a friend again. I will probably never be as close to him as I was to Sherri. But then I will probably never be as close to Sherri as I used to be either. At least now I have someone to talk to about some things anyway. Sherri and I used to tell each other everything. I know I could never tell anyone about what happened between us. Especially not a guy!

Wednesday, June 8, 1983

I went on my first official "date" last night. Steve and I went to the movies. It was an incredibly stupid movie, but I had fun anyway. Steve kept making these funny remarks about the characters. He was much funnier than the show. He has a clever sense of humor. We're going biking again today. I guess I'd better get ready. He'll be here soon. Bye!

Thursday, June 9, 1983

Sherri called last night while Mom and I were at the grocery store. She left a message with Dad. She told him to tell me that she'd had a fight with her parents and that she needed to talk to me. It was too late to call when I got back home though because Mom and I went to have an ice cream cone at the Polar Bear afterwards. So I still don't know what the fight was about. I'll bet it was mostly Sherri's fault. She's been really upset about breaking up with Mark. Whenever she gets that way, she takes it out on everyone else. Too bad school is out. There's no reason why she couldn't talk to a school counselor. At least this is a normal teenage problem.

Friday, June 10, 1983

Sherri just called. I found out why she was fighting with her folks. They found out that she was having sex with Mark. I didn't know they were actually doing it. Damn! How could she do that? I can't believe it. I knew he was no good. I wonder if Steve knows about it. Knowing guys, he probably does. I guess I'm the last to find out. I can't believe this. She's probably pregnant now and will have to get an abortion or have a baby. Oh god! How could she be so stupid?

Sunday, June 12, 1983

Steve came over to swim again today. He didn't know about Sherri and Mark either. I'm really surprised though, the ways guys talk. They act like they've just won a trophy if they get a girl to have sex with them. How stupid! All they ever think about is sex.

Wednesday, June 15, 1983

I just reread my last entry. I'm beginning to think that all I think about is sex. One night of sex and my whole life has changed. I can't quit thinking about how good it felt when Sherri touched me. Sometimes I touch myself to see if I will feel tingly all over. It feels good, but it's a lonely kind of feeling good. Why did Sherri start all that with me and then run away? That was so unfair! Especially since she refuses even to talk about it. I feel so alone now. So isolated from everyone. If it weren't for Steve, I wouldn't have any real friends at all. I can't even talk to most of my more casual friends any more. The things they like to talk about seem incredibly stupid to me.

Thursday, June 16, 1983

Steve came over today. I found out that he likes the Tourists too. I'm going to see if he can come with Dad and me to some of the games. Unfortunately the Tourists are playing a bunch of games out of town right now. They're going to be in Charlotte for a while.

Sunday, June 19, 1983

Steve's family left yesterday to go on vacation for several days, so I'm back to solo swimming and biking. Too bad Sherri isn't a biker. She likes to swim sometimes, but lately, she doesn't seem to want to have anything to do with me. I think she's looking for a new boyfriend. She's not likely to find one hanging out with me. I don't go to the places where guys hang out. I'm just not interested in dating. I'm confused enough as it is.

Friday, June 24, 1983

Steve is back in town, and so are the Tourists. Dad said that it would be all right if he goes to the game with us tonight. I can't wait! I just love baseball. I wish we could have a girls' baseball or softball team here in Spruceton. They just started a girls' softball league in Asheville, but Spruceton doesn't have a division for my age group. Someone from the planning committee came to my school last year to find out if there were any girls interested in playing. Apparently there weren't enough of us though, because when they announced the teams in the league, they said that there hadn't been enough interest to start an adolescent division in Spruceton. That figures. Most of the girls at school don't seem to be interested in anything except hanging out at the mall, wearing make-up, or dating. Sometimes I really feel like a misfit. I'm not interested in any of those things.

It doesn't help either that I don't have a southern accent like most of the people at school. But my family is from Ohio, so they don't have a southern accent. They're the ones that taught me how to speak English therefore I don't have an accent either. Maybe if I hung around people who are from here I would have one anyway.

Sherri and her family are originally from New Jersey, so they don't have an accent either, at least not a southern one. I think it's hysterical when they say "you's guys." Anyway, that's probably one of the reasons Sherri and I became best friends. We both felt a little different from the other kids who grew up here. We look different. We talk different. We've always felt as though we were from a different planet. Now I'm beginning to wonder if Sherri and I are even from the same planet.

Maybe I'm really an alien. Maybe I'm adopted. No, that's stupid. I fit in fine with my parents. It's the rest of the world that makes me wonder. Except for Steve. He's not too bad. He's from Charlotte, so that's kind of like being from around here, but not exactly. He has only a slight southern accent. He told me that he was trying to get rid of it though because of wanting to be a lawyer. I'm not sure what his occupation has to do with it, but whatever. I guess maybe he's afraid people would think of him as a hick if he went somewhere else to practice law. I'll have to ask him some time where he plans to live when he gets out of law school.

Sunday, June 26, 1983

So much for my great summer of baseball. The Tourists are terrible this year! They lost four of the last five games they played. Steve went with us to the last two. That was the only thing that made the games fun. He and Dad started telling each other jokes. Those two seem to get along really well. Dad even told me that he thought that Steve was a good choice for a boyfriend. I wouldn't exactly call him a boyfriend. He's really just a good friend. He's coming over to swim today. He's a really good diver. He can do all kinds of cool flips and stuff.

Monday, June 27, 1983

I guess I was wrong about Steve not being a boyfriend. He kissed me today when we were out by the pool. It was okay, but not as soft as Sherri's kisses. Plus he tasted kind of sweaty. It definitely didn't make me tingle all over. Maybe that happens only with your first kiss. I guess I'm rather ignorant when it comes to sex. I just never thought about it much before. You see these sex scenes in movies all the time, but they don't tell you that sex makes them feel warm and tingly when you're actually doing it. Maybe the library has some books on it, some that aren't as stupid as the films they show in school.   Those are really about starting your period and all that puberty stuff. They're pretty boring.

Tuesday, June 28, 1983

I went to the library today to look up sex. Oh my god, was that ever a mistake! While I was looking in the card catalog, this really cute guy came over. I nearly died. I flipped the cards to another spot so fast I ripped one. I know I must have turned forty shades of purple. I'm sure he could tell I was blushing. He gave me a strange look.

Wednesday, June 29, 1983

I went to the library again. This time I managed to look up sex in the catalog.   There were a lot of books, but I narrowed it down to three. When I went to find them in the stacks, there were people in the aisle, so I kept going. When they left, I went back and pulled out one of the books. I can't believe they keep books like that in the library! There were all these pictures of naked people. They were only drawings and not real photographs, but still.   I was so embarrassed I couldn't even check any of them out.

Thursday, June 30, 1983

I have decided to find out about sex firsthand.   I'm not quite sure how to tell Steve, but maybe I can just hint around some. We're supposed to go biking today. We'll see what happens.

Later--Steve is either very shy or very stupid. I dropped a couple of hints today about being curious about everything. But he didn't get it. Well, maybe he got it, but pretended not to because he doesn't like me that way. He hasn't tried to kiss me since that first time. That was three days ago. Maybe I didn't do it right. Oh great! One bad kiss, and now he's going to dump me. I'm not about to try looking up books on kissing though. I've learned my lesson with libraries!

Friday, July 1, 1983

Steve and I had a long talk today. He said that he really likes me, but he just wants us to be friends. I asked him if it was because I didn't kiss him right. He said that I kissed fine, but that he just didn't want to get serious with anyone right now. I told him that was okay with me. I didn't really like it anyway. Kissing him was kind of like kissing a brother or something. It's hard to explain really, particularly since I don't even have a brother. It wasn't anything at all like kissing Sherri.

Monday, July 4, 1983

The Fourth of July is great! Especially when you get to see cool fireworks. Dad, Mom, Steve, and I went to the Tourists game tonight. After the game, the Asheville Fire Department set off a fireworks display at the baseball park. It was awesome!

One of the guys running the display got hurt though. He didn't get burned or anything. He just tripped on something and cut his head really bad on a wooden platform. It was pretty gross when he came walking by us with blood streaming down his head. I thought I was going to lose my dinner.

Friday, July 8, 1983

We're leaving tomorrow to go to the beach. I can't wait. I'm going to miss Steve though. Sherri, too, even though I don't see her much anymore. She's dating some guy named Larry. He's nineteen. She's sixteen now, but I'm still kind of worried about her after what happened with Mark. I found out that her folks were upset with her before, not because she was having sex with Mark, but because they weren't using anything to keep her from getting pregnant. She now has her own supply of those rubber things. How disgusting!

Saturday, July 9, 1983

So far the trip is great! We drove over early this morning and checked in as soon as they would let us.   After lunch we went swimming in the ocean. It's so neat to hear the sound of the waves. I love it here. I wish I could live near the ocean. Of course, I like the mountains too. I guess I'll have to buy two houses when I'm older — one on the coast and one in the mountains. Too bad there aren't any towns in North Carolina that are near both. Well, I'm really tired, so I'll say goodnight.

Sunday, July 10, 1983

I met a cute guy today when I went to play video games at the arcade. He has black hair and soft brown eyes.   He's kind of short, only a couple inches taller than me. His name is Jimmy or Timmy. I'm not sure which, but I was too embarrassed to ask him to repeat it. Of course it was so noisy in the arcade, I probably wouldn't have understood him even if he had told me a second time.

Monday, July 11, 1983

His name is Jimmy. One of his friends called him, just as I walked up to him today. Talk about good timing. He's from Newark, New Jersey. He's seventeen. His family comes here every year, only they usually come in August.   He's really cute. I think he kind of likes me. He said that he wants to go for a walk on the beach with me, if I'm interested. I think I am. I don't feel as relaxed with him as I do with Steve, but then I've known Steve for a couple years, even though we weren't good friends before.

Tuesday, July 12, 1983

Oh god, can Jimmy ever kiss! Tonight we went walking along the beach. It wasn't dark yet. When we came to a really isolated spot, he pulled me to the ground and started kissing my lips and face. I hardly knew what was happening. At any rate, I got tingly again! Now isn't that bizarre? I got tingly when I kissed him and when I kissed Sherri. Maybe I'm just attracted to people from New Jersey. Or maybe people from there know how to kiss better. No, that's stupid!

Anyway, I finally got myself together enough to tell him that I really needed to get back before my parents came looking for me. They don't exactly know Jimmy well enough to let me go away with him for a long time.

Wednesday, July 13, 1983

I think things are going too fast for me. Jimmy took me back to the same place this afternoon. After we kissed for a few minutes, he pulled my bathing suit down to my waist, and started kissing my breasts and running his hands all over my body. I told him to stop. He didn't at first, until I forced myself up from beneath him. He looked surprised and said, "I'm sorry. Are you a virgin? I didn't realize."

"Not really. I just don't like to go this fast."

He kind of laughed. "Okay, I'm sorry. It's just that we have so little time, and you are so beautiful."

No one has ever told me I was beautiful before, at least not anyone who isn't related to me, and that hardly counts.

Relatives will tell you that you are beautiful, even if you look like a toad.

Thursday, July 14, 1983

I'm really confused. Why is it that everything Sherri did to me felt so wonderful? It didn't feel all that great with Jimmy today. We went back to the same spot on the beach. This time Jimmy asked permission to kiss me. Then he asked if he could touch my breasts.

When I said, "I guess so," he began pulling my bathing suit down. I thought he was going to stop at my waist like he did before, only he didn't. He kept tugging on it until it was down to my feet. I stepped out of it, feeling very naked and very nervous. Then he took off his trunks. I didn't dare look at him below his chest. I think I would've fainted.

I said, "I am a virgin."

He smiled. "I know. It's okay. It won't hurt."

But it did hurt. Oh, god! I can't believe I let him do that to me. I can't believe I'm not a virgin anymore. Well, I guess I've now gotten my second lesson in sex. Somehow I think I was better off without it.

Friday, July 15, 1983

I went with Jimmy again today. I don't know why. I guess I thought I had to. We have only a few days left, and he has such soft brown eyes. We had sex again. It didn't hurt as much, but it still didn't feel good. I really don't understand. Maybe having sex with guys is like eating raw oysters or drinking coffee. Dad says that you have to acquire a taste for those things.

Saturday, July 16, 1983

I wonder how long it takes to acquire a taste for sex. Personally I think I'd rather not try any more. I'm glad we're leaving tomorrow. I haven't had much fun at the ocean this year. I'm going tonight with Jimmy to walk on the beach. I know he will want to have sex. He always does. Maybe that really is all guys think about.

Sunday, July 17, 1983

Jimmy looked sad last night when we went to have sex for the last time. I didn't think he'd ever get off me. He gave me his address in Newark, and I gave him mine. I don't think I'm going to write him though. I'd just like to forget everything that happened at the beach this year.

Monday, July 18, 1983

I thought I would be glad to get home, but I'm not. I'm glad I don't have to see Jimmy anymore. It makes me kind of sick to think about what he did to me. It wasn't anything like I thought it would be. I thought sex was supposed to feel wonderful. Maybe there is something wrong with me after all. I thought that I would feel good, but I don't. I feel embarrassed and angry with myself for letting him touch me.

Later-- I'm back. Steve just called. He wants to go biking soon, but I don't know if I can face him right now. I think I'll go over to Sherri's house.

Friday, July 22, 1983

I told Sherri about Jimmy. She thought it was great that I'm a woman now. Frankly, if that is what it takes to be a woman, I would've rather stayed a girl.   Personally I think she's just glad not to be the only one who feels rotten. She and Larry are having sex now all the time. I can't say that I am surprised. I really don't know what she sees in it. It's pretty gross if you ask me.

Monday, July 25, 1983

I'm glad Steve and I decided to be friends. I don't think I could stand to live near a guy I had sex with. At least I can be pretty sure I won't see Jimmy again. Maybe I can talk my parents into going somewhere else for our vacation next year.

Friday, July 29, 1983

I got a letter from Jimmy today. I nearly threw it away without opening it. It was rather boring. He didn't say much of anything. He can't spell worth a flip either. I don't know why I let him touch me.   I thought it would feel good, the way touching Sherri felt good. But it didn't. I can't really explain why it was so different. I just know it was. Oh god, I was so stupid to let that creep touch me!

Sunday, August 14, 1983

School will be starting again soon. I can't believe how much I've changed since the beginning of the summer. I don't even feel like the same person. I feel sad inside. My parents keep asking me if I'm okay.   What am I supposed to tell them? I feel like saying "Hell no, I'm not okay! I lost my virginity this summer."

They'd probably be very understanding. They are pretty cool. They might even offer to supply me with rubbers. Oh please! But how could I ever tell them that I'd really rather touch girls than guys? I don't know if they could understand that.   I'm not sure I understand it, for that matter.   I guess there really is something wrong with me.

Maybe I really am an alien or a lesbian. I suppose that's pretty much the same thing. I don't know. I don't particularly want to try to look that subject up in the library.   I would die if anyone saw me reading a book about that. For that matter, I'm not sure anyone has ever written about it.   I suppose someone has, but I don't know who would.   Doctors? Psychologists? Lesbians? Oh well. I guess I'll never know because I'm not going to risk looking it up.

Thursday, August 25, 1983

School starts Monday. The whole summer has come and gone. Maybe I will be a little more disciplined with my journal writing once school starts. It got a little too painful to think about what I was feeling inside. I've been trying to forget this summer ever happened. The only good thing that happened was that I got really strong from biking so much. With the way the rest of this summer has gone, I'm surprised my bike didn't break down.   I would have really been in trouble then.

Thursday, September 15, 1983

School is okay, so far. I'm kind of annoyed that I don't have any classes with Sherri or Steve.   Oh well.   I didn't spend much time with either of them this summer, at least not after our family vacation.   I knew they would want to know why I was so down all the time, and I didn't want to talk or think about Jimmy any more.   So I just kind of quit doing things with them.

I have some pretty decent teachers this year.   Mr. Stevens, my Geometry teacher, is really funny.   He makes math a lot of fun. Ms. Sparrow is pretty cool too.   She teaches

English. She's a feminist.   We're not supposed to call her "Mrs." or "Miss." She is "Ms. Sparrow." I like her. My favorite teacher though is Miss Evans, the new P.E. teacher.   She's kind of quiet, but she's very nice. Sometimes she seems sort of scared of the students.   I think she has already picked up on my athletic ability. She wants me to join the tennis team. I told her I would think about it. Tennis isn't one of my best sports. I'm already in the German Club. My German teacher, Mr. Hofstader, is very serious about German.   Oops! I'm supposed to call him "Herr Hofstader."   I think I might join the Drama Club too. There's so much to do this year!

Monday, September 19, 1983

    Miss Evans appointed Missy Staves and me to be her P.E. assistants for our class. We're supposed to help her get the sports equipment out to the field, take attendance, and keep track of everyone and everything. I feel good about it. It makes me feel as though she trusts me. I like that. I feel kind of like a junior teacher or something. Well, that's all for today. I just thought I'd make a note of that. My parents think it's neat too.

Friday, October 21, 1983

    So much for being more consistent with my journal writing. Maybe if I had Mrs. Haze again this year, I would do better. Then again, I may just be doing too much.   Between tennis practice in the afternoon and homework at night, I barely have enough time to eat and sleep. I already had to drop out of Drama.   That definitely required too much time and energy.   It wouldn't help if I dropped out of the German Club, since it meets during school hours, and I'm not about to drop tennis. I love it! Miss Evans is a lot of fun now that she has begun to open up. I can tell she likes me. I think I might even be her pet.

Monday, November 28, 1983

I hate it. I was fine all through Thanksgiving vacation, until last night. Then I started feeling horrible. I was sick to my stomach and running a fever. Why didn't I get this virus Friday? Then maybe I wouldn't have to miss school today. We were supposed to get our school pictures back. Not that I really care about pictures, but I don't like to miss school. Not this year anyway. It's too good!

Tuesday, November 29, 1983

Something really weird happened today. After school I had to go back to my homeroom to pick up my pictures, since I wasn't there to get them yesterday. I had them on top of my books when I went to tennis practice. Miss Evans saw them there and asked if she could have one so she could remember her "star tennis player."

I couldn't believe it. I didn't think she was serious at first and told her so. I mean, I'm hardly the star of the tennis team. Anyway, she said that she is always serious. I told her that wasn't true because I've seen her smiling and laughing a lot during P.E. and at practice. Then she said that she didn't know she was being watched so closely. I know my face turned red. I'm not sure what that was supposed to mean.

Thursday, December 8, 1983

I'm glad I spent so much time on my bike this summer. It's helping me with tennis. I can play for hours without getting worn out. Just think, when the school year started, I barely knew how to play tennis. Now I'm pretty good. I have even won a few sets off the best players on the team. Not bad, huh?

Friday, December 16, 1983

Today was the last day of school in 1983. It's hard to believe the year is nearly over. I've been so busy. I've barely had any time to think. Of course, after last summer, that is a good thing. All that stuff with Jimmy seems more like a bad dream now. Fortunately he stopped writing me after just two letters. I never answered them, so I guess he got the message. Either that or he found someone else to have sex with. At least it's not me any more.

Friday, December 30, 1983

We just got back from my grandparents' house in Virginia. It snowed about six inches while we were there. It hardly ever snows that much here at Christmas time. I think that's why my parents make a big deal about going to Virginia every Christmas. They miss the white Christmases they used to have in Ohio. I was only three when we moved here, so I don't really remember any of that.

I like the snow at Christmas time, but I'm glad to be back home. I have to sleep on the foldout couch when we go to my grandparents' house. It's kind of a lumpy old thing so it's hard for me to sleep. Besides, I like being back in my own house with my own bedroom walls surrounding me. I'll be even happier to go back to school Monday. I miss it.

Thursday, January 19, 1984

We're supposed to have an intramural tennis tournament this weekend. Unfortunately they're predicting snow, so it might get canceled. I hope not. I've been looking forward to this tournament for weeks now. My tennis game has improved so much. I'm anxious to get into a tournament of some kind, so I can play some different people.

Sunday, January 22, 1984

As expected, they canceled our tournament. Bummer! I really wanted to play. Oh well. Instead I just hung around the house all weekend. I read a lot and watched a little bit of television. I watched this one movie that was really strange. It was about these two women athletes. I think they were lesbians, but then one of them ended up with a guy. I'm still not sure I understood it completely. I felt really bad for the woman who was left alone. She probably felt the way I did when Sherri kept dating Mark after that night we spent together.

I'm really confused about a lot of things, but I don't know what to do about it. I don't know who to ask for help. I can't think of anyone who would understand how I feel. Not one person. I guess I just need to forget about sex until I'm older. I know I don't want any more boyfriends, at least not any time soon. And Sherri doesn't seem to want to have a lot to do with me outside school.

Tuesday, January 24, 1984

The tennis tournament has been rescheduled for this weekend. Yay! I can't wait. It's probably a good thing I have to though, since I have two tests this week. I'd better get back to studying. Bye!

Sunday, January 29, 1984

I came in third place in the tournament. Not too good, but not too bad either, since there were a lot of players. I wonder why some of those kids aren't on the school tennis team. A couple of them were really good, and I didn't know they even played tennis. They would probably get even better if they joined a team. I can see a lot of improvements in my game since I joined.

Miss Evans is such a good tennis coach. I really like her. She doesn't yell at you when you screw up. She just asks you how you could improve on the shot you missed. Then she walks you through the improvements you've mentioned, while giving you other pointers. She never makes me feel stupid for making mistakes.

Tuesday, February 14, 1984

Today is Valentine's Day. Will you be my Valentine? Oh brother! I sound like Mr. Rogers. "It's a wonderful day at Stepford High. Will you be my Valentine?" They're having a dance Friday night at the school. Nobody has asked me to go, but I wouldn't want to anyway. I think that kind of stuff is stupid. I thought it was funny though when Miss Evans asked me if I would be there. She looked pretty disappointed when I told her I wouldn't. I told her that I'm not the social type, and that I don't date much. She said that she didn't really date either. It was very strange. I kind of got the feeling there was more to the conversation than what was on the surface. Don't ask me what though, because I'm clueless.

I have wondered if she might be a lesbian because she isn't married or engaged to anybody, but that doesn't necessarily mean anything. Maybe she just hasn't found "Mr. Right" yet. Oh please! I think I'm going to throw up! Somehow I can't imagine Miss Evans getting married. It doesn't fit her personality. I just can't picture her draped over some man's arm, and I certainly can't picture her letting a guy do to her what Jimmy did to me. God, that makes me sick to my stomach just to think about it!

Monday, February 20, 1984

Damn, damn, and double damn! I overheard someone talking about the Valentine's Dance today. They said that Miss Evans was there and that she looked really good. Well, actually the guy said that she looked "smokin' hot!" Now I wish I had gone just to see her. I wonder what she was wearing. Surely not a dress. I think I'd die if I ever saw her in a dress. She just isn't the type, but maybe that's because I'm used to seeing her in her P.E. clothes. I really wish I could have seen her. I wonder if she actually danced.

Wednesday, February 22, 1984

I asked Sherri about the dance. She told me that Miss Evans was one of the chaperones. Maybe that's why she asked me about it. Sherri also told me what she was wearing. Now I really wish I had seen her! She had on black dress pants with a gold and black shirt that shimmered in the lights. I bet she looked good. Sherri thought so.

Sherri also thought my questions were suspicious. She teased me about having a crush on Miss Evans. I don't know whether I do or not. I really like her a lot. I love to talk with her and be around her. Does that mean I have a crush on her? I don't know. Maybe it does. So what if I do?

Friday, February 24, 1984

We have another tournament this weekend. This one is not as big as the last one. It's only for the players on our tennis team. The coaches are trying to get us in shape for the spring. I like it when we have these tournaments though, because I get to see Miss Evans on the weekends too.

Tuesday, February 28, 1984

I didn't do very well in the tournament. I kept taking my eye off the ball. I need to make sure Miss Evans sits somewhere else next time. She was right in my line of vision when I was at one end of the court. I kept looking at her instead of the ball. That is not the best way in the world to impress the woman. It certainly isn't the best way to play a good game of tennis.

Tuesday, March 6, 1984

No school today because of snow. I think I'll go biking. I will probably freeze to death since I don't have a very good jacket for biking. Most of the ones I have are either too light to keep out the wind, or they're too heavy and bulky to wear on a bike. I have good gloves though. They make my hands downright hot after a few miles. I hope the roads aren't icy. They look all right in this neighborhood anyway.

Tuesday, April 3, 1984

I've been making a list of things I would like to get for my birthday. One of which is a nice pen to use when I write in my journal. It seems like all the pens I get for school like to make ink blotches all over the place, including on my hands.
"A pen! A pen! My kingdom for a good pen!"
Geez, I think I've been reading too much Shakespeare this semester. I decided to do my British Literature paper on Shakespeare, so I've been reading all his plays. Methinks I'm beginning to talk and think in Elizabethan English. Zounds! What next? I guess I'll have to start wearing tights and short tunics. I certainly wouldn't be caught dead in one of those long gowns the Elizabethan women wore. I'd trip and fall down a long, winding staircase and bash my head on the floor

at the bottom. Well, that sure is a gruesome thought. I'll just stop for now before this gets any worse. Bye!

Thursday, April 26, 1984

I am now sixteen. At least I can say that I've been kissed! I'm still not dating anyone though. I wonder if I'll ever find someone who cares about me so much that they won't be able to live without me. I guess I'm crazy, but I want something more than a casual relationship. I want a love that is deeper than the ocean, higher than the sky, and all that sentimental stuff. I don't know if I'll ever find anything like that. Maybe it exists only in love songs. I sure hope not.

Thursday, May 10, 1984

What a bummer! Today I heard someone say that Miss Evans isn't coming back to Stepford next year. She's such a good teacher! I was really getting close to her too. Who's going to coach the tennis team next year? How can she do this to me? She's the best teacher I've ever had. I can't believe she's quitting.

Friday, May 25, 1984

School's nearly over, and I'll never see Miss Evans again! She told me that she got a job teaching in Kentucky. What's so special about Kentucky? I can't believe she's actually going to leave. Why is she doing this? She's my favorite teacher! I wish there were some way I could talk her into staying, but I don't suppose she would change her mind just for my sake. It's not like my opinion would make any difference to her.

Sunday, June 10, 1984

I am so bored now that school is out. What is really bad is thinking about next year. I know it won't be nearly as much fun. I still can't believe Miss Evans is leaving. I don't even know if I want to be on the tennis team any more. It just won't be the same. Maybe I'll just bike and swim myself to death this summer. I won't have to worry about next year if I'm dead. I guess that's kind of a stupid thing to say.

Monday, July 2, 1984

I'm getting worse all the time with this journal. Maybe I should just throw it away. It was nice when I was younger, but it seems more of a nuisance now. Besides, what is there to write about? There are only so many ways you can say, "I went biking today. I went swimming. I read a book."

Mom asked me yesterday if I were okay. I told her that I was just bored and missed school. She gave me some standard mother responses: "Why don't you go over and see Sherri? And whatever happened to your friend Steve?"

Oh, please, Mother, try not to be so maternal! She makes me crazy sometimes.

Friday, July 6, 1984

We're leaving tomorrow to go on our family vacation, back to the beach, of course. What a major bummer! I really don't want to go. What if Jimmy is there? Yuk! Maybe I should get sick, so I won't have to go at all. I don't want to ruin my parents' vacation though. I know they really like going. Too bad I can't get them to change locations. But I wouldn't know how to go about doing that without giving them a reason why. Besides it's probably too late to get a room anywhere else. These places are usually reserved months in advance.

Monday, July 9, 1984

So far, so good. No sign of Jimmy. Maybe his family isn't coming until August. I'm trying to enjoy the beach, but I can't shut out the memories of last year. I have been avoiding the arcade and that one spot where he used to take me. Yuk! I can't stand to think about it.

Wednesday, July 11, 1984

God I hate this! Every time I turn around I see someone who looks like Jimmy. I'm really getting tired of having a heart attack every five minutes. I want to go home. I really am beginning to feel sick. My stomach stays tied up in knots. I don't know if I can endure a whole week of this. Please let this week come to an end!

Thursday, July 12, 1984

Good! We're going home a few days early. Dad got a call about an urgent meeting about some possible buyout or something that he has to attend. He offered to go back by himself, but I'm ready to get out of here anyway. Dad was worried about disappointing us. Well, Mom may be disappointed, but I'm definitely not.

Tuesday, July 17, 1984

This summer is really boring, but I'm not interested in going back to school either. I'm too depressed. I don't even care much about sports this year. I've been watching tennis on television, but that just makes me think about the fact that

my favorite teacher won't be at Stepford next year. She was so
nice. They'll never find another tennis coach as good as she is.

Thursday, July 19, 1984

    I don't believe it! I ran into Miss Evans today at the mall.
I thought I was going to die on the spot. I've really missed her
since school got out. I thought for sure she'd be gone by now.
She told me today that she isn't moving until the middle of
August. She asked me if I wanted to have lunch with her at
McD's, so I did. I don't even like the place. I just wanted to be
with her. I got a coke and some fries. When she ordered a
salad and water, I asked if she were on a diet. She said, "No,
I'm vegetarian."
    I told her that McD's was a strange place for a vegetarian
to eat. She said, "Yes it is, but it was the only place I could
think of where a teenager might like to eat."
    I said, "Nice try, but frankly I hate this place."
    She cracked up laughing. Then she got up, threw her
stuff in the trash, and said, "Come on, let's find some place
where we can get some real food."
    So then we went to this neat little restaurant. It looked
like something leftover from the 70's. There were beads
hanging in the doorways and a couple of lava lamps on one of
the counters. Each table had a small cactus plant and a candle
on it. The candles were shaped like mushrooms, peace signs,
and stuff like that. It was kind of funky really.
    I never even knew a place like that existed in Spruceton
until today. I can hardly believe it can stay in business in this
part of the world. There must be a lot of former hippies that
live in the nooks and crannies around Spruceton. I can't
imagine who else would visit such a restaurant. But then,
Miss Evans is not a former hippie, and she eats there. Then
again, she's not from around here. She's from California.
That's a far cry from Spruceton, North Carolina. Anyway,

Miss Evans ordered a vegetarian Mexican dish. We split it because there was so much food. It tasted good, kind of spicy though.

I found out that she likes biking, so I asked her if she'd like to go riding with me tomorrow. She's got an appointment, but she's going to call me later to set another time. I wonder if she will though. Maybe I should not have asked. I mean, come on, she is a teacher, and I'm just a student. She was probably just trying to be polite when she said that she had an appointment. God, I feel stupid now!

Friday, July 20, 1984

Shock of shocks! Miss Evans called me today when she got back from her appointment. We're going biking tomorrow. I can't wait. I'll never sleep tonight. This is going to be great! I just know it. I can't believe this is actually happening.

Saturday, July 21, 1984

What a day! Miss Evans, I mean, "Anna," and I rode to this really beautiful spot, way up in the mountains. We took lots of water with us and a picnic lunch. When we first got there I dropped to the ground and lay there gasping. A couple minutes later Anna sat down next to me and lay back on the grass. She was within six inches of where I was. Is she ever beautiful! Her eyes are really green. I mean, really green! I almost asked her if she had tinted contact lenses. I don't think she does though. I don't think she even wears glasses.

I had so much fun with her. We talked about everything under the sun. We laughed a lot. I love the way the sun made her hair shine. Her face was shining too. I don't think all of it was from the sweat either. She looked as though she were really enjoying herself — with me, no less!

She invited me to go to a tennis tournament with her. Martina Navratilova is going to be in Charlotte all next week. That's about as close to Spruceton as she will ever get, I guess. Mom already okayed it, but she wants me to check with Dad too, just in case he has some objection. She thinks he'll approve, since I'll be going with my former tennis coach. Unfortunately I have to wait until he gets home from work to find out for sure.

Later--This is really great! Dad said yes too. I'll never get to sleep tonight. Of course, I said that last night, and I went to sleep right away. I didn't know that being happy required so much energy.

Monday, July 30, 1984

Life is so good! I could just scream or sing or something! Not only did Martina win the whole damn tournament, but I also got to spend every day for a solid week with Anna. She's great. She is so much fun.

I hope August 18th never comes. That's when Anna is supposed to leave for Kentucky.   I don't want to think about it. Not yet. We still have time to be together. I don't want to ruin it by getting sad now.

I can't wait to see her again. I love the way her face lights up when she sees me. I can't stand it! I love her. I know I do. I don't care if that means I'm crazy. I hope that's not a terrible thing to say. I don't really care if it is. I just can't help myself. She's such a wonderful person. How could I not love her?

Tuesday, July 31, 1984

I wanted so badly to kiss Anna today. We went on another picnic and bike ride. After lunch, she stretched out on the grass and lay there looking at the view of the mountains. I sat down next to her. She was lying on her side, facing away from me. When she turned to look at me, I got the most incredible feeling. She gave me this look that made me tingle all over. I started to lean towards her. I knew I was about to kiss her, but I stopped myself just in time. I can't imagine what she would've done if I hadn't stopped myself. Then I closed my eyes and tried to pretend that nothing had happened. I sat there for a few moments, afraid to move. When I finally opened my eyes again, Anna was wiping her eyes. I asked her what was wrong. She said that she just had something in her eye. I think she was trying not to cry. I'm not sure why. Unless it's because she felt the same thing I felt. If she did, she may be as afraid of it as I am.

Wednesday, August 1, 1984

Today Anna and I had lunch at the vegetarian restaurant again. Then we went for a long walk around Lake Thomas. We stayed there for hours. I told her about what happened with Jimmy. Her eyes filled with tears. When I asked her why she was crying, she said, "Because he hurt you."

I told her that I had hurt myself by being so stupid. Then I told her about Sherri. She had a strange look on her face after that. Maybe I shouldn't have said anything. Maybe she doesn't share this feeling after all. Oh please let this be all right. I love her. I'll die if she doesn't kiss me soon. I wonder what she would do if I kissed her. Oh god! I hope I'm not crazy for feeling this way. I know she's five years older than I am, but I still love her. Please love me, Anna.

Thursday, August 2, 1984

Anna and I were supposed to play tennis today. We never made it though. She had forgotten her racket, so we went back to her house to get it. I asked her to show me around. I just had to see where she lived. It's a neat little house. It has a brick fireplace in the living room. There's just one bedroom and bath. It's really small, but then she lives alone so she probably doesn't need much room. It isn't actually hers anyway. She's just renting it. I nearly croaked when she showed me her bedroom. She has a big waterbed with built-in bookshelves.

We spent all day talking at her house. Then she fixed supper, and we ate by candlelight. She's very romantic, I think, and beautiful. She's definitely beautiful, especially in candlelight. I LOVE HER SO MUCH!

Sunday, August 5, 1984

Well, it finally happened. Anna kissed me, or actually, I guess I kissed her first. It was all so quick and I can't believe I did that, but I love her so much. She has such green eyes, such soft lips. I can still feel her lips on mine. I can still feel her soft hand on my face as she looked deeply into my eyes and kissed me back. I'll never forget that moment. God, I love her!

Monday, August 6, 1984

I had a real scare today. I thought for sure I was in trouble. I haven't told my parents yet that my new friend Anna is also Miss Evans. I didn't think they would understand. So today when Dad asked me about the "mysterious Anna" I have been spending all my time with, I choked. Then he winked and said, "Are you sure you're not sneaking off with a boyfriend somewhere?"

I nearly died! I could not believe he said that. I glared at him and said, "Would you like for me to call Anna so you can talk to her yourself? She's a friend from school. I introduced you to her awhile back."

He laughed and tickled me. Then he said, "I'm just playing with you, honey. I'm a nosey old parent who likes to know what his kid is up to."

Then I blurted out, "She's leaving in a couple weeks, and I may never see her again!"

He was so sweet. He put his arms around me and told me that he understood how I felt because he lost a few best friends in high school too. If he knew how I felt about her though, I don't think he would say that. But I can't tell him.

I guess I was just really emotional because I didn't get to see Anna today. She had to go to Kentucky for a meeting. She won't be back until tomorrow. I may die by then. I love her so much. I can't let her leave.

Tuesday, August 7, 1984

I never knew that love could be like this! I know that what I experienced with Jimmy and Steve was not love. One was sex; the other was friendship. This is love. I love Anna so much I could burst into a million pieces! And she loves me too. She told me so today. We spent all day at her house talking about everything and nothing. It was wonderful. She is wonderful.

Wednesday, August 8, 1984

I made Anna cry today. She is very sensitive. After we kissed again, I asked her if she would like to touch my breasts. She looked at me with so much love and said, "Oh, Allie, I love you so much. But I can't accept your offer, as much as I would like to. You are so young. I must refuse for your sake."

"Why for my sake? I want your touch. I want to feel your hands all over my body. I want you to love me."

"Allie, I just can't. You need time to be a teenager, and I need to avoid attracting the school board's attention. I'm not sure about the laws in this state, but I think that I could be arrested just for kissing you. I want more than anything to touch you, Allie, but I don't want you to get hurt. If anyone found out about us, there would be a big scandal. I really don't think that would be good for you or your family. That's why I'm moving to Kentucky."

That nearly killed me. I started crying then. I begged her to stay in Spruceton. I told her that I loved her more than anyone. I told her that I didn't care what people thought.

She said that she didn't care what people thought either, but that it was a little more complicated than that. She said that we have to wait until I'm older, until I can make a decision as an adult. Then she cried. I could kill myself. I love her so much. I know that being with her is what I want more than anything. Nothing in my whole life has ever been any more clear to me. I can't live without her. What will I do when she leaves? She can't leave! She just can't. I've got to find some way to talk her into staying.

Friday, August 17, 1984

Anna is leaving tomorrow. I tried to talk her into staying, but she has already signed a contract with the school in Kentucky. Besides she's thinks it for the best if she goes away for a while so I can have time to be a teenager. Who cares about being a teenager? I just want to be with Anna.

We've been together every day this past week. We've done a lot of talking. We'd talk all afternoon, and then she'd have to pack all evening. I just can't stand it. Why can't we be together? We love each other. So what if she's five years older than I am? People get married with bigger age gaps than that. Why can't we get married? And who cares how old I am? I know girls my age who have gotten married. What's the difference? What a stupid world this is! Why can a sixteen-year-old girl marry a grown man, and yet I can't marry Anna? What is the difference?

Saturday, August 18, 1984

I can't believe she's going to do it. She's actually going to leave me. I'll never survive. She says that she'll come back for visits, but how will I survive between visits? Oh god! I am so miserable. How can she do this to me? How can she just walk away from us?

Wednesday, August 29, 1984

All I can do is think about Anna. I miss her so much. My parents keep asking me if I need to see a doctor. I'm so depressed. I write her every day, but it's not the same as holding her. I miss her kisses. I miss her laugh. I miss the way her eyes smile at me. I even miss the way her hair smells. I miss everything about her!

Thursday, September 13, 1984

School's okay, I guess. Sherri is in my American History class. She sits a couple rows away though, because we are seated alphabetically. I hate when teachers do that. I guess it would be all right if your best friend's last name was close enough to yours. Unfortunately there are too many people in this class whose name starts with "L" or "M." Oh well. We're not that close any more. She's interested in dating guys and

I'm not. All I'm interested in is being with Anna. Since I can't do that, I don't really care about anything else.

Sunday, September 23, 1984

   Anna called last night to tell me that she will be in town soon. God, I miss her. School is so boring without her. I'm not even taking P.E. this year. I'm sure not going to be on the tennis team. It's too hard. I miss her so much. I write every day then mail my letters once a week. She does the same. I just wish she would move back here.

Saturday, November 24, 1984

   I couldn't sleep last night, so I got up and turned on the television. I ran across a very strange movie that had just started playing. It was called *The Fox*. It was about a lesbian couple who were living out in the country somewhere up north, just the two of them. Then this strange man appears on the scene and seduces one of the women. When the other woman is killed in an accident, the man takes the woman he seduced home with him away from the life she shared with her female lover.
   It was all very strange, and I got the feeling that the man felt as though he needed to rescue this woman from being lesbian. Yet the woman didn't seem convinced of her need to be rescued from her lesbian lover. On the contrary, she was very sad when her female lover died.
   It kind of reminded me of that other movie I watched about the female athletes. Why does one of the women always seem to end up with a man? I don't get it. Now that I've met Anna, I can't imagine being interested in a guy again. I was never really very interested in guys to begin with. Just curious. Anyway, I think my curiosity about guys is a thing

of the past. Why should I want anyone else now that I have Anna?

Sunday, December 16, 1984

The long lost journal writer strikes again. I gave up trying to keep a diary regularly this year. Whenever I have time to write anything that isn't school related, I write a letter to Anna. Instead of telling a diary about my daily life, I've been telling Anna everything. Writing to her a lot makes not seeing her a little easier.

Anna will be here soon for the holidays. I haven't seen her at all since she moved to Kentucky in August. The trip she planned in September got canceled because there was something wrong with her car. She couldn't come back during Thanksgiving break because she had to go to a basketball tournament. She's coaching basketball at her new school. I think she's had a rough year so far. I know I have.

Friday, December 21, 1984

Anna will be here tonight. I can't wait! She's going to stay in a hotel in town. She's supposed to call when she arrives. It has been so long. I'm almost afraid to see her. What if she's changed a lot? I know that she cut her hair recently because she didn't have time to take care of long hair. I hope I like it. I hope that is the biggest change in her. I just don't know what to think.

Sunday, January 6, 1984

Anna had to go back today. We were together every day except Christmas. I begged my parents to stay here for the holidays. I couldn't stand the thought of going to Virginia while Anna was here. Grandpa got sick anyway, so it turned out to be for the best. He doesn't like to have visitors when he doesn't feel well.

Anna is so wonderful. Her haircut looks good on her. It's really short, but she still looks the same for the most part. Except that she looks tired. I don't think she is doing very well in Kentucky. I wish she'd come back to me. I wish she'd come home. I bought her a silver identification bracelet for Christmas. I had her name engraved on it.

She gave me a copy of Martina Navratilova's book, *Tennis My Way*. She's knows I'm not playing tennis this year, but she still wanted me to have the book, since I like Martina so much. She understands why I don't want to play on the team this year. She admitted that she was relieved when she found out she wouldn't have to coach tennis this year. Tennis seems to be a painful reminder to both of us of our time together last year.

Friday, February 15, 1985

I got a Valentine card from Anna today. It was pretty, but sad. I sent her one too. Mine was more on the cute and cuddly side. I wanted to make her smile. I hope she got it on time. The mail seems to run so slowly between here and Kentucky. You'd think that we were separated by 3000 miles rather than 300.

Thursday, March 7, 1985

Anna will be coming home soon for spring break. She sounds really tired when she calls. I'm beginning to worry about her. She's been sick a lot this winter. I think she's very unhappy where she is. I wish she would come back here. She would probably be better off.

Monday, March 25, 1985

It snowed eight inches last night, so we don't have school today. The roads haven't been plowed yet, so Mom couldn't get to work either. We've been sitting around staring at the ice crystals on the windows. Nature has some really cool ways of doing things. It's like artwork. All these thousands of tiny crystal patterns make a beautiful decoration on the glass. It's very creative.

Wednesday, April 10 1985

Anna and I had fun during spring break. She still looks worn out though. How can she do this to herself? I'll be glad when school is out. She's talking about moving back here for the summer. I hope she does. Kentucky isn't good for her. She needs to come back here and rest. She never should have moved there in the first place.

Wednesday, April 17, 1985

I would probably enjoy school more this year if Anna were here. Nothing is very much fun without her. Even biking reminds me of her. I do it anyway. I need some way to burn up my excess energy.

I've been drawing a lot lately. Mostly I draw pictures of Anna. She gave me her biggest school (teacher) picture. I gave her mine too, though I had to give her the second biggest one since my parents got the biggest one. Anyway, the first picture I drew of her was based on her school picture. She still had her hair long when it was taken.

She is so beautiful. I really miss her. Being without her is the hardest thing I've ever done. One of the worst things about missing her is that I can't talk to my parents about her. I can't even leave her picture out on my desk. I bought a nice frame for it, but I have to keep it hidden in the drawer unless I'm alone in my room. I detest having to keep our love a secret. But there is no other way. I just don't think people would understand.

Tuesday, April 23, 1985

This school year is really beginning to drag. I think it's because I miss Anna so much. We haven't been writing every day, but we still write a lot. She calls every weekend too. One time I asked her how much her phone bill was. She just laughed and said, "Don't ask." Our talks must cost her a fortune. She also sends me stamps so I can keep writing her every week. I sure do miss her.

Friday, April 26, 1985

Well, today is my birthday. I'm now seventeen. Just one more year. Then I will be old enough to be with Anna without getting her in trouble. I wonder what she was like when she was seventeen. I hope she was happier than I am.

My parents bought me some clothes. They also got me a gift certificate from Waldenbooks. We're going to go to the Asheville mall tomorrow so I can pick out some books. Now I just need to remember some of the titles my teachers have mentioned.

Saturday, April 27, 1985

I got my birthday present from Anna today. She sent me a sterling silver necklace with a locket shaped like a heart. It's really pretty. I was glad mom was at work when it got here. Anna always omits her last name on the return address, so my parents won't figure out that she's Miss Evans. But I'm still glad I didn't have to open her present when anyone was around. Dad was home at the time, but he was taking a nap when the mail was delivered, so he didn't see the package either. I'm going to wear it all the time underneath my shirt. That way I'll be the only one who knows it's there.

Friday, May 3, 1985

We had a special assembly at school today for juniors and seniors. They're trying to get us ready for college. Mrs. Sarens, one of the school counselors, said that the juniors need to start looking at colleges now. It's hard to think about something that seems so far away. I mean I have another whole year of school left.

Monday, May 20, 1985

It won't be much longer until school is out. Anna gets out sooner than I do, but the teachers have to stay for another few days. She'll be coming home on Stepford's last day of school. I can't wait! I miss her so much.

Tuesday, May 28, 1985

Anna will be home soon. She has already made arrangements for a hotel room until she can rent something for the summer. I can't wait to see her. I miss her hugs. When she puts her arms around me, I feel so safe. I feel as though nothing can hurt me. I wonder if she feels that way when I hug her.

Saturday, June 15, 1985

Life is so much better now that Anna's back. We spend most of every day together. I pretend that I'm going out with different friends all the time. Fortunately Mom is working part-time again, so she's gone a lot in the afternoons. Sometimes Anna comes over here to go swimming. She sure looks good in a bathing suit.

Thursday, June 27, 1985

Anna and I went biking today. I love the way my body feels after a hard ride. It feels strong and tired. I get so tired I usually fall asleep afterwards. After our ride today, we went back to Anna's place (she's renting a small cottage for the summer). When she was taking a shower I was nearly overcome by the desire to see her naked. I resisted though. I didn't know what Anna would think about my watching her take a shower. She's so beautiful though, and I really would like to see her body.

I want so badly to go beyond our safe cuddles and kisses. I'm afraid she thinks I'm still too young, despite the fact that I feel ten years older than I did last year. I can understand why Anna didn't want us to get sexually involved last summer. She's so wise. And I really was a bit immature. I'm not sure if she feels we should continue to wait. I'm afraid to ask. I don't want to make her cry again.

Anyway, after our showers we hung out in the living room. I was still wishing I could see her naked. Then she started reading aloud from a book that explains how to go about choosing a college. Boring! I realize that she is trying to help me and I appreciate it. But the last thing I wanted to do at the moment was to read aloud from a boring old book. It was really hard for me not to go farther than kissing today.

Speaking of books, she let me borrow a book on sexuality. It was all about accepting yourself and your sexual preference. I think she's trying to tell me something. We had gotten into this big discussion about homosexuality the other day. I told her that I wasn't a lesbian because I don't hate guys. She said that she didn't hate guys either, but that she is definitely a lesbian.

Anna has never had sex with a guy. Somehow she figured out that she was a lesbian when she was fourteen. But then her aunt is lesbian so she knew more about it. She even told her parents then. They told her that she was a little young to make a decision like that, but that it was okay with them if she were. They also told her that it would be okay if she changed her mind later. She didn't though, and she's twenty-three now.

She seems so sure about who she is. I guess I'm not even sure what a lesbian is. When I hear people talk about lesbians at school, it doesn't sound like a good thing to be. I had gotten the impression it had a lot to do with hating men, which I don't. But Anna didn't seem to think so. Perhaps I should've gone to the library to research it after all. But now I don't have to. I can just read Anna's book. I think I should start immediately.

Monday, July 1, 1985

I finished reading Anna's book about homosexuality. It was actually about lesbians in particular. It was a collection of "coming out" stories. Anna had to explain the title to me when she gave it to me, because I didn't know what these people were supposed to be coming out of. I guess the Gay Liberation movement of the seventies didn't impact western North Carolina in a big way.

Although Anna did say that there is a rather large and visible community of gay people in Asheville. Maybe if I had grown up there I would know more about it by this time. Spruceton is rather small. I can't imagine that there are very many gay people here, but Anna says there are probably a lot of kids at school who may or may not know it yet, but will eventually figure out that they are gay. I certainly can't think of any that might qualify.

When I gave Anna her book back, I asked her to let me borrow another one that sounded a little more interesting. It is called *Lesbian Sex*. She told me that I should probably wait awhile before I read that one. So I borrowed another book of coming out stories. It's pretty cool to read about all these people's lives. About how they figured out they were gay, and what they chose to do with that realization.

I asked Anna where she bought all these books because I've never seen anything like them at any of the bookstores I've been in. She said that she bought them in California and New York. Apparently there are lots of gay people in those states and lots of bookstores and shops that are owned by gay people. I simply can't imagine that. She also said there was a bookstore like that in Asheville. She promised to take me there some day. I can't wait!

Tuesday, July 9, 1985

I've been thinking a lot about being gay. The books I've been reading have made me realize that being gay is not necessarily a bad thing. It can certainly be a difficult experience, but it doesn't have to be bad. I'm even beginning to get over my dislike for the word *lesbian*. I really didn't like it at first because of the way I have heard it spoken at school. But I realize now that those kids at school don't have a clue as what being a lesbian is all about. Not that they really have a clue about much of anything.

When I look at Anna, I see a strong, beautiful woman. A woman who could have a dozen guys if she wanted them. But she doesn't want them. She doesn't hate them or even dislike them. She just isn't sexually attracted to them. That makes sense to me now.

Anna is such a wonderful person. I just can't get over the fact that she loves me. She has so much going for her. I hope I'm not holding her back from getting a great job. I hope she doesn't wish she could find a woman her own age. Of course, I'd probably die if she did find someone older, but I feel kind of selfish sometimes. But she certainly seems happy to be with me, and she's so giving and patient. I really need to concentrate on doing nice things for her. She deserves it.

Thursday, July 11, 1985

I'm doing better about giving to Anna. I've been giving her back massages to help her relax. I also cooked supper for her last night. She has been teaching me stuff about vegetarian cooking. It's not hard at all. I think I like it better than cooking with meat anyway. I hate touching raw meat. It feels all gooey and squishy. Yuk! And it stinks too!

Monday, July 15, 1985

I asked Anna today if she wished she had found an older woman to be her girlfriend. She looked at me very seriously and said, "Allie, I love you. I don't need an older woman. But if you feel as though you need a younger one, just let me know. I will step out of the way."

I thought I was going to cry. I couldn't believe she would make that kind of offer. Why on earth would I need anyone besides her? She's nearly perfect, and she's so good to me. I just don't want to hurt her. What would happen to her if anyone found out that we love each other? She'd probably be put in jail. I guess we will just have to be very careful until I turn eighteen. At least that is less than a year away. I can hardly stand the idea of her going back to Kentucky, but I guess I'll survive, if that's what she has to do.

Tuesday, July 23, 1985

My parents are going to the beach next week. I told them that I really did not want to go this time. Last year was bad enough, having to deal with memories of Jimmy. I really couldn't stand to go now and leave Anna behind.

My mother was so funny when I told her I didn't want to go. She said, "Well, I suppose this is one of those sudden spurts of independence you teenagers are famous for. We'll have to line up some people you can call, in case you need help. Get Sherri or one of your other girlfriends to spend the nights with you, so you don't get scared."

I'm a little shocked that they're going to trust me that much. Of course, it's not like I'm going to throw a big party or anything. It was too funny when she told me to have one of my "girlfriends" spend the night. I nearly choked!

Thursday, July 25, 1985

Anna is going to stay with me while my parents are at the beach. I'm glad. It'll be fun. We won't have to say "good-night," and then go our separate ways. This is so exciting. I'm having a difficult time acting normal around my parents. I'm afraid they'll get suspicious if they see how happy I am about them going to the beach without me. There's so much I can't tell them about how I feel. I don't like that, but I don't know that there is anything I can do about it.

Monday, July 29, 1985

My parents left yesterday morning, and I am having so much fun already. Anna and I went to Asheville today. I've been dying to go to the lesbian bookstore there. It's really cool. It's called Malaprops. It's not just a lesbian bookstore though; it's a feminist bookstore. Really there are books of all kinds there, but there is a section towards the back of the store that is all about gay people. There are even a bunch of novels written about, and by, gay people. It was so cool! I couldn't believe my eyes.

There's a neat cafe downstairs too. Anna and I went down there and ate bagels with cream cheese. The people in the store were really interesting. I could tell that a lot of them, male and female, were gay. I've never seen so many gay people together in all my life. It was great! I felt as though I belonged there, even though I didn't know a soul there besides Anna. People were so friendly. They all seemed very intelligent too — like Anna.

It made me wish even more that I lived in Asheville. Spruceton seems like light years away from there, even though it's less than thirty miles away. It's more like thirty years away, thirty years behind the times, that is. Too bad my parents didn't move there when we came down from Ohio. But if they had, I might not have ever met Anna. Now that's a horrible thought.

Saturday, August 10, 1985

It was great having Anna over while Mom and Dad were gone. It was like being married or something. Except that we didn't actually have sex or do anything more than we normally do. Being with Anna is so different than being with Jimmy. He pushed me into things. Anna, I think, is trying to steer us clear of getting sexually involved.

We kiss and hug each other, but she has never tried to push me into doing anything beyond that. I wonder sometimes if she's actually sexually attracted to me, since we never really do anything. We did hold each other all night though. That was wonderful.

We slept in the spare bedroom because there's a double bed in there. I wish we could live together all the time. What do lesbians do anyway, since they can't get married? I guess I'll ask Anna about it. She'll probably give me a book to read. She is so cute that way.

Sunday, August 11, 1985

I knew it! Sure enough, Anna loaned me the book on alternative lifestyles she just bought in Asheville. I cracked up. It's really interesting reading though. There's a whole section that describes how people have told their family and friends that they're gay. I don't think I could ever tell my parents. They'd probably be okay about it, but I'm sure they would want to know more, and I can't tell them about Anna. Not yet. She could get in too much trouble.

Monday, August 12, 1985

Yes! Anna is thinking about staying here this year. She's definitely not going to teach at Stepford, but she's gotten a job offer in Madison County. She says that she can live here and commute to work. Please let it happen! I can't stand the thought of her going away again. That was so hard. I was miserable without her.

Tuesday, August 13, 1985

Anna and I had our first fight today. God I was so stupid! Anna was asking me what I was going to do about college. I told her that I didn't really care about college, that all I want is to be with her. That definitely didn't go over well. She told me that I needed to make plans for the future and not waste my life. She's right, I guess, but I don't want to move far away from her, and there isn't a college in Spruceton. Going away to college is the last thing I want to do, once I'm old enough to be with Anna openly. She told me that she would kick my butt if I don't make an appointment with a guidance counselor as soon as school starts. Of course, she wouldn't really do that, but she's very serious about all this college stuff. So I promised her I would go as soon as possible.

Thursday, August 22, 1985

Anna is staying! She's already accepted her new teaching position. We're going house-hunting today because she can't stay in the cottage past August. It will be fun to look for a house with her. She wants to find a two-bedroom house, so there will be more room. I hope that means she wants me to move in when I turn eighteen.

Saturday, August 24, 1985

We found a cute little place. It has two bedrooms, one bath, and a stone fireplace. She's going to use one bedroom as a library. The house is tucked up in a cove, very private and quiet. I love it! I wish I could move in with her. That would be great. Then we could be with each other all the time. Or at least when we weren't at school.

Sunday, August 25, 1985

School starts next week. I'm excited, mostly because I know this is my last year. It's not that I care much about being a senior, but I do care about turning eighteen. Just eight more months. Too bad it isn't just eight more days. Sometimes I feel as though I'm spending all my time wishing that time would hurry up. I think I'm ready to leave home now. I really don't think that waiting until I'm eighteen is going to make any difference.

Tuesday, September 3, 1985

I'm taking German III. Herr Hofstader's eyes lit up when I came into class the first day. He said, "Fraulein Katz! Guten Tag! Es freut mich, Sie zu sehen."* He's so funny. He really likes it when a student enjoys learning German.

I'm also taking Comparative Governments, Senior English, Trigonometry, Art, and Contemporary Classics. I think this year will be fun. At least I don't have to worry about spending all my time crying and missing Anna.

* "Miss Katz! Good day! I am glad to see you."

Friday, September 6, 1985

I went to see Mrs. Sarens today. We talked about going to college, the pros and cons of dorm life, etc. I told her that I'd prefer to stay nearby and commute. So we talked about that too. She gave me catalogs for a bunch of the schools in this part of the country. She told me that I should have no trouble getting a scholarship, since my grades are so good. I'm going to talk to my parents tonight and see what they have to say about all this stuff.

I haven't gotten to see Anna today because she had a meeting that lasted all afternoon. Oh well. At least I know she's here. I bet she will save a lot of money on phone bills this year. Of course, she'll spend it all on gas, driving to the next county every day.

Sunday, September 8, 1985

Oh great! Anna's former lover is coming to stay with her next weekend. I can't believe it! Anna was surprised too because she hadn't heard from her since they graduated from college. Apparently she called Anna's parents and got her phone number from them. She's got a lot of nerve! Where's she going to sleep? Anna has only one bed. I can't believe this is happening!

Friday, September 13, 1985

Anna's old lover, Sarah, showed up today. She was on Anna's front porch when she got home from work. I can't believe she just appeared like that out of nowhere. Who does she think she is? Anna didn't want me to come over until she had a chance to explain about us. What a wonderful Friday evening I have had!

Saturday, September 14, 1985

I met Sarah today. She doesn't look like much. I hated the way she looked at me when I arrived at Anna's house. She looked me up and down then said, "Boy, you really are robbing the cradle with this one!" I nearly laughed out loud when Anna punched her on the arm. I know that must have hurt because Anna is really strong. I just said, "Very funny!"

Sunday, September 15, 1985

I really don't like the way Sarah keeps saying, "Remember when we used to... " and then proceeds to ramble on about all the stuff she and Anna used to do in college. God she has a lot of nerve! Anna doesn't look too happy about it either. She keeps glaring at her.

What did Anna ever see in this woman? I wonder how they met. Sarah probably seduced her. I don't particularly want to ask about it though. I've heard enough about what they did together, which is practically everything under the sun. Fortunately Sarah is leaving tomorrow morning.

Monday, September 16, 1985

Good riddance, Sarah! May I never see your face again. Now I have Anna to myself again. I missed being alone with her. Sarah never let us have a private moment. I wonder if that woman ever shuts up. As soon as Anna gets home today, I'm going over there. Uh, oh. I guess I'd better get going. She'll be home soon. Bye!

Tuesday, September 17, 1985

I wish I could keep my big mouth shut. I am so stupid sometimes! I asked Anna how she ever got together with someone like Sarah. That was a big mistake. She told me that I had no right to talk about Sarah that way, and that I don't know her and shouldn't judge her by one uncomfortable weekend. I just left after that.

I'm afraid to see her again. What if she wants to get back together with Sarah? After all, I am only a teenager. Sarah is her age, and they used to be lovers. I wonder if Anna is still in love with her. I wonder if that's why Anna has not made love to me. Oh god! I sure hope nothing happened between them while Sarah was staying there. I don't think I could handle that.

Wednesday, September 18, 1985

I can't believe it! Anna sent me a dozen roses! I'm glad my mother was at work this afternoon. I don't know where to put them. I can't let my parents see them. The card says, "I'm sorry I was such a jerk. Love, Anna." She wasn't a jerk. I was the jerk! I think I'll ride over to her house and wait for her to get home. Where am I going to put these roses?

Thursday, September 19, 1985

Anna and I had a long talk. She apologized for jumping my case. She explained that she was really uncomfortable all weekend because of Sarah. After Sarah left, Anna wanted to forget the whole thing. She just kind of lost it when I brought it up. I have a feeling there's more to it, but I don't want to pry. She'll tell me if she wants to. If not, then it's none of my business. I want to know more about it, but it is not worth risking another blow-up. I apologized too for being such a brat. Now I'd better start working on some homework, or I may flunk my first test of the year.

Friday, September 20, 1985

Anna finally explained some things about Sarah. She met her in college during her freshman year. When she went to the first women's basketball game, Anna overheard someone talking about the lesbian "jocque." Not knowing any other lesbians, Anna was anxious to find out more. So she listened until she figured out who they were talking about. Then one night she ran into her in the locker room so she introduced herself. Two weeks later they were lovers. They stayed together for two years and then broke up. Why Sarah suddenly decided to visit her, Anna doesn't know.

So now I know how they met. I think I'd rather not know any more. But I'm not sorry Anna told me. She doesn't talk about her past very much. In any case, it is not very comfortable listening to the story of how your girlfriend met a former lover. I don't think I want to know how many more there were or who they were. Until Sarah came into the picture, I hadn't even thought about Anna having lovers. It just never crossed my mind. I guess because she never talked about it.

Monday, September 30, 1985

Less than seven months until my 18th birthday! I can't wait. I'm still looking at schools, and talking with Mom, Dad, and Anna about it all. I may go to the university Anna attended. It's in Tennessee. It sounds really good, and it isn't all that expensive. The only problem is that I don't know what to tell my parents about the dorm. It would be a long commute, but I want to live with Anna. Oh well, there's still time to figure it all out.

Tuesday, November 5, 1985

I can't wait until February. I'll be going to visit Denisson University, so I can make a final decision about school. Of course, I don't have a clue about what I want to study, but I'll have time to figure that out later. Anyway I'm going with Anna and some girls from her high school. I told my parents that I was going with Miss Evans and two girls from Mitchell High School. They knew Miss Evans had left Stepford, so I had to explain that she was teaching at Mitchell now. I told them that I ran into her recently, and that we started talking about college and a trip she was going to take to her old school. I don't like telling them only part of the story, but I see no other way. She'd be in serious trouble if the school board found out that she's dating a former student, a female student at that. This really stinks, but there's nothing I can do about it. I tell my parents the truth about everything else. This is just too important and too dangerous a situation to be that honest. I can't take the chance.

Thursday, November 14, 1985

Anna called me tonight to tell me that a friend of hers was killed yesterday. She was really upset about it. I wish I could be there with her. She's there all by herself with no one to hold her while she cries. Damn! I hate hiding our relationship. If it were Sherri who had called, or a boyfriend, my parents would let me go over there to be with them. But how could I explain about Anna without explaining about us?

Friday, November 15, 1985

Anna left today to go to her friend's funeral. I'm really going to miss her these next few days. I wish I could go with her. I hate that she has to face this alone. It's just not fair. I'm tired of hiding how I feel about her. I should be with her during this time. Instead I get to stay home and pretend that I'm an innocent teenager who doesn't know anything about love or happiness.

God I wish time would hurry up. I'd run away and live with Anna, but I know she would send me back home. She doesn't want to mess things up between my family and me. But she isn't messing things up. I am. I just want to be an adult now. What difference does it make if I'm seventeen and a half or eighteen? Six months isn't going to change how I feel about her. Six months isn't going to make me any more ready to leave home.

It's not that I don't care about my parents. I care about them a whole lot. I just don't know how they would feel about my love for Anna. That's why I have to wait until I'm eighteen. Then it won't matter what they think. It won't matter what anyone thinks. I'll be an adult then, and I'll be able to make my own decisions.

Friday, November 22, 1985

I have to go to Virginia for Thanksgiving break. I'm really annoyed about it too. We're going now though, so we don't have to go at Christmas. That's good. It's just that it is inconvenient right now to leave Anna. She's still upset about losing her friend. I wish I could just stay here with her while my parents go. Unfortunately, I don't have much of a choice. I can't tell them about Anna, so I can't explain why I need to stay here with her.

Friday, December 13, 1985

I can't believe it! Sherri just called to tell me that she's pregnant. Sometimes she is so stupid! Surely she could've waited one more year. Six months, for that matter. She doesn't know for sure if she should have the baby. She definitely doesn't want to marry Ted or whatever his name is. She's been seeing him for only three months. Apparently she's been seeing a lot of him. Much more than I'd ever care to see. I'm glad I don't have to worry about such things. Poor Sherri! I guess I should've seen it coming, but I thought she was being careful. What a way to end your senior year. At least she's not due until June. It's a good thing she already had her senior pictures taken.

Friday, February 14, 1986

Anna and I ate a wonderful candlelight dinner tonight, to celebrate Valentine's Day. I asked her about that time, two years ago, when she asked me about going to the Valentine's Dance. She didn't say anything for a long time. Then she laughed and said, "What I really wanted was to ask you to go with me to the dance. Instead, all I was allowed to say was, 'Are you going?' I knew you weren't, but I had to say something about it."

Then she told me that she feels frustrated because she wants us to be able to go out to eat, or go for a walk around the lake, without having to be so careful. She also told me that she'd like to skywrite "I love my Allie Katz!" for the whole world to see. I know how she feels. I don't like having to sneak around either. It makes me feel dishonest, and I am not a dishonest person. I don't like feeling that our love is a horrible secret that must be kept. It is the most wonderful thing that has ever happened to me. It doesn't seem fair that I should have to keep it a secret.

Wednesday, February 19, 1986

Tomorrow we leave on our trip to Anna's school. I can hardly wait. The best part is that I get to be with Anna for three whole days. I'm kind of excited about being on a college campus. It will be nice to be around some older people. I get tired of hanging around immature high school students.

Sunday, February 23, 1986

Well, I guess we really screwed up this time. Damn! Just a couple months away from my birthday. While we were at Denisson, one of Anna's students walked into the dorm room and caught Anna and me with our arms around each other. We had just been kissing. I have no idea how much she saw or what will happen now. I hope she keeps her stupid mouth shut! Anna better not get fired. Oh god, I can't believe we were so careless!

Monday, February 24, 1986

I haven't heard anything about the college weekend fiasco yet. Of course, Anna won't be home from work for another hour. I think I'll go over and wait for her. I can't stand the suspense. I hope she doesn't get into trouble over this. It's all so incredibly stupid.

Later--Nothing happened today, so maybe Tina didn't tell anyone. I sure hope not. This is terrible! Anna is a nervous wreck. She was trying to act calm, but I could tell that she was really upset on the inside.

Tuesday, February 25, 1986

Still no news. Anna is starting to panic. She's talking about resigning her job now before everything blows up. She thinks that there may not be as much publicity if she is no longer teaching. She's concerned about what it will do to my family. I told her that was not important, since the only reason my parents don't know about us is that I didn't want to make trouble for her. I told her too that she was being ridiculous because she didn't know for certain that anything had been said about it. She agreed that it would be better to wait and see if anything happens.

Thursday, February 27, 1986

I nearly croaked today. Cindy Smetner came up to me at the lockers and asked me if I had been with Miss Evans at the lake last week. I didn't know what to say at first, but then I realized that I'd better act cool and say something. Finally I said, "Oh yeah, Miss Evans. I ran into her there so we talked about Stepford and stuff. You know."
She smiled and said, "Yeah, Miss Evans sure is a good P.E. teacher. I wish she'd come back so they could get rid of the old bag that is teaching now."
I said, "Yeah, definitely."
I have never even had "the old bag" for a class, but I didn't know what else to say. I didn't want to act suspicious or anything.

Friday, February 28, 1986

It finally happened. Anna got called into the principal's office today (now that's an odd thought). He told her that Tina Washington had come to see him and told him that she had seen her with her arms around a female student. She told him that she had seen her cousin Trish there and had given her a big hug when she told her about her engagement. This actually did happen, although it was earlier in the day. She's pretty sure he believed her, but she's still worried about it.

Anna had already called Trish to let her know what was happening in case the school decided to check up on her. Trish was cool about it and didn't mind backing her up. I hope that is the end of this whole stupid thing. It isn't anybody else's business anyway.

Wednesday, March 12, 1986

So far, so good. Nothing else has been said about the college weekend fiasco. I guess we're safe. I sure hope so. They would have done something by now, though, surely. What would be the point in waiting this long without taking any action?

Monday, March 31, 1986

Less than a month until my eighteenth birthday. Yes! School is a lot more exciting now. So much is happening all at once. I got my graduation announcement order form yesterday. Mom is making a list of all the relatives who should get one so we will know how many to order. It's during times like these when I wish my parents' families were a little smaller. I'm going to have to address a thousand envelopes! Okay, so probably not nearly that many, but still.

Saturday, April 26, 1986

Hurray! It finally got here! It took long enough. I'm now eighteen, and I can no longer get Anna into trouble. At least, I don't think I can. Happy birthday to me! I am now an adult. And just as I thought, I don't feel any different than I did yesterday, so what did having a birthday prove to anyone? At least now I should be able to move in with Anna. She hasn't said anything about it though, so I guess I'd better try to find out if she actually wants me to live with her.

Sunday, April 27, 1986

Anna and I had an argument of sorts today. She told me that we still can't be open about our relationship for several reasons. For one thing, homosexual acts are illegal in North Carolina, so the number of people who know about us should be few. Another problem is that she's still teaching high school, and I am still a high school student. That kind of thing would not be well received in the community. There would be a big scandal. People would think that she had seduced me while I was a minor. It's even possible that the scare we had earlier with Tina would be revisited.

Of course, she's right. I guess I hadn't thought about anything except turning eighteen, so I would be considered an adult. I can be so dense sometimes. I didn't realize that it is actually illegal for gays to have sex in this state. Who made up that stupid law? No one has the right to tell me who I can or cannot love. That's ridiculous!

Tuesday, April 29, 1986

Wow! Anna finally let me borrow her *Lesbian Sex* book. I've read only the first few chapters and I'm very freaked. It's very exciting. I'd like to try some of these things. Hmm. I think I'll go now. It's time to learn more about this lesbian stuff. Later!

Thursday, May 1, 1985

Help! This book I'm reading is blowing my mind. I can't believe people write so freely about something so personal. My god! I can't imagine doing some of those things. On the other hand, I get all tingly reading about some of the things lesbians do. I'm not even kissing anybody, and I'm getting tingly all over. It makes me want to run over to Anna's house and jump into bed with her right away. Only I really don't know if I could try those things unless she started it.

Now I know why Anna was so reluctant to let me borrow this book. She finally agreed because she figured I wouldn't read it all, if I couldn't handle it. I not only read it all, I went back and reread parts of it. One thing I know for certain. I am a lesbian through and through. Reading the books on heterosexual sex was embarrassing, and even kind of boring. But not this book.

Between the two "coming out" books I read before, I learned enough to know that being lesbian doesn't have anything to do with relationships with men, good or bad. It has to do with loving women and wanting to be loved by women. With this book, I'm finding out how to go about loving women. Love between two women is very sexy and beautiful. It has absolutely nothing to do with men. Where do people get such silly ideas anyway?

Saturday, May 3, 1986

Now I understand what people mean when they talk about fireworks. I had my first orgasm today. I had no idea that was what sex was supposed to be like. It definitely wasn't like that with Jimmy. Anna is amazing. What is even more amazing is that she showed me how to make her feel that way too. I nearly freaked. She is even more beautiful then. The look on her face was incredible. I have never seen anyone look like that. Oh my god! It was so wonderful. She's so wonderful.

I can hardly believe we finally made love. I have wanted so badly to make love to her, and to have her make love to me. I had no idea it would be that powerful though. Wow! I just couldn't stop myself. I was so excited from that book.

When I went over to Anna's I had planned just to talk about the book, but I couldn't do it. I sat Anna down on the couch and opened my mouth, but nothing came out.

She smiled at me and said, "Yes, what is it?"

But I couldn't say anything. Finally I just leaned over and kissed her. I started with her lips, but that wasn't enough. I kept kissing her all over her face and neck and ears. She was wearing a button-down Oxford shirt with the first two buttons undone, so I just kept on kissing her down to where the first button was buttoned. And then I actually had the nerve to unbutton that next button.

Anna didn't protest, so I kept right on kissing and unbuttoning and kissing some more until her shirt was completely undone. Then I looked at her and said, "Anna, I love you, and I'm ready for this. I am lesbian, and I really want to make love to you right now. More than I've ever wanted anything in my life."

She looked at me with tenderness, but no tears. Then a fiery look appeared in her eyes, and she whispered, "Oh Allie, I want you too."

Then she kissed me like she has never kissed me before. She kissed me as though she wanted to devour me. It was then that I knew for sure that she felt the same way I did. So I opened her shirt wide and began running my hands over her bare skin. I caressed and kissed her soft lovely breasts and stomach. Anna caught her breath when I did that.

Then I stopped and pulled my T-shirt off and unhooked my bra. Anna was braless at the time, so I didn't have to fumble with that. Then I stood up and pulled my shorts and underwear off, and Anna pulled hers off too. It was the most amazing moment I have ever experienced. That split second before our naked bodies touched. Oh my god! I'm tingling all over just thinking about it. Then it was like some awesome dream — even better than the movies — where we made love to each other for hours totally oblivious to the rest of the world. What a day!

Monday, May 5, 1986

I'm so glad I finally got up the nerve to make love to Anna. She is so wonderful. She doesn't seem to be sorry about it either. In fact, our love has deepened because of our lovemaking. It's not at all like it was with Sherri. I was kind of afraid it would be, even though I know that Anna is definitely a lesbian, and Sherri isn't. Sherri was just playing with me, and it got out of hand.

My relationship with Anna is so different. We finally sat down and talked about the lesbian sex book. It took a couple of tries before we could talk about it without winding up making love ourselves. I find it very hard to keep my hands off the woman. She's so irresistible. Not that I'm trying to resist her. It's so much easier to talk about sex with her now that I know a little bit firsthand. Besides there's less tension in the air now that we've gone ahead and actually done it.

Tuesday, May 13, 1986

I'm more ready than ever to graduate from high school and move in with Anna. I love that woman so much. I can hardly believe anything is as beautiful as our lovemaking. There certainly is no one more beautiful than Anna especially when she is experiencing an orgasm. She really blows my mind. I find it hard to express in words. I just want to hurry up and move in with her. I want to spend my whole life with her, and I'm ready for that life to begin now.

Saturday, May 17, 1986

Congratulations to me! I've not only been accepted by Denisson University, but I've also been awarded a full scholarship. Things are looking good. Anna's thinking about going back to school too. She wants to get her master's degree. I wonder what you do with a master's degree in P.E.

Monday, May 19, 1986

The lady never ceases to amaze me. I knew Anna liked to read a lot. That much is obvious, but I never dreamed that "Miss Evans, the P.E. teacher," was planning to become "Dr. Evans, the Literature professor." She majored in Literature and P.E. No wonder she's a walking library! And here I thought she meant she was going to get a master's in P.E.

Sometimes I wonder if I have spent most of our time together talking about myself. I keep getting these little surprises. It's not that she's doesn't talk. It's just that she doesn't talk about herself very much. She answers any questions when I ask. I just don't seem to ask enough questions. I guess I'll never get bored with her though because I'll never know when she's going to come up with some other interesting tidbit about her life.

Monday, June 2, 1986

Well, school's out, and it should be okay to move in with Anna. Only now I have to tell my parents. I'm pretty sure they'll be okay about it, but I'm still kind of scared. They've always told me not to judge people by their race or religion or anything like that. This may be their big test to see if they really meant it. I can see it now. I'll just sit them down, and say, "Okay, Mom and Dad, pop quiz time! Did you know that your one and only daughter is a lesbian? Five seconds. Beep! Time's up! What's your response?"

Tuesday, June 3, 1986

Anna and I had a long talk today. I decided to tell my parents tonight. I'm scared. Anna offered to be here with me, but I told her that this is something I have to face on my own. Besides, if they freak out, I don't want them to know who she is. It isn't her fault. She certainly did not make me a lesbian.

She gave me a book to give to them if they're interested. I swear, she really is a walking library. Where was she when I was trying to learn about sex at the public library? I feel kind of sorry for my parents. They probably haven't even gotten over the shock of their "baby" graduating from high school. I wouldn't want to be them right now, any more than I want to be me (which isn't very much).

Later--Well, I did it. I told them. They looked surprised but not devastated. Mom said, "Well, honey, we rather suspected this when you weren't very interested in boys. I suppose your friend Anna was your first love."

That about floored me. I said, "How did you know?"

Dad said, "Allie, it was written all over your face. It was in your eyes, and in the fact that you were never home. Then when she moved, you were depressed for months. It was obvious that something was going on inside you. We kept trying to get you to communicate with us, but you really shut us out. It is okay, you know. We love you for who you are. You're our daughter."

We all hugged a lot and cried some. Then I told them about Sherri. Well, not in detail or anything. They gave each other a funny look and said, "Sherri?"

I said, "Yeah, but I guess she got over it."

That reminds me, Sherri is due any day now. I really need to call her. I haven't seen her since graduation, and she was looking very pregnant then. It's too late to call tonight though.

Anyway, back to my parents. Dad asked me who I was seeing now. He smiled when I said, "Anna." He said that he suspected she must be back in town because at the end of the school year, I was instantly cured of my "melancholy."

They really want to meet her. They want to know all about her. I'm supposed to invite her to dinner. How should I warn them that they've already met her? Maybe they won't remember her. Oh well, I'm really tired of hiding things from them. I want them to know everything, but I've got to tell them the right way. Not tonight though. Right now I need to call Anna, so she can relax. She told me to call her, even if it got late, so I'd better do that before it gets any later. Good night.

Wednesday, June 4, 1986

Anna is coming over tomorrow night to meet my parents. She agrees that we need to come clean with them. She's willing to take the blame and consequences should anything happen. At least I'm old enough now to move out. We can run away together if necessary, but I think things are going to work out all right.

Later--I talked to my parents again about Anna. First, I reminded them about Romeo and Juliet, and forbidden love, and all that stuff. They told me to "cut the corny crap and just tell them whatever it was I was trying to tell them."

So I did. I told them that Anna is Miss Evans, my former P.E. teacher, and that she is five years older than me. When I explained why she decided to transfer to another school, they said that it must have been difficult for her. I told them about how we accidentally ran into each other at the mall and how things went from there. I also told them that we didn't get sexually involved until after my eighteenth birthday.

Anyway, the long and short of it is that although they were stunned, they said they understood. Then they told me a long story about my Uncle Philip. He fell in love with a sixteen-year-old girl when he was in college. Even though they tried to wait until she was old enough to get married, she ended up pregnant with his child. When she told her parents, they had Philip arrested for statutory rape. He offered several times to marry the girl because he really cared for her, but her parents refused. After serving a short term in prison, he was let out on parole. By the time he was released, though, the girl had married someone else. Even then he offered to help pay for the care of the child, but the couple refused. Six months later, Uncle Philip committed suicide.

I was freaked when they told me all this. I knew Dad's brother had died young, but I always thought he'd been killed in a car wreck or something. The family always referred to the incident as "Philip's accident." I had no idea he shot himself. How awful!

Anyway, because of that Mom and Dad vowed that they would never forbid me to see anyone unless I was in some kind of danger from this person. They admitted that they probably would have counseled me against seeing someone, male or female, who was so much older. But now that it seems that our relationship has lasted, they agreed to support us in any way they could.

Whew! I am exhausted. These intense talks are wearing me out. I'm excited though too, because now Anna can get to know my parents. I should probably call her before I go to bed. She will sleep better if she knows everything is okay.

Thursday, June 5, 1986

Anna and my parents really hit it off tonight. It was cool to see them cracking each other up and having fun. I love it! My parents asked her a lot of questions about her family. I learned some things I didn't know. For instance, her real father is gay. He and her mother got divorced when she was really young because he could not pretend any more. Her mother remarried a few years later, so she could stay at home with Anna and her older brother. I also learned that she has a younger sister, who is still in high school. She is really her half-sister though. It's amazing how much I never asked Anna. I have so many questions now. I want to know everything about her. She told me some stuff before about her dad, but apparently I have been confusing him with her stepfather. I think I'm going to have to refigure everything.

Friday, June 6, 1986

I've been packing all my stuff so I can move in with Anna. Dad's going to borrow our neighbor's pick-up tomorrow and haul everything over. I'm excited, but kind of scared too. I'm actually moving out on my own. Then I will be going to college in less than three months. Even though I've been waiting forever for this moment, it's kind of frightening now that it's arrived. It's almost too much change all at once.

Anna is going to help me look for a summer job. She's going to teach summer school so she can earn some extra money before she goes back to school. She's already saved a little bit of money from the three years she has been teaching.

I'm not sure how though, with the phone bills one year, and the gasoline bills the next.

She's really incredible though. She spends very little on clothes and food. Although she drives to work, she bikes nearly everywhere else. Her luck in finding inexpensive housing is amazing. She says that she has a system, but she hasn't explained it yet. Maybe she will when we go house hunting in August. I can't wait until we have more time together. Just think, this time tomorrow night, I'll be sleeping in her arms. Mmm. That's a nice thought.

Monday, June 9, 1986

It didn't take long to move my junk over here, but it is taking forever to unpack it. My parents let me have the dresser from the spare bedroom for my clothes. Anna has an extra bookshelf I can use for my books. We're both going to sleep in her bedroom, so we can keep the other room for use as a library. It's only logical, since we both love books so much. Besides I don't need my own bedroom. The whole point of moving in with Anna is so we can live together. Why would I want a separate bedroom?

Maybe when I'm as old as my grandmother I will feel differently. She made my grandfather move into their guest room because now that's he retired he gets "in her space." She actually said that! I think she's been watching too much television. She's starting to sound like a teenager.

Thursday, June 12, 1986

I got a job. I start working Wednesday. This is my first real job. I babysat some in junior high, but this is different. I'll have a regular paycheck and everything. I'm going to be working at the Polar Bear ice cream shop. It's a small store with just a pick-up window. The best thing about it is that it is very cold in there because of the ice cream machines. They keep the air conditioning cranked up. That will be great because I hate to be hot.

Celia, the girl who is going to train me, is seventeen. She says that all the kids from the high school hang out there, so there's never a dull moment. She's been there for almost two years already, and she loves it. I'll be getting paid $3.50 an hour. That's fifteen cents over minimum wage. The owner is starting me out at that rate because I'm a high school graduate with "excellent grades." He wants another responsible person in charge of opening the store in the mornings. Celia closes the store at night. Anyway, it sounds kind of neat. I think I will like it.

Anna is sleeping right now. She's so beautiful. She has to start back to work Monday. We didn't have very much time to "play house," as Anna calls it.

Wednesday, June 18, 1986

Work is okay, but I sure miss Anna. She feels the same way. She gets home before I do because she leaves earlier. We don't get to see each other from 7:00 a.m. until after 5:00 p.m. most days. That's too much time away from her. At least I don't have to leave at night.

Anna has massaged my feet the last couple of nights. They've been sore from standing on them all day. There are stools to sit on when there's no one around, but that doesn't happen very often. We've had a steady stream of business, so far. It's been really hot lately. The best thing about working at P.B. is that it's always cool in there, no matter how hot it is outside. We don't have air conditioning here at the house. But we're completely covered by the shade trees, so it stays pretty cool in here with just the windows open.

Saturday, June 21, 1986

Mrs. Mackey just called. Sherri went into labor last night around midnight. She finally had the baby about an hour ago. Anna and I are going to the hospital tonight to see them. I can't believe she actually went through with it. I can't believe Sherri is a mother. That's just too weird!

Monday, June 23, 1986

Sherri will be leaving the hospital today. She and the baby are doing fine. I haven't really gotten a good look at him yet. Both times I went to the hospital to see them, he was in the big room with all the other babies. Of course, he was on the other side of the room away from the window. Oh well, I'm sure I'll see him later.

Friday, June 27, 1986

I just got off work. Anna isn't home right now. She had to run errands and buy groceries. She's been teaching me a lot about cooking. I think I like eating vegetarian foods all the time. She's such a good cook. She asks me what my favorite dishes are then she makes them without the meat, using all healthy ingredients. Yum! Unfortunately, I have put on weight since I moved in. I think that's because I have less time to bike. About the only biking I get to do these days is riding back and forth to Polar Bear. It seems to rain all day whenever I'm off work.

Oh, I think I hear Anna's car. I need to help her with the groceries, so I'd better go now. Bye, little journal. You've been with me through a lot, haven't you?

Monday, June 30, 1986

You know, I fail to see the attraction Celia has for P.B. She's really very young for seventeen. I know I wasn't like that. I did some stupid things, but I wasn't a flirt, like she is. I guess she's the kind of person who fits in high school. I never felt like I did. I enjoyed my classes, but not the stupid dances and the social games.

Well, I need to get going. Mom and Dad are coming over for dinner. I can't wait. I've hardly seen them since I moved out. Working thirty hours a week takes up a lot of time. When I'm not working, I want to be alone with Anna. We never have the same days off, so all we have are bits and pieces of the day together.

Tuesday, July 1, 1986

Mom and Dad came over last night for supper. They brought over some records they used to play when they were dating. They taught us some old dances too. Anna actually knew some of them. It was a riot. I could not believe my eyes when I saw Mom and Dad "cutting the rug," as they called it. Dad and Anna danced together. It was so much fun! I had no idea they could be so hilarious. I think they're going through a second adolescent phase. I'm glad they like Anna. Of course, I really don't know what there would be not to like. She's as perfect as anyone I've ever met. Sometimes I wonder why she puts up with me. I guess I ought to be glad and not worry about it. I just got lucky.

Monday, July 7, 1986

Sherri came over today with the baby. He's cute. He loved Anna's rocking chair. So did Sherri. They don't have one at her parents' house. I haven't gotten her a baby present yet, so I think I'll take some of my next paycheck and buy them one. Every mother needs a rocking chair, right?

Tuesday, July 8, 1986

Anna and I talked about how we could help Sherri with Teddy. I still can't believe she named that baby after his father after he treated her like a leper. He didn't even offer to pay for an abortion. I'm awfully glad he didn't though. Teddy is so sweet. It's not his fault his father is a jerk. You can tell that Sherri really loves him — Teddy, that is, not his father.

Anyway, Anna wants me to see if Sherri would like for us to babysit one night a week so she can have some time to herself. I'm going to call her later today. Maybe I'll see if she can bring him to see me at P.B. Those two would be a lot more interesting than the idiots that hang out there.

Friday, July 11, 1986

I finally got in contact with Sherri. Every time I called, the line was busy. They must take the phone off the hook when Teddy is asleep. Anyway, Sherri is going to bring Teddy to P.B. today. I can't wait. He's so cute. I think Sherri was glad I called. She's supposed to come by as soon as I open this morning. She doesn't want to keep Teddy out in the hot sun. Can't say that I blame her. I wouldn't want to be out in the hot sun either.

Saturday, July 12, 1986

Sherri and Teddy came to see me yesterday. It turned into a sideshow. Everything was fine until some guys on loud motorcycles pulled up. You'd think they'd never heard of mufflers. They started picking on Sherri, saying stuff like,

"Let me take a turn nursing," and "I bet I could make one of those with you." They were real jerks.

Finally, Sherri turned to them and said, "Frankly boys, I've had enough of guys like you. You have only one thing on your minds."

One guy said, "Yeah, sex!"

Sherri said, "No, you don't think about sex. That's something any animal can do by instinct. The only thing you guys have on your mind is air!"

I cracked up laughing at that. So did Sherri. The guys just looked at her and said, "Bitch!"

What a witty comeback. I could've laughed all day about that one. Only it got really busy, so Sherri left with Teddy. That girl sure has guts!

Monday, July 14, 1986

Today is our day to babysit Teddy. I really like that kid. It will be fun to entertain him while Sherri's gone, though I'm not quite sure what we're going to do with him. I haven't really spent much time around babies. Anna knows a little more about babies than I do, but she hasn't been around them for a long time. She thinks that he'll probably just sleep a lot, since he's still very young. I suppose we'll do all right. How hard can it be?

Tuesday, July 15, 1986

Sherri didn't leave Teddy with us after all. We all got to talking about what happened at P.B. and lots of other things. We lost track of time. It was fun. Sherri let Anna and me play with Teddy while she just watched and talked all evening. I have to admit that I was kind of embarrassed when she started nursing him. It's really amazing what happens to a woman's body when she has a baby. Sherri's breasts are really full now.

Friday, July 18, 1986

Tomorrow is our second anniversary. Exactly two years ago, I ran into Anna at the mall. I'd really like to do something special for Anna, but I don't know what. Maybe I'll buy her some flowers. She loves flowers, but we've both been scrimping this summer, so we haven't gotten any lately. Speaking of school, there's only one month left until I start college. I'm excited.

I should probably stop writing and go clean the house. I've been a real slob all week. Anna's pretty neat. I usually am too, but I do have my messy days. I sure don't want to have to clean the house on our anniversary. Especially since I had to arrange to have the day off. I'm going to work Tuesday instead. Anna and I will have the whole day to ourselves.

Sunday, July 20, 1986

Wow! I had a wonderful time yesterday! I got up early and rode my bike to the florist to get some flowers for Anna. I found a really pretty arrangement with lots of lavender-colored flowers. Anna's favorite color is lavender. Mine is blue. Always has been, ever since I was little.

When I got back, Anna, whom I left in bed supposedly sound asleep, had decorated the house with banners that said things like "Happy Anna-versary!" and "I love you, Allie!"

On the coffee table was an envelope with my name written on it. Anna was nowhere to be seen. I opened the envelope and pulled out a little card. On the front was a drawing of two teddy bears playing with some alphabet blocks. Inside, the bears were sitting there smiling. They had put the letters together to spell, "I love you beary much." It was so cute! Anna had written a note inside that read, "Come back to the bedroom, my love. I want to share the fantasy I had about you two years ago."

That got my attention. So I walked to the bedroom and slowly opened the door (I had forgotten all about the flowers by that time). There I saw Anna lying on the bed on her stomach. She was propped up on her elbows reading something. She was very naked. She looked over her shoulder and said, "Ah, you're back. Come over here and sit down. I want to read something to you."

I laughed at that. "Your fantasy was to read to me?"

"Right! Come over here, silly. I want to read the fantasy I had about you on July 19, 1984. Then I would like to act it out with you, if you're interested."

I couldn't believe what she wrote about me. I would have melted on the spot, had I known back then what she was thinking. As it was, we both got so excited we ended up making love most of the day. It was wonderful. I can't begin to describe the ecstasy. Talk about reaching new heights! The woman is incredible. I love her so much!

Monday, July 21, 1986

I just read yesterday's entry. I made myself excited all over again. I forgot to finish writing about what we did the rest of the day, so I will now. After our little excursion into ecstasy, I led her into the living room (I made her close her eyes), so I could give her the flowers. She kind of squealed when she saw them. I could tell she liked them. Later we went to the restaurant where we had our first date. Little did we know what a wonderful thing was about to happen because of that day.

Tuesday, July 29, 1986

Sherri and Teddy came over last night. Somehow I think Sherri doesn't like to leave him, but she does like to show him off. He was pretending to be a drink-and-wet baby last night. It was kind of funny. I changed his diaper. Then he was hungry and wanted to nurse. Two minutes later, he was soaked again. I knew the kid was short, but not that short!

Friday, August 1, 1986

I think I will be glad to quit working at P.B. I guess it's okay for a first job, but the kids that hang around there are so immature. It's hard to believe I'm only a year or two older than they are. It seems more like five or six years' difference. I hope when I go to college I will find people who are more like me. Sometimes I feel like a real misfit around people my age. Anna said that she never quite fit in at high school either. Unfortunately, she also said that college wasn't much better for her. That doesn't sound very promising.

Saturday, August 2, 1986

Yes! I got a raise today. David, the owner of P.B., said that he really appreciated my hard work and good attitude. He said that I was the best worker he's ever had. He apologized to me for not giving me the raise earlier. He was going to put it on my last check, but he forgot. He's going to make it retroactive and add my back pay to my next paycheck. Woohoo!

He also said that he wanted me to come back next summer, if I can. I told him that I didn't know if I'd be in this area, but that I'd let him know if I were. He also said that if I came back, he'd start me at a dollar more an hour. As it is, I'm already making $4.00 an hour. Not bad for just pushing ice cream.

Sunday, August 3, 1986

Sherri and Teddy are coming over again tomorrow. I really enjoy their visits. Sherri is beginning to look happy for the first time in a long time. I'm really glad for her. She said that she might be bringing a friend along. I bet she's found a new boyfriend. I hope he isn't a creep. She's had enough bad luck with guys already.

Tuesday, August 5, 1986

Well, I'll be damned! Sure enough, Sherri and Teddy came over last night, accompanied by a friend. I didn't think too much about it when I saw that it was a woman. But then Sherri said that they were going to go out and actually leave Teddy with us. While that surprised me a little, I was even more surprised when Sherri looked over her shoulder as she was walking out the door and said, "It's been a long time since I've gone out on a date."

Then she winked at us and walked out the door hand-in-hand with Carol, her "friend." I nearly died. Anna and I looked at each other and cracked up. Then we both rushed out the door yelling stuff like, "Have a good time!" and "Don't do anything we wouldn't do."

Carol yelled back, "In that case, don't expect us until tomorrow morning."

We thought she was joking. When they returned, Teddy, Anna, and I were crashed out on the living room floor.

Thursday, August 7, 1986

Carol is a real clown. She, Sherri, and Teddy came over again last night. We had fun. We all played cards until late. Fortunately summer school is over, so Anna no longer has to get up early. We have a lot more time together now. She even bikes to P.B. to see me every day. I think she kind of likes me (smile).

Anyway, we didn't all play cards. Teddy giggled, smiled, and spit a lot. As much as that may sound like a tobacco-chewing, drunken old man playing cards, that wasn't the case. He did try to eat the jokers though. He's so cute!

I like being close to Sherri again. It feels really good. I never realized how much I missed her when we went our separate ways. I guess I was too wrapped up in self-pity because Anna was so far away.

Monday, August 11, 1986

Sherri, Teddy, and Carol came over again. We had fun. After Teddy fell asleep, we turned off all the lights and lit some candles. Then we all just cuddled and talked. Well, we cuddled in couples, not all four of us together.

It's kind of weird to see another lesbian couple kissing. It really turns me on though. I don't feel like that when I see a girl and a guy kissing. I see that all the time at P.B., but it doesn't have the same effect. Those kids are kind of like magnets. They just keep getting stuck together at the face because their hormones are so strong they overcome any opposing forces. There doesn't seem to be any real intimacy or relationship. It's as though heterosexual coupling is just another symptom of adolescence. You know, like pimples!

Wednesday, August 13 1986

One more week at P.B. I'm quitting a little early, so I can have some time to pack and catch up on my rest before we move. Anna has already packed the stuff we don't use every day. I'm excited about going to college, but I'm also kind of scared.

Friday, August 15, 1986

Sherri, Teddy, and Carol came over again. They're talking about moving in together soon. Anna told them that they were welcome to have any or all of the kitchen stuff she has already packed. We rarely use any of those things anyway. Sherri doesn't really have any stuff for living on her own. Carol is twenty-one and has been living with her older sister, so she has a few things, but not many. They're so cute together. I'm going to miss them when we leave. Too bad they can't move with us. I ought to talk to Anna. Maybe we could persuade them to move with us.

Sunday, August 17, 1986

Anna picked out our new apartment today. It's in a duplex that is vacant on both sides. We are trying to get Sherri and Carol to move with us. Sherri's not working right now anyway. Carol is an assistant manager in a fast food restaurant. She should be able to transfer easily enough.

They're planning to help us move, at any rate. Carol's father has a pick-up with a long bed and a topper. He said that we could use it as long as we return it with a full tank of gas. Sounds like a good deal to me. Anna is going to drive the pick-up. Carol, Sherri, and Teddy are going to haul some stuff in Carol's car. She's going to put Anna's bike rack on it and take our bikes too. I'm going to drive Anna's car, so I have to learn how to drive a stickshift between now and the twenty-fifth.

Monday, August 18, 1986

I thought I was going to wet my shorts laughing today. Anna took me to a big parking lot to teach me how to drive her five-speed. It was so funny! I'm beginning to get the hang of it, but starting out is a riot. It's easy once you get going. I like it better than an automatic. We're going to practice again tomorrow after I get off work. It will be my last day at P.B. Yes! I will be glad to get out of there. I like the money, and I don't mind the job for the summer. But I sure as hell don't want to make a career out of it.

Tuesday, August 19, 1986

I did much better driving today. I stalled out only once. Not bad for a rookie, right? And, NO MORE POLAR BEAR! You can't tell I'm excited, can you? Me, neither. I managed to save $550.00 this summer. I'm going to keep it in savings to use while I'm in college. I may buy a new bike, though, because my old one is worn out. I've had it for over seven years now. That's not too long really, but I've put an incredible amount of miles on the poor thing, and it wasn't even an expensive one to begin with. I think I'll go down to the bike shop and look around. I need to clean this messy house first though. Then I need to figure out what I am going to fix for supper tomorrow night. My parents are coming over for a farewell dinner.

Thursday, August 21, 1986

Mom and Dad came over yesterday. We had fun, as usual. It was quieter that normal though. I think we were all thinking about how much we are going to miss one another. My parents told me to call them collect every weekend. They want to know how we are doing. They also want to visit, once we get settled.

Mom is coming over today to take me to look for a new bike. Dad just got a raise and promotion, so he offered to help out with my new bike. Unfortunately, he has a meeting today and won't have any time off before we leave. Oops! I hear Mom's car coming up the drive now, and I'm not even dressed yet. Gotta go!

Friday, August 22, 1986

My parents decided to pay for my new bike. They said that they had expected to help me buy my first car. But I never got very interested in driving, so they figured it was only fair to buy me a nice bike. I could hardly disagree. I picked out a purple 18-speed mountain bike. It has much better brakes than my old bike. It's a much better bike altogether.

I'm sure going to miss them. Too bad they can't move with us too. Dad's job is just too good though, and the house is nearly paid for. Mom told me that they're thinking about buying a beach cottage so they can take lots of vacations without paying motel rates. That would be great. I know they love the ocean.

I seem to be rambling on and on. I don't know if this journal has improved my writing skills or if it just gives me a forum for self-expression. I do know that it helps me to see that even when things are bad, they tend to get better. Maybe not right away, but eventually. In any case, I sure enjoy it. Thanks, Mrs. Haze. Keep telling your students about journals. They do help. A lot.

Sunday, August 24, 1986

Tomorrow is moving day! I can't believe we're really going to do it. Of course, it's impossible to disbelieve it when you walk around this box warehouse. I don't think I have ever seen so many boxes! Of course, I've never really moved before. At least not that I remember. I was too little to remember moving here from Ohio. Anna has so many books! That's the one disadvantage of our book addiction. We ought to be able to win a bodybuilding contest by the time we finish moving all these boxes of books. Those things are heavy.

Friday, August 29, 1986

Whew! Moving to another state is a real project! I can't believe we're nearly moved in already. Anna is a one-woman moving crew. She picked out a nice apartment for us too. Once again I missed finding out how her system works. But she had lots of free time once summer school ended, and I was still working. Oh well, maybe next time. I thought at first that fireplaces were the key, but this place doesn't have one.

So anyway, we're moved in, and Carol has been job-hunting. She has an interview for an assistant manager's position here in town. It looks promising. I hope she gets it so they can stay here. Sherri and Carol both like the area, and there's a big yard where Teddy can play. The apartment isn't in a big complex. It's just one duplex set under some nice shade trees, well away from the road.

Sunday, August 31, 1986

I'll sure be glad when Sherri and Carol can move next door. I really miss our privacy. Carol got the restaurant job, so now they're negotiating with the landlady to rent the other half of this place. She said that she doesn't usually rent to people with children, but she's considering it since there is just one, and there is no husband to suggest that "more will be forthcoming."

What is wrong with this woman? I mean it isn't like the tenants in the other half of the duplex are going to complain. Anna thinks the landlady might be worried about a lawsuit, if Teddy got injured on her property. At any rate, the landlady is supposed to tell them tonight. Please let them get it! I want my Anna alone for a change.

Later--The answer is "yes!" As long as there is only one child. What does this woman think Sherri's going to do? Run down to the baby store and pick up another one? Take two, Sherri, since they're so small. Some people!

Tuesday, September 2, 1986

Sherri, Carol, and Teddy went back home to pack. We're going back this weekend to help them move. They will have Carol's father's truck, so we can get it all in one trip easily.

Meanwhile, Anna and I have started classes. I'm taking standard freshman classes: English, Algebra, World History, Biology, and Psychology. That's seventeen hours, including the Biology lab. I don't want to overdo it the first semester. Besides, I want to spend some time with Anna. She's taking two night classes.

It's funny to think of Anna as an English Lit major. Until this summer, I had no idea that she had a double major in college. She said that the P.E. had been more for fun and that she hadn't planned to teach it at first. I still have a hard time thinking of her as anything but a P.E. teacher though. I guess I will get used to it.

Monday, September 15, 1986

My Algebra class is totally boring. The professor is so full of himself that I can hardly stand it. At least I aced my first test. English is interesting. We're doing a lot of foundational grammar stuff, review really, and then we're going to start writing. Well, gotta go! I have a history test tomorrow. Yuk! I hate memorizing all that stuff. I like reading biographies of famous people in history, but dates and wars are so boring. My teacher was in the army during WWII. He brings it up all the time, even when we're discussing a different time period. His mind wanders a lot. So does mine once he starts talking about WWII because I know that stuff won't be on a test.

Saturday, September 20, 1986

Sherri, Teddy, and Carol seem to be doing well in their new home. Teddy is growing like a weed. Carol is doing well at work. Frankly I don't see how she can stand to work in fast food. I don't think I could stand to smell the grease all day. But at least she has a job that pays pretty well. I'm glad Sherri doesn't have to get a job while Teddy is this young. She enjoys him so much. She has talked about getting a job later, but not until he's older. She says that she doesn't want to miss out on all the new things he's learning every day. Babies are pretty amazing creatures. I had no idea they could be so interesting.

Monday, October 27, 1986

My how time flies! School has been really hectic. I'm doing fine though. I'm getting all A's so far. I like college a whole lot better than high school. One of the things I like best is that you don't have to have a pass when you leave class.

Plus, you have more choices as to what classes you take and when you take them. If you don't want to have early morning classes, you don't have to. Pretty cool, I think. I'm not much for mornings anyway, though I think Anna is more of a morning person. At least more so than I am.

Wednesday, November 12, 1986

I haven't had a lot of time to write in my journal lately. I have been really busy with my classes. Anna and I started playing tennis again too. We both need the exercise after a week full of studying. I miss doing my journal, but I have a lot of writing assignments in my English Comp class, so I'm getting plenty of practice. Last week I had to spend fifteen minutes describing a tree in minute detail. I picked this really strange looking tree in our backyard. It has lots of interesting twists and turns in it. I had fun writing about it. Maybe that kind of writing is something I could start doing in my journal for practice. For now, I get enough practice in my classes.

Monday, November 17, 1986

I really wish Sarah would jump off a cliff! She tracked Anna down again and is coming for another visit. Shall I leap for joy? I don't know why Anna agreed to let her come here. She knows I don't like Sarah. I wonder sometimes if Anna still loves her. I wonder who broke up with whom. She never said exactly.

Thursday, November 27, 1986

Guess who's coming for dinner? Yep, you guessed it, Sarah. I could puke! Maybe I will, right in the middle of the table. That would teach her. Unfortunately, it would also remind everyone how young I am. Not a good idea. Even so,

I wish she weren't coming. At least I had the brains to invite Carol, Sherri, and Teddy too. That should help anyway. Anna seemed really glad I suggested it. Who knows? Maybe she doesn't really want to see Sarah, but she hasn't the nerve to tell her so. It seems she has the courage to say or do anything, except when Sarah's around. Then she gets very quiet.

Friday, November 28, 1986

Last night was certainly entertaining. Sarah was rather shocked to find a full house when she arrived. Anna had not warned her that we were having other people over too. Sarah recovered well, however. I could almost hear her saying to herself, "Hmm. Plan B, I guess."

She sure is manipulative. I don't trust her any farther than I can throw her. Considering that she is several inches taller than I am, that wouldn't be very far. I'm not certain, but I think she was flirting with Sherri right under Carol's nose. I wouldn't do that if I were Sarah. I've been seeing signs of an explosive temper in that one. She said something kind of mean to Sherri the other day. She apologized later, but it didn't look very promising. I hope they don't break up. Then again, if she doesn't treat Sherri right, I'd rather they did break up. Of course, Sherri would be in bad shape if they did, since she's not working. Ugh! She'd probably have to move in here again.

Sunday, November 30, 1986

Never a dull moment around here. Sarah was over again for dinner, only not here exactly, next door. Apparently, Sherri invited her. This does not look good. I wonder if she's trying to move in on Sherri just so she can get close to Anna again. I really don't like the looks of things. Especially since I heard Sherri and Carol fighting this morning.

I'm glad Anna and I don't fight like that. We hardly ever fight. I'm glad, too. I don't think I could handle it, if we did. My parents got along really well. I guess I've always assumed I would get along with whomever I married. I'm glad we don't fight a lot. Life is too good to mess it up like that.

Later--I asked Sherri what was going on between her and Carol. She said that Carol is trying to read things into what isn't there. I told her that if she were referring to Sarah, then it is likely that things really are there. I also told her that if Sarah is moving in on her, then it is probably because she's trying to get close to Anna. I got a dirty look for that remark. Sherri told me that I was just jealous. Of whom, I wonder? Sarah? Yeah, but only in connection with Anna, not Sherri. I don't give a damn who Sherri sleeps with, as long as they treat her right. I don't think Sarah would. I think she's using Sherri. I don't trust her at all.

Monday, December 1, 1986

Welcome to another episode of "As the Stomach Churns." I'm really getting sick of all this. Carol and Sherri are still fighting. Sarah has been over there three nights in a row. Frankly, I don't blame Carol for being angry. Sherri is acting like a jerk. She's still trying to pretend that nothing is going on. Right! What really gripes me is that Anna won't talk about any of it. She just says, "It really isn't any of my business."

Like hell it isn't! Sarah is her friend, and Sherri is mine. We can't just let them screw everything up. What if Carol leaves, and Sarah moves in? Then Sarah can get back to Plan A, namely stealing Anna. This is not good for my sanity. Go away, Sarah!

Thursday, December 4, 1986

I knew this was going to happen! Carol moved out last night. In the middle of the night, no less. Nice timing, girls. She made such a racket that it woke Anna and me. We never did go back to sleep. I can't believe she did that. What on earth is Sherri supposed to do now?

Friday, December 5, 1986

Apparently, my question about Sherri has been answered. Sarah moved in today. What is this, anyway? Am I writing the script for this damned soap opera or what? Well, I'm not going to let Sarah have Anna. No way!

Sunday, December 7, 1986

I really need to get control myself. I jumped on Anna's case last night, and accused her of wanting Sarah back. I have never seen her that upset before. I thought she was going to explode. Instead she just clenched her fists until her knuckles turned white. Then she said, "How old will you be before you begin to see that I really love you and only you? I could have Sarah back right now, if I wanted her. She has been telling me that ever since she tracked me down last year. I do not want Sarah. I want you."

"Now I'm going to go ride my bike until I collapse. By the time I get back, hopefully, you will have grown up enough to carry on a rational conversation. In the meantime, I really need to go let off some steam. I love you, Allie."

Then she left. She said a lot more, but I can't remember it all. I'm afraid my brain shut down. I want to stop being jealous, but I don't know how. I really love Anna, and I honestly think I would die if I lost her. I would at least be miserable as hell.

I love her so much. Damn it! Why do I do these stupid things? Anna is such a wonderful person. Sometimes I have a hard time believing she is real. I know she isn't perfect. She gets moody and stuff especially just before her period. But somehow she always does the right thing. She always says the right thing.

Oh god! I hope she doesn't get in a wreck while she's out. What if she dies remembering me as a jerk? Oh please come back, Anna. I need you and I want you. I'll try to do better.

Tuesday, December 9, 1986

I feel as though I'm living in a war zone. Carol came back yesterday and let herself in with her key. She found Sherri and Sarah in bed. Nice touch, girls. It sounded like Carol was going to kill Sarah so Anna and I went over there and got her calmed down somehow. I could tell that she had been drinking a lot. She ended up passing out on our couch. What a nightmare!

Anna is blaming herself for this whole situation because she let Sarah come and visit again. I keep telling her that she didn't know this would happen. She keeps saying that she should have known, but I don't see how. Neither of us knew Carol drank that much or had a horrible temper. We both knew Sarah was manipulative, but I never dreamed it would get this bad.

Monday, December 15, 1986

Anna and I finally got a quiet evening to ourselves. We've been playing counselor to Sherri and Carol all week. Anna refuses to speak to Sarah right now. She's mainly concerned about Sherri and Teddy. She has even offered to start working again in order to support Sherri until she can get on her feet. She doesn't want her in the awkward position of having to depend on another unreliable lover for a home for herself and Teddy. Of course, I also think she wants to avoid having Sherri move in with us. We both value our privacy and our time alone. We need lots of it and a third and fourth party just wouldn't work.

Wednesday, December 17, 1986

I'm trying to deal with my anger towards Sarah. I have to keep reassuring myself that Anna and Sarah are not going to get back together. One side of me knows this is true. Unfortunately, there's another side of me that is a little on the crazy side. It keeps imagining Sarah and Anna in bed together. That's when I really lose it.

I've decided, though, that whenever I start to get upset or jealous, I will go ride my bike until I'm too exhausted to throw a temper tantrum. Then I can try to talk to Anna like a rational human being. She has always answered my questions honestly, so I know I can trust her to tell me the truth.

I want to talk to Anna about all this tonight when she gets home from class. I just hope we don't have to referee again. I'm really tired of this nonsense. Anna and I have spent so much time listening to Sherri and Carol gripe and complain about each other that we haven't had time for ourselves. I'm beginning to see why Anna kept saying that it wasn't any of our business. After all, there isn't anything I can do to make Sherri act sensibly. She's so stubborn. I've never been able to reach her when she has made up her mind about something. She refuses to see or hear anything else.

Thursday, December 18, 1986

I took my last exam today. I wasn't sure I was going to make it through finals week with World War III going on next door. I've really enjoyed my classes so far, but I'll be glad for some time off. We have four weeks before we have to start classes again. Yes! College is much better than high school.

Friday, December 19, 1986

Anna and I have been having some long talks lately. Of course, I'm probably doing most of the talking. I really want to get over this jealousy thing. I know Anna loves me. How can I miss it when it is so evident every day of my life? She has told me that she loves me and wants to spend the rest of her life with me, if I will have her. I would be an idiot if I didn't take her up on it. Of course, sometimes I think I am an idiot. I can't figure out how someone with such good grades can be such an empty-headed fool at times.

Anyway, Anna told me that she has a very special Christmas present for me this year. I have no idea what it is, but I have a feeling it is not a regular kind of present. I can't wait to find out, and yet I'm kind of scared too. I don't know why exactly. It may have been the tone of her voice when she told me about it. It seemed as though it were painful to talk about somehow. Yet she also seemed glad about it. I don't know what to do about a present for her.

Saturday, December 20, 1986

I went Christmas shopping tonight. I went into a dozen stores before I finally found something I thought Anna would like. It is a really nice edition of *A Tale of Two Cities*. Of course, it doesn't really express my feeling for her, but gifts rarely do. I just hope she likes it. I know it's one of her favorite books.

Tuesday, December 23, 1986

Christmas is almost here. I can hardly wait. We may even get snow tomorrow night. Now that would be great. I'm trying to do a lot of pleasure reading during Christmas break. I haven't been able to read much lately because most of my spare time has been spent refereeing and trying to get my own thoughts together. At least things have finally calmed down over there. Carol quit her job and moved back to her sister's house. Sherri and Sarah seem to be getting along okay. I still see Sherri a lot (when Sarah is working), but Sarah has made herself scarce. That, I think, is because Anna told her off. I'm not sure if it will be permanent, but I'm glad for the peace and quiet right now. At any rate, Sarah seems to be thoroughly engrossed in her new job and in Sherri and Teddy. She's actually good with Teddy, according to Sherri.

Sherri told me that Sarah has wanted a child for a long time, but she didn't want to have sex with a man in order to get one. Apparently she tried that once before with a gay friend, and it wasn't very successful. Somehow I can't see Sarah pregnant or nursing.

Wednesday, December 24, 1986

Anna and I are going to begin our celebration of Christmas tonight, since Mom and Dad are coming tomorrow afternoon. I'm making some vegetable soup in the slow cooker. Anna is going to bake some bread. I can't wait. The smell of the soup cooking is marvelous. It makes me feel warm and cozy inside. What really smells good though is Anna's bread when it is baking. That has got to be one of the most wonderful aromas in the world. Hurry up Anna and come home. I'm getting very hungry. She had to go to the store because she was missing an ingredient for her bread.

I'm getting really excited. I still haven't a clue as to what Anna is giving me for Christmas. I heard her wrapping something earlier today, but I don't know if it was my present. I wrapped hers last night and put it under our little tree.

Later--Dinner was wonderful. Anna makes the best whole grain bread. The soup was good too, if I do say so myself. We had dinner by candlelight as usual. Then Sherri and Teddy came over and invited us to their side of the house. We were warned that Sarah would be there.

We went over and had a really decent time together. Sarah was very loving and attentive to both Sherri and Teddy. I saw a gentle side to her tonight that I never would have dreamed existed. She has always seemed so hard, kind of like burnt bread. Tonight she looked more like one of Anna's tender dinner rolls with butter melted on top. I don't think it is just the season either. Something seems to have changed on a deeper level. It's a nice change. This new softness of Sarah's lets her physical beauty show through. Even her eyes look kinder. Anna noticed it too.

Thursday, December 25, 1986

Merry Christmas! I opened my Christmas present from Anna. Never in a million years would I have figured out what she had for me. The first present I opened was a blank book, like the ones I use for my journals. Only instead of containing a journal, it was filled with poetry, all written by Anna. The second present was a bundle of spiral-bound notebooks. These were Anna's journals from the past seven years of her life. She began keeping a diary as part of a Freshman English writing project. Apparently it was something she enjoyed doing because she never stopped. Last night she wrote the final entry then wrapped them all up for me to read.

In a card she wrote, "You have been puzzled by me for a long time so I thought it was time to share these books with you. I'm not really such an enigma, you know. I am simply a human being like you. I have deep emotions too, some of which threaten to wash me away in a flood of passion. I have fears and insecurities that are sometimes difficult to control. I hope that in reading these, you will come to know me better. I just hope you don't decide that I'm not so special after all. Merry Christmas, my love. Your Anna."

Later--I've been reading Anna's journals all day. It's hard to quit. I feel as though I'm meeting Anna all over again. I've decided to let Anna read my journals too. Hopefully we will come to understand one another better through this exchange. I hope she doesn't find mine boring and stupid. I write some of the dumbest things sometimes, but I never thought anyone would read my journals. Oh well, here goes. Goodbye diary. Hello Anna!

Part Two:
Anna's Journal

Monday, September 17, 1979

My name is Anna Karen Evans. I was named after my father's favorite literary character, Anna Karenina. I received this appellation on January 16, 1962, which was, of course, the day of my birth. My father was in the middle of teaching his Tolstoy class when my mother called him to go to the hospital. They never made it to the hospital, however, as I decided to make a surprisingly quick entrance into the world. My older brother Peter had been somewhat reluctant it seems, so my mother thought there was no need to rush with me.

Somewhere along the way, my brother and I switched personalities. He is now the bold one, while I am the shy one. Many times I have wished that I had not left the womb. Many times I have wished that I could go back. Every time I had to do an oral report, every time I had to meet new people, every time I had to try something new, back to the womb I would long to go.

I don't why I have been so shy all of my life. I am pretty average looking, so it isn't as though I have been teased about my physical appearance. I have blonde hair and green eyes. I take care of myself with good food and exercise, so I'm very healthy and physically fit. I inherited an excellent genetic code. My father is a genius; my mother is extremely intelligent. Perhaps my problem is that I got too much of a good thing. My intelligence has sometimes brought me alienation.

I've never overcome my shyness, though I am getting better at hiding it. I still tend to blush easily. I still get sweaty palms when I read aloud in class. I still avoid speaking in public whenever it is possible to do so without jeopardizing my grades.

Like many shy people, I enjoy solitary activities, such as reading and writing poetry. I like to read many different kinds of literature. What I read usually depends on my mood.

What I write depends on my mood as well. Sometimes I write poetry; sometimes I write prose. I write nonsense too, occasionally, just for comic relief. I don't usually allow anyone to read my writings (except assignments that teachers have to grade). My personal writings are far too private. I don't like to expose my thoughts and feelings to the scrutiny of others. I guess I am afraid of being rejected. Who isn't?

Wednesday, September 19, 1979

I have often tried to figure out the reason for my many fears. The only thing I can think of is that my fear may have something to do with my sense of "otherness." I have always been so different from everyone around me. I learn faster than most people. That, I'm sure, is a result of my excellent intellectual heritage. But why do I cry so much more than others? I can hardly blame that on adolescence, since it started earlier, much earlier in my life.

Another aspect of my "otherness" is related to my sexuality. I am a lesbian, and in spite of other people's attempts to make me ashamed of this part of myself, I am proud to be who I am. It is not easy to grow up being a lesbian though. All the books I read, all the movies I watch, and all the images I see exalt heterosexuality as the pinnacle of human experience. Yet in spite of all this, I have never been attracted to the idea of a heterosexual relationship. I guess that makes me a perfect Kinsey 6.

Thursday, September 20, 1979

When I was in the ninth grade, I had a crush on a girl named Stephanie. She was on the track team. I wanted to be on the track team too, but I was afraid to try out because of my height. I didn't think they would want such a short person on the team. All the runners I knew at the time were long and lean. While I am lean enough, I will never be long, not at 5'2".

Stephanie, on the other hand, was both. She looked like a runner. She carried herself like a runner. She always moved as though she knew precisely where she was going. She was headed for the finish line, and nothing and no one could stop her. I used to watch Stephanie running track after school. I sincerely doubt that she even knew I existed though, since I never had the courage to introduce myself. I was afraid she wouldn't like me if she found out I was gay.

At the beginning of my sophomore year, I learned that Stephanie had moved during the summer. I was devastated. Not so much because of my love for Stephanie, but because I had allowed my fear of rejection to hinder me from doing something I really wanted to do. I got over the crush soon enough, but I promised myself that I would never again allow fear to keep me from acting on my feelings.

Then halfway through my junior year, which was also my senior year because I graduated a year early, I met Tammy. She was a new student who had just moved to California from Eugene, Oregon. My homeroom teacher asked me to show her around school. So I did, and we became friends right away. She was shy at first, but I think that was mostly because she was new. She felt out of place in southern California. For some reason, I was not shy around her. I felt comfortable with her from the very first day. Perhaps I was trying so hard to help her overcome her feelings of awkwardness that I never had a chance to feel awkward myself.

Whatever the reason, we became best friends in a matter of days. Then one weekend we sneaked into an R-rated movie together. There were, as usual, many heterosexual love scenes. Putting myself in the leading man's shoes, I imagined what it would be like to kiss the leading woman. That didn't work very well, so I started fantasizing a full-blown love scene of my own, starring Tammy and myself. What startled me out of my private reverie was the touch of Tammy's hand on mine. We had been taking turns using the armrest situated between our seats, but suddenly we were sharing it instead.

I glanced at Tammy out of the corner of my eye to find her staring at me. My heart did a somersault. I turned and looked directly into her eyes. A spark leaped from her eyes into my heart, where it lit a fire that threatened to consume me. I leaned over and asked her if she'd care to spend the night at my house. She said that she could if she called her mother first.

We left the theater immediately and phoned her house. Then we went to my house, greeted my parents, and went straight to my bedroom. I locked the door after we went inside. Then I turned Tammy around, looked into her eyes and said, "Am I imagining things, or are you a lesbian?"

Tammy smiled. "Well, sort of, I guess. What about you?"

"Hell, yes. Why didn't you tell me?"

"I was afraid to. When I lived in Oregon, my mom and I lived in a small community of lesbians. Everything was very open there. I didn't know what to expect when we moved here."

"I suppose it would have been rather strange if you had introduced yourself as the new lesbian in town. That was a stupid thing for me to say. I'm just shocked. I never suspected."

Don't feel bad. My mom tells me I'm the most unlesbianlike lesbian she knows. But I can't help it. It's not like I try to hide it."

By this time the fire in my heart was beginning to get a little impatient. Finally I said, "I have to tell you something, but you have to promise not to laugh."

"I would never laugh at you, Anna."

"It's just that I have never acted on my sexual feelings before. I don't really know what to do. I have only read about lesbian love in a book my aunt gave me when I told her about my feelings."

Tammy admitted that she didn't know much either, except through talking to her mom and her friends. So we began where all lovers do — with gentle touches and probing kisses. As the night continued we learned a lot about each other and ourselves. As the months passed, we learned a lot about lesbian lovemaking.

I cannot say that Tammy and I were in love, although we definitely experienced passion. I think we were simply two young lesbians in need of a safe place to explore our budding sexuality. We filled this role for each other for about five months. Then Tammy and her mother moved back to Oregon. I've not seen her since, though we still write occasionally.

Friday, September 21, 1979

Now that I have written about my background, I suppose I should start writing about my present life. I haven't really wanted to write about my current feelings because I'm not doing very well these days. I'm a freshman in college, and I really miss my family. I knew I would get homesick, but I was hoping I would get over it quickly. I don't have any friends yet, so that doesn't help. I call my parents on the weekends, but I try not to talk long because I'm in Tennessee, while they're out in California. That can get expensive.

My roommate, Denise, is a pleasant enough person, but she is so man crazy it nauseates me. I can't spend very much time with her. Though I'm only seventeen, and she's twenty, I feel much older. I thought for sure that once I got to college I would find mature friends. I haven't had any luck thus far.

College is certainly not what I expected. My classes so far have been a repeat of high school. My faculty advisor told me to set aside two hours of study time for every hour of class. What a joke! I would have to work hard to stretch it out that long. Perhaps it will be more of a challenge as the semester continues.

Monday, September 24, 1979

Monday has come at last. I am not supposed to make journal entries on the weekends, according to my English professor. I'm not sure why, but I'll follow her guidelines for now. I have to write at least three times during the week. I guess I'll have to find something else to do on the weekends.

I talked to a couple of girls in the cafeteria today. They looked athletic, so I thought that they might be lesbians. Wrong! They are not even athletes. They just wear sports clothing for appearance's sake. I find that rather unfathomable.

Wednesday, September 26, 1979

I think I need a room to myself. Sharing a room with Denise not only drives me crazy, it also leaves me no time when I can be sure that I will not be disturbed. My body misses Tammy. For that matter, it misses me too. I really miss sleeping in the nude. Dorm life takes a toll on your love life, even if you have only yourself to love.

I hope I am not setting myself up for major embarrassment. Perhaps Dr. Miller is a speed-reader, and as she flips through our journals, she gathers information to use against us. Now that's a frightening thought. It makes me want to write so illegibly that she wouldn't be able to understand what I'm saying. Or I could write so small that she couldn't decipher it quickly.

Friday, September 28, 1979

I'm glad it's Friday. Denise is leaving for the weekend. I can sleep stark raving naked two nights in a row. Perhaps I should just lock my door, and spend the whole weekend in the nude. That sounds like fun. A little excessive maybe, but fun just the same.

Monday, October 1, 1979

I wish I could find some lesbian friends. I wouldn't even care if they were already coupled. I just need to be around some women who feel as I do so I can talk. I think Denise would freak out if I told her about my sexual preference. She's probably one of those idiots who think that gays go around attacking people of their own gender. Where do people get such bizarre ideas anyway? Obviously they think gay people have no taste.

Wednesday, October 3, 1979

I think I would like to see if I could get a different room. I wouldn't mind something smaller as long as it was a single room. I can't take much more of Denise and her whining. I don't think I could've picked a worse roommate if I had advertised for one. Even the way she sleeps makes me crazy. She doesn't snore exactly. She sucks in air between her teeth, which is much more annoying.

Thursday, October 4, 1979

I found out today that there's a waiting list for single rooms. I suppose I'll just have to suffer. Maybe Denise will go away every weekend. I am definitely not cut out to be celibate. What I miss more than anything else is cuddling. I miss the hugs and kisses of a lover. I don't necessarily miss Tammy. I just miss the little expressions of intimacy we shared. I miss the long talks. I miss having someone to do things with. Someone to go places with. It is ironic, though, because I am such a loner most of the time. I guess I can take being alone only so long.

Monday, October 8, 1979

Dorm life is about to drive me crazy. I'm having a hard time tolerating the stereo next door. If they must play their music loudly, why can't they at least wear headphones? That way they can damage their own eardrums, while leaving others in peace.

While I'm bitching about dorm life, I might as well mention the food. You'd think that a university of this size would have a few options for vegetarians. If I mention the lack of vegetarian fare to anyone, I invariably get the response, "Oh, but they do have a nice salad bar."

Do people really think that vegetarians want to eat salad all day every day of their lives? They must think we are just a bunch of rabbits. Well, I am feeling a little caged at the moment, and my nose is beginning to twitch. Maybe I should just hop on over to the cafeteria and nibble lettuce for a while.

Wednesday, October 10, 1979

I hereby declare this "National Bitch About Dorm Life Week!" Another thing I hate about dorm life is sharing a bathroom with a bunch of beauty queen candidates. One of the first mornings I was here, I had to brush my teeth in the communal bathroom because Denise was monopolizing the basin in our room. Still half asleep, I stood before the mirror, brushing away. Suddenly my mind was jarred into acute and painful consciousness by a clattering noise coming down the hall. It kept getting louder and louder. Then it came around the corner and invaded the bathroom.

I stopped in mid-spit and looked into the mirror. Into the bathroom came a woman carrying a huge cosmetic bag. When she started dumping out a bunch of bottles and tubes, I thought, just for a split second, that she was about to perform a chemistry experiment. But oh no, she started putting all that gunk on her face! Now I don't have anything against make-up. It was the method she used for applying it that befuddled me. Essentially she painted it on like a second layer of skin. I wouldn't have been surprised if she had taken a putty knife out of her bag and started using it to apply the stuff like spackle.

Unable to resist temptation, I took a close look at her face, as surreptitiously as possible, of course. It was a perfectly normal face, at least in the places that hadn't yet been covered in gunk. However, the normal face quickly lost ground, until suddenly — well, not really suddenly — until eventually, there emerged from the bathroom, a painted, plasticene woman. This woman looked so unreal I could hardly believe it. She looked like a mannequin. I concluded that the gunk monster had won that battle.

Friday, October 12, 1979

I'm going camping this weekend all alone. Just me, my bike, my camping equipment, and a good book or two. I can't take dorm life any more. I'm beginning to wonder if I'm cut out to be a college student. I don't have a problem with the classes or the homework, but I do have a problem with living in the dorm. I don't like living is such close quarters with all these people. I can never find a quiet place, a place of solitude. Solitude is something I need in large doses. If I can't find a little peace and quiet in the campground, I may as well give up trying and go back to California.

Monday, October 15, 1979

Camping was wonderful. I usually prefer to go a little more primitive, but I stayed in the state park camping area this time. I don't like going out too far by myself in a place where I don't have reliable contact people. If something happened to me, nobody would know for a long time. I don't even think Denise would know what to do if I didn't return on schedule. Besides, there's a good chance she wouldn't notice my absence. I am rather quiet and unobtrusive when I'm here. But then reading and writing don't require a lot of sound effects. Though I would have a hard time proving that theory in the library here.

Tuesday, October 16, 1979

I got a letter from my brother Peter today. He said that he remembered how lonely he was during his first semester in college, so he wanted to let me know he was thinking about me. That was sweet of him. We've always been pretty close. We did not fight much at all when we were growing up, though I'm sure I got on his nerves when I was little. I know my younger sister Christine was particularly talented at annoying me.

In some ways, Peter reminds me of our father (our biological father, that is, not our stepfather). He looks a lot like him, and he talks like him. I wish I knew my real father better. I was three when he and Mom divorced. I saw him after that, but not a whole lot. He lives somewhere in New York. Perhaps I should try to visit him, since I'm much closer now. This may be the only time I live this close to him. Thanksgiving is coming up soon. I think I'll call home and get his number. I wasn't planning to go all the way to California, anyway, but I definitely don't want to hang around the dorm during the holidays.

Wednesday, October 17, 1979

I think word has gotten around that I am intelligent. Unfortunately, Denise is in one of my classes. She asked me what I made on our last test. When I told her I got a 99, she nearly dropped her teeth. Then she asked me what my high school G.P.A. was, so I told her. Now the entire dorm seems to know.

This morning, while I was brushing my teeth (in the communal bathroom), in walked the Painted Plasticine Woman and her sidekick, Gunk Monster. She took one look at me then said with a smirk, "Oh gee, I've never seen a brain brush its teeth before."

I just smiled and said, "That's okay, you're the only person I've met who carries her face in a bag."

I gave one final spit and left. I just love dorm life.

Thursday, October 18, 1979

Life has taken on a new dimension now that I've been labeled as a "walking encyclopedia." I have perfect strangers (well, strangers anyway) approaching me with homework questions. Perhaps I should start a tutoring service and charge fifty dollars an hour. That might encourage everybody to do their own thinking. What's really ridiculous is that the questions I'm being asked are so easy that even if I didn't know the answers already, all I would need is five minutes of library research to find the answer. Thank you ever so much, Denise!

Friday, October 19, 1979

It has started to get chilly, but I think I'm going to go camping again this weekend. I need some time to do my own homework. I think I'll booby-trap my campsite. I'll keep a bucket of water poised above my tent door. Then if anyone tracks me down seeking help with their homework, I'll just yank on the rope and *voila*! Wet intruder.

Monday, October 22, 1979

I got my father's phone number and address from Mom last night. She isn't sure it's current, but it's the only one she has. I'm going to call next weekend, I think. I haven't heard from him in a long time. I wonder why he doesn't call much any more. He used to write and call fairly often until I started junior high. Then he really slacked off. I haven't heard from him in a couple of years even though he's paying for my education through a trust fund.

I've been thinking about him a lot lately. He always seemed so sad to me. When he used to visit, he would put a smile on his face, but I knew that was only for public display. I could tell he was really unhappy. Yet I didn't dare ask too many questions of someone I saw only once or twice a year. I was afraid he might not come back at all if I got too nosey.

I detested the toys he gave me. Not because there was anything wrong with them, but because they were such a poor substitute for a father. I wonder if he actually thought he could buy us off like that. I wanted a father, not possessions.

Wednesday, October 24, 1979

I got a letter from Peter today. He called Mom the same night I did. When he found out that I wanted to talk to Dad, he decided he'd better talk to me first. Apparently they write and call each other often. He told me that the reason Dad quit coming to visit was that he was afraid we would reject him once we were old enough to understand who he was. Peter didn't get very specific. All he said was that Dad would be delighted to hear from me, but that what he had to say may be a bit of a shock, so I should prepare myself. I'm so glad that I now have to wait until the weekend to find out. Nothing like a little suspense. Maybe he's a drug dealer or something. No wonder he could pay so much child support!

Friday, October 26, 1979

I'm not going camping this weekend. I'm going to call my father tonight. Then if I am still capable of it, I will spend the remainder of the weekend in the library. I have a research paper I need to finish writing. I got next to nothing done on it last night because of all the interruptions. I have to go to the library to study anyway. Otherwise I can't get any of my homework done. I sincerely doubt that the mind mooches know the way to the library.

Monday, October 29, 1979

Peter is such a riot. He had me worried for no reason. I finally reached Dad Sunday morning. He was ecstatic to hear from me. He apologized profusely for not staying in contact with me. He explained that he wanted a relationship with Peter and me, but only by our choice. I told him that it might have been a good idea to let us know that instead of just cutting off communications with us and then waiting to see if we ever tracked him down. We both started crying. I guess geniuses do stupid things in their personal relationships just like everyone else.

Speaking of relationships, I also found out that Mom and Dad got divorced because Dad is gay. That was the mystery Peter warned me about. That was the reason Dad drifted out of our lives. He was afraid we would be ashamed if we learned the truth about him. I can't believe Peter thought I would not be able to handle that juicy tidbit. I laughed at first when Dad told me. Then I had to explain quickly because I could tell that I had hurt his feelings.

He got really quiet then he said, "Honey, I'm not joking."

"Dad, I'm sorry. It's just that Peter wrote and warned me that talking to you might be a shock. I figured you had some horrible, dark secret to tell me. I had you pegged as being involved in something nefarious."

"So it's okay with you?"

I couldn't stop myself from laughing again. "Okay? Dad, I'm a lesbian. Shall I throw stones from my lavender-tinted glass house?"

He was thrilled. I heard him pull away from the phone and say, "Hey Buddy, guess what? My daughter's a baby dyke!"

Then he asked me if I had a lover. He was dismayed when he learned that I don't even know any other lesbians on campus. Anyway, he's sending me a picture of himself and Buddy, his lover. He's also going to send a plane ticket, so I can visit him during Thanksgiving break. I'm really looking forward to meeting Buddy. From what Dad said about him, he sounds like a colorful character.

Tuesday, October 30, 1979

I'm really excited about going to visit Dad. I think I need to have a talk with Peter. Apparently Mom never told him that I'm lesbian. I guess she figured I would tell him, and I figured she would. Neither of us did so he still doesn't know. I told Mom about my feelings the first year Peter went off to college, but I guess it never came up when he came home that summer, and I really haven't seen him much since then.

Thursday, November 1, 1979

Not only did Dad send me a picture of Buddy and himself, he also sent me a copy of his first novel. He has been writing under a pseudonym so we wouldn't discover his books accidentally and freak out. He warned me that it was pretty erotic, but he was sure I was mature enough to handle it. If I like this one, he's going to send me his other three published novels.

I think it's really cool that Dad is a published author. Mom mentioned years ago that he was a writer, but I had no idea that he had published anything other than musty old tomes. I wonder if Mom knows about the novels.

Friday, November 2, 1979

I just talked to Dad on the phone. He made all the necessary arrangements for Thanksgiving. I'm going to leave campus as soon as class gets out on Tuesday the 22nd. Dad will pick me up at the airport at JFK that evening. I'll be flying back Sunday evening. I'm really looking forward to my trip. Right now, though, I need to go to the library and do some research. Tomorrow I get to start Dad's book.

Monday, November 5, 1979

My research paper is nearly complete. I'll be glad when I'm done with it. I have a test tomorrow, so I need to review my notes before I go to bed. I've been having a difficult time getting to sleep lately though. I'm getting so anxious about my Thanksgiving trip. I can't believe I'm actually going to spend all that time with my real father. It feels strange after not hearing from him for several years.

Wednesday, November 7, 1979

I saw a couple of lesbian suspects today. They were playing tennis. I stopped and watched them briefly from afar. Since I'm not that good at tennis, I didn't want them to ask me to play with them some time. I wouldn't mind taking up tennis again, but I would have to do a lot of practicing before I would feel comfortable playing against anyone. But then, it's rather hard to get in a good practice session by yourself.

Friday, November 9, 1979

I'm going camping again tonight. I've had about all I can take of this campus. I'm really getting perturbed with the way people gather in the library to gossip. I think I might check into getting a private study carrel. So far, the only place I have found where I can study without constant interruptions is the campground. Too bad I can't just stay out there all the time. At this point, I think I would rather live in my tent than in this dorm. Unfortunately, I may not be able to go camping much longer. My sleeping bag isn't warm enough for really cold weather.

Monday, November 12, 1979

Camping was great, but I got cold this time because my coat was too thin. My sleeping bag was adequate, surprisingly enough. I enjoy the privacy and solitude, so I want to go as long as I possibly can. Perhaps I should ask Mom to buy me a heavy winter coat for Christmas. That would help immensely.

I got my airline ticket today in the mail. I'm getting more and more excited about Thanksgiving. I guess I'd better stop thinking about it though. I need to study for my Psychology test. Memorizing my itinerary will not be very helpful, I'm sure. I don't think my teacher is interested in knowing how much time I will have to change planes in Atlanta. I still can't figure out why I have to fly down there in order to catch a plane to New York. It seems rather stupid to me. When I mentioned it to Denise, she said, "Honey, if you die while you're living in the South, you'll have to change planes in Atlanta just to get to heaven."

Wednesday, November 14, 1979

I'm glad I took my Psych test before I got sick. I feel like death today. On second thought, I don't think I feel that good. I haven't been able to keep anything down since breakfast. I don't think I like being sick here. If you can't get up to do something for yourself, there's no one who can do it for you. Where's my mother when I need her most?

Friday, November 16, 1979

Denise left this morning to spend the weekend elsewhere. At least I can have some privacy while I try to regain my strength after this bout with the flu. I put a "Do not disturb!" sign on my door. Underneath it I wrote, "I am very contagious." Otherwise the mind mooches would knock regardless. So far they haven't bothered me.

Instead a woman named Debi slipped a note under my door. It read, "I'm sorry to hear that you're sick. If I can do anything, just leave me a note on your door. I'm a nurse. Room 211. Debi."

So I left her a note saying, "I could use some decent food. Please come in when you have a moment. Thanks, Anna."

Around 3:00 p.m. I heard a faint knock, then the door opened, and an inquisitive face peered in at me. In the sweetest sounding southern accent, she asked if she could come in. I said, "Sure, as long as you're Debi."

She smiled a gorgeous smile and slipped into the room, carefully closing the door behind her. We talked for a little while before I dispatched her to the nearest health food store for some vegetable soup. She's definitely a nurse. She has a gentle nature. It was pleasant to have someone helping me for a change. I hadn't realized how much it had drained me emotionally to have to answer everybody's questions or go out of my way to avoid them. I wish I knew how to get them to leave me alone.

Debi was so sweet and helpful. I paid her for the soup and the freshly baked bread she bought me, but she wouldn't take any money for gas. She said that she was going out anyway, so I needn't bother. Unfortunately her act of kindness (or perhaps it was the flu) has triggered a serious case of self-pity and depression. Debi made me realize how lonely I am. I really would like to have a friend or two. I think I will at least send Debi some flowers for being so kind. I can't really think of any other way to express my appreciation.

Monday, November 19, 1979

I sent a small basket of flowers, with a note of thanks, to Debi's room. I don't know if she has received it yet. I hope she doesn't get offended that a woman is sending her flowers. I certainly don't mean it in a romantic way, just a friendly and appreciative way.

I'm feeling healthy again, at least physically. I'm still a little on the depressed side. I'm glad I'm going to Dad's house for Thanksgiving. I don't think I could stand to hang around here by myself.

Mom called yesterday to see how I was doing. She knew I had been sick, so she just wanted to make sure I was getting well. She was worried about me. I miss her a lot, but California is way too far away to go for a long weekend. But the semester will be over before you know it, and I'll be flying home for Christmas.

Monday, November 26, 1979

I had a blast in New York. Dad lives on Long Island, but commutes three days a week via train to New York City to teach his Literature classes. I managed to finish his book on the plane trip. It was really good. He gave me copies of the other three. He's working on another book right now, but it will be several months before it is finished.

Tuesday, November 27, 1979

I really enjoyed talking with Dad. We had a long talk about his little vanishing trick. He said that he was doing what he thought was best. He didn't want us to be ridiculed for having a "fairy" for a father. I think he must have suffered a lot over the years. He didn't seem to want to talk about that though. I'm glad I have the chance to get to know him now. It hurt deeply when he stopped calling and visiting. I was afraid I was the reason for his sadness. Now I know he was sad because he was lonely and depressed. He missed us, but he knew he could not pretend to be someone he wasn't. I still think he should have told us. I could have handled it. It would have been a lot easier to know the truth than to be left wondering, blaming myself for his abandonment.

Wednesday, November 28, 1979

I went for a bike ride today. When I came back, I ran into Debi in the hall. She thanked me for the flowers. She had gotten them last Tuesday, but didn't have a chance to come by until after I left for New York. She invited me to go with her to the basketball game Friday night. Her boyfriend is on the team. I'm not very interested in men's basketball, but there will be a women's game first. I love to watch women's basketball.

Monday, December 3, 1979

I finally discovered another lesbian. Her name is Sarah Jacobs, and she's the freshman star of the women's basketball team. She's pretty good looking too—wavy blonde hair, athletic limbs. She is, of course, long and lean. And she can sure shoot hoops! While I was sitting in the gym waiting for the game to start, I overheard two guys talking about the lesbian "jocque" on this year's team. From their conversation, I learned her name and jersey number. So I scoped her out, watched her every move, and lusted a lot! Seriously, though, I would at least like to get to know her well enough to find out if there are any other lesbians here. There must be, but I have no way of finding them. I certainly can't assume that all female athletes are lesbians.

I called Dad to tell him about Sarah. He told me to corner her and not let her get away until she gave me the names of at least five other lesbians on campus. I reminded him that she too is a freshman and may not know any more lesbians than I do.

"Oh, no," he said. "There is a big difference. She's a known lesbian, and you're not. Women will flock to Sarah the way you are planning to do."

He does have a point.

Wednesday, December 5, 1979

I saw Sarah Jacobs in the cafeteria today. She was eating a hamburger, so she's definitely not vegetarian. That's not a problem though, as far as I'm concerned. She was sitting with two other women, both from the basketball team. They look like they might be lesbians too, though they may not have figured that out yet.

Thursday, December 6, 1979

I saw Sarah again today. She was walking across campus. I really want to approach her, but I don't know how to go about it. This reminds me of the situation in high school, when I was trying to meet Stephanie. Only this time I'm not going to let the woman get away. Knowing for certain that she's a lesbian makes it easier, but I'm still nervous about it. I'm not very good at meeting people. I do all right once I'm in the situation, but thinking about approaching someone who doesn't know me scares the hell out of me.

Tuesday, December 11, 1979

This is the last week of classes. Finals start Monday. I'll be glad when it's over. This has not been the best semester of my life. I still haven't figured out what to do about Sarah. I think I need to get Dad to coach me. Maybe I can talk him into coming down and orchestrating a meeting between Sarah and myself. He's awfully good at that in his books. Perhaps it would work in real life.

Wednesday, December 12, 1979

I biked for a long time today. It was sunny and fairly warm, so I took advantage of it. I stopped by the tennis courts again to watch that same pair of women. I actually watched them up close this time. I even shagged a stray ball for them. I think they might be lesbians, but it's so hard to tell. It could just be wishful thinking.

Friday, December 14, 1979

Now that the semester is over, I no longer have to keep a journal. I like it though, so I want to keep writing when I can. I think I will splurge and throw in an occasional Saturday or Sunday entry. How positively daring of me! Sometimes I amaze even myself.

Monday, December 17, 1979

The game Friday night was okay. Unfortunately Sarah was injured, so she rode the bench. Ah well. Next time, I suppose. Next semester actually. I just hope Sarah returns. I will be really perturbed if she leaves before I get up the nerve to talk to her.

Well I suppose I should do some studying. I had two tests today. I have one tomorrow, and two Wednesday. Then I will be finished. I'll be flying out of here Thursday. It will be strange to be in California again. I bet it will be warm. I think I like the climate here better. I like the cool weather. I hope it snows next semester.

Wednesday, December 19, 1979

All right! I'm finally finished. I can't wait to get out of here. Denise is leaving tonight. I'm really glad I have one last night alone. I'm going out to eat with Debi and her boyfriend, Mike.

Thursday, December 20, 1979

Debi and Mike are going to drive me to the airport this afternoon. I'm actually going to be sweating tomorrow. Traveling by jet can be so strange. One day I'm cold and shivering in Tennessee; the next day I'm in Southern

California, sweating by the side of the swimming pool. Talk about two different worlds.

I've decided not to write in my journal over Christmas vacation, unless I get really bored. Since I can't imagine that happening, this is most likely my last entry until 1980. It's hard to believe it will be a new decade when I return.

Monday, January 14, 1980

Back to my journal at last. I definitely did not get bored over Christmas break. Peter was home too, so we did some catching up. He was floored when I told him I was a lesbian. He said, "Well, cool! I have a radical dad and sister too."

I told him that I didn't think either of us was trying to be radical. We are just being who we are. If that seems radical, it is only because our society has placed undue emphasis on heterosexuality as the norm.

Anyway, we had a good talk. Mom asked me a lot of questions about Dad. She was very interested in my New York trip. I think she still cares about Dad. I can imagine how difficult it must have been for my parents to face all that. Dad told me that he still loves Mom, and that he never would have left her if his homosexual feelings had not made it impossible for him to stay. He has never cared for any other woman.

If it weren't for the fact that they both seem happy now, I would feel that it was all very tragic. I'm certain it felt that way during the break up. They're both such decent people. I've never heard either of them criticize the other in any way. On the contrary, they speak highly of each other. I wonder if Dad will come around more now that I know everything. Maybe my parents can renew their friendship. I hope so.

Tuesday, January 15, 1980

In a way I'm glad to be back at school. I enjoy studying. I think I may even have at least one class to challenge me this semester. I'm taking a couple of literature classes, which will require a lot of reading. I'm not really sure what to major in, but since I am merely a freshman, I suppose that decision can wait. In the meantime, I think I'll go say "hello" to Debi. This is her last semester.

Wednesday, January 16, 1980

Today is my eighteenth birthday. I realize this is supposed to be a watershed moment, but it rather loses its punch, I think, when you graduate from high school early. Too bad I don't have anyone to share it with me. Dad sent a check and a letter with my birthday card. He told me that if I decided there was nothing for me here, he was sure the "Big Apple" could provide plenty of forbidden fruit for me.

I may take him up on it, but I think I need to stick it out here for a year at least. After all, it's not completely bad. I like the moderate climate, not too hot or cold. I'm afraid I'd freeze my California butt off in New York!

Thursday, January 17, 1980

I got a birthday card today from Mom, et al. I also got one from Tammy. I'm surprised she remembered. She's still in high school. Her letter made me realize just how different our lives are now. There are some disadvantages to graduating early.

I think I might continue the practice of weekday journal entries, even though it is no longer an assignment. That, in itself, is a discipline. Sometimes it is difficult to hold off until

Monday, but I think it is good to do so. I'm sure I would be more morose on the weekends. At least on the lonely ones.

This semester has shown one improvement so far. The stereo level has been more tolerable. Perhaps I just lucked out last semester and got assigned to the same hall as somebody whose life ambition was to be a disc jockey. At least I don't live in one of the co-ed dorms. I've heard that they're even more rowdy.

Friday, January 18, 1980

There's a basketball game tonight. I think I shall go and lust after Sarah Jacobs. Better take a towel along, since my drooling gets a little excessive sometimes. Speaking of towels, I'd better get my P.E. clothes out of my gym locker. I really need to include them in my laundry tomorrow. Oh dear. You know your life has reached a deplorable level of boredom when you start writing about your laundry. Time to stop writing before I launch into a descriptive essay on sharpening my pencils or combing my hair.

Saturday, January 19, 1980

Okay, okay, so I'm breaking my first commandment of journal writing. But you've got to hear, excuse me, read this one. At last, something worth writing about! I think I am still in shock. Are you sitting down? Good. Here goes. I went to the women's basketball game, right? I lusted after Sarah Jacobs, right? Am I going too fast for you to follow? No? Good. Is the suspense killing you? Too bad.

You will recall, I presume, the exciting news that I needed to retrieve my gym locker's contents in order to provide a full load of laundry and prevent myself from being inducted into the World's Smelliest Athletes Society. Little did I know how significant a bundle of dirty clothes would become. Ha! I love it!

If you haven't died of curiosity yet, keep reading. It only gets better. Of course, it could hardly get worse, right? You are so impatient for a journal, you know that? What do you mean you've been waiting for months to read something interesting? You are a rude little journal, aren't you? Okay, okay, I'll finish.

I trotted my drooling self over to the locker room after the game. I knew it would still be unlocked, since the players have to use it. Well, just as I rounded the corner where my locker is, I ran smack-dab into Sarah Jacobs herself in the flesh. And when I say "in the flesh," I truly mean in the flesh! She had just taken a shower and discovered that her cute little teammates had swiped her clothes. What children! All I can say is, "Wow! What a body!"

As we quickly disentangled our limbs, I said, "Oh! You're Sarah Jacobs."

I know, I know. You're saying to yourself, "Quick thinking, Anna." But seriously, what do you say to a naked lesbian? Especially if she's been the star of your fantasies for the past couple months.

She said curtly, "Yes, I am."

Then she proceeded to fumble for several minutes with the combination lock on her locker, until she realized that it was not her lock, though it was her locker (part two of the practical joke). Suddenly, we heard peals of female laughter coming from the next aisle. Then several feet were heard sprinting out the back door.

"Do you need some help?"

"I'm afraid so. My friends seem to think that it will be funny if I have to walk bare-assed back to my dorm in the cold. I don't suppose you have any spare clothes on you."

"Ah, the damsel in distress. Yes, certainly, my lady, I also have a trusty steed waiting outside to whisk us away. But I suppose I must clothe you first."

I tossed her the dirty sweats from my locker.

"I'm afraid they may be a little aromatic. I was just coming to escort them to the land of Maytag, where they were to be flogged by the cruel tyrant, King Tide."

Sarah laughed. "Well, at least I get to be rescued by a humorous knightess in shining armor."

As she dressed (yes, I admit it, I watched every move she made), she said, "So I'm Sarah Jacobs, damsel in distress, and you are?"

"Many apologies," I replied. "Any knightess worth her mettle should know enough court etiquette to introduce herself. It's just that I don't often get this pleasure--I mean, this has never happened before. In any case, I'm Anna Evans."

"Nice to meet you, Anna Evans. I'm glad it has been a pleasure for someone besides my funny friends. Frankly, it has been a bit embarrassing for me. I don't suppose you would care to help me get even."

"Sure. Though I'm afraid I couldn't view it as revenge. They did me a favor, you see."

"Excuse me? Don't tell me my knightess in shining armor is actually a co-villainess."

"Oh, no. It's just that I've been trying to find a way to introduce myself to you without coming on like an awestruck fan. I've been watching you play all season. You're really good."

"Gee, thanks. Should I autograph your sweats before or after I wash them?"

"Don't bother washing them. I think I'll preserve them as they are, for posterity's sake."

"With me in them?" She asked with a mischievous twinkle in her eye.

"Actually, I prefer you without the sweats." (I can't believe I said all this!)

"I take it then, Anna Evans, that your observation of me has been more than a purely athletic appreciation."

"Definitely. I, well, I heard that you are a lesbian. Is that true?"

"Very true. And yourself?"

"Need you ask after this conversation?"

Sarah really laughed then.

"No, I guess not. I have to admit that you have a unique way of introducing yourself."

"Me? You're the one who flung yourself `bare-assed' into my arms. Or have you forgotten that part?"

"Jesus, I was sure trying to, but I guess I won't live that down for a long time."

Then the awkwardness of the situation descended upon the conversation, rendering us momentarily speechless. Finally, Sarah said, "So, do you want to get some coffee or a coke? After I change my clothes, that is."

"Sure. Do you want to meet me somewhere, or shall I follow you to your room and have the pleasure or watching you change your clothes again?"

"Jesus, you're bold!"

"Actually, I'm neither."

"Neither what?"

"I'm neither bold nor Jesus."

She cracked up at that one. Then she invited me to her room to watch or not watch but at least to wait while she changed into some better smelling togs.

"Here, have some smelly sweats," my damsel said, throwing my odiferous attire in my face. "I can't say that I blame you for banishing them to King Tide's tyranny, but they sure spared me the awkward experience of streaking across campus. I don't think that sort of thing is in vogue any more."

"At least not at this time of the year."

Once she was fully dressed and no longer quite so vulnerable, I retrieved my shyness and stuttered, "I-I'm sorry about teasing you about all this."

She laughed again. She seems to laugh a lot. Of course, she may have just been embarrassed still. Then she said, "That's okay. But seriously, you will help me get revenge, right? I can't let this slide."

"Oh sure. Why not? I'm not much of a prankster, but I suppose there's a first time for everything. Do you have anything in mind?"

"Not yet. Let's go conspire over coffee."

So we went to an all-night diner. She ordered coffee. I got hot water for the herbal tea bag I had stuffed in my jacket pocket. We stayed there for a couple hours. We left only because we were both so bleary-eyed we could hardly see. Neither of us is accustomed to staying up late.

Needless to say, I slept until noon today. I probably would've slept longer if Denise hadn't come in and slammed the door. She'd just had a fight with her boyfriend. I can't say that I was very sympathetic.

Monday, January 21, 1980

I saw Sarah across campus today. I don't think she saw me though. But that's all right, I'll see her some time soon because we have to execute our plan to even the score. It's so nice to have a friend. It's especially nice knowing that she's lesbian.

Tuesday, January 22, 1980

Sarah came by my room today while I was in class. She left a note on my door asking me to come to her room at 6:00 p.m. tonight. I'll have to look closely at my social calendar to see if I can squeeze her in. Oh good! I see that she's in luck. I am free tonight at six.

Thursday, January 24, 1980

Sarah is pretty certain now who the pranksters were. She wants to wait awhile though, until they relax their guard. She wants them to think she's not going to pay them back. Our plan will work much better if we maintain the element of surprise. She wants to get together after the game tomorrow night. It's an away game, but she said I could ride in her car, if I don't mind getting there early. I can just bring a book and read while I wait. I have lots of reading to do anyway.

Monday, January 28, 1980

This weekend was fun. I enjoyed being with Sarah. She laughs a lot, but I think that deep down she has a lot of hurt. I get the feeling that her family life is not very good. She's a bit older than I am, even though she's a freshman. She worked for a few years after high school. I'm not certain, but I think she's twenty.

Well, I really need to study for a test now, so I guess I'd better shut up about Sarah. Thinking about her won't help me on my biology test.

Thursday, January 31, 1980

We worked out the details of "Operation Revenge." Tomorrow is the day of reckoning. I can't believe I'm actually going to go through with this. I hope I'm not going to regret agreeing to help Sarah get revenge. I don't exactly have a reputation for being a practical joker. I'm not particularly interested in acquiring one now.

Friday, February 1, 1980

Ha! We got them bad. They never expected Sarah to have an accomplice, so we caught them completely off guard. During the last part of the game, I went into the locker room to set everything up. Sarah was, of course, still playing so they didn't suspect a thing.

All three of the pranksters invariably shower in consecutive stalls, so it was easy to set them up. I ran a long, thick wire through the hooks of the shower curtains, looping it around the curtain rods. When they were all lathered and shampooed, I pulled the wire with all my strength, and yanked the curtains down.

Meanwhile Sarah stood there with a Polaroid camera snapping away. She has one of those cameras that develops the film immediately. It was so funny to see the looks on their faces. Sarah is keeping the photographs as a form of blackmail. She told them that if they try any other cute stunts, she would post the photos in strategic places around campus.

They agreed to a truce. Then we helped them put the curtains back up so they could get the shampoo out of their eyes. I have to admit that I had a good time. I've never done anything like that before, and I doubt I ever will again. Still it was funny, and it did work. Of course, it was rather titillating to see all three of them "bare-assed" too. Personally I think Sarah's body is the most attractive, but then I think I'm getting more and more partial in that department.

Monday, February 4, 1980

What a weekend! Apparently I wasn't the only lonely lesbian on campus. Sarah has no lover either. Though I suppose I should say that she had no lover. I'm afraid she does now — me! I think I was beginning to forget how good it feels to be with a woman. I've been flying solo for so long.

Too long! But, oh how sweet is the re-initiation into the world of lesbian love. I can tell Sarah knows a thing or two. She's rather wild, which is totally opposite of Tammy.   With Tammy, I spent a lot of time drawing her out. With Sarah, I have to worry about keeping up with her. I think she's been with a lot of women. I hope I can live up to her past experiences.

Wednesday, February 6, 1980

Sarah's roommate is leaving for the weekend this Friday. I am going to spend the entire time with Sarah. I'm really looking forward to it. It's difficult for us to express our feelings towards each other when our roommates are around. Her roommate knows she's a lesbian, but we still don't feel comfortable around her.   My roommate doesn't know anything at all about me. Of course, I wonder sometimes if she knows anything at all about anything. Behave yourself, Anna! You must at least try to be nice.

Friday, February 15, 1980

I can't believe I'm slipping up on my journal writing. Well, perhaps I can believe it.   I'm afraid I'm a little preoccupied. I guess it's just one of those things. Those who can, do. Those who can't, write about their laundry.

Monday, February 18, 1980

Unfortunately both of our roommates were around for most of the weekend. Luckily though, Denise had a date with her boyfriend last night. So while Denise was away, the dykes did play! Sarah is such a fun lover.

Tuesday, February 19, 1980

I have a research paper that needs to be written. I think I hate school now. I really want to be with Sarah. I think I'm in love. I know I'm in lust anyway. It's not quite the same thing, but it will have to suffice for the present. It's infinitely better than being alone all the time. Being with Sarah is so different from being with Tammy. With Tammy, I felt as though I was gently leading her. With Sarah, I feel as though I've totally lost control. I just fly along behind her barely holding on for dear life.

Thursday, February 21, 1980

It's not the easiest thing in the world to study when Sarah keeps running her hand up the inside of my thigh. When we went to the library today, we found a study carrel vacant, with no one else nearby. That was a big mistake. I got very little accomplished. I'm getting the distinct impression that Sarah isn't the most studious person. She's here on an athletic scholarship. Apparently sports are all she cares about. Oh well, I guess you can't have brawn, beauty, and brains all in one body.

Denise will be gone this weekend. What a tragedy. I guess I'll just have to invite Sarah to stay with me. I've given up trying to study on weekends when we have a chance to be alone. It's a good thing our weekly schedules are so varied. I would not be able to study otherwise.

Monday, February 25, 1980

I think Denise is beginning to suspect that my relationship with Sarah is not limited to giggles and boy-talk. Well, Denise, it is time to grow up and face the real world. Not all women throw themselves at men's feet. Some of us throw ourselves at women's feet. Personally I have higher aims in life. I throw myself at women's breasts. Anna, you are very naughty!

Tuesday, February 26. 1980

Denise definitely suspects something. She was hinting around about how "masculine" Sarah is. To begin with, she isn't masculine; she's athletic. There is a difference. This society has such stupid ways of categorizing people. We're all lumped together into two groups, male and female. If a male isn't muscular, or doesn't walk with a swagger, he's effeminate. If a woman isn't prissy, doesn't wear make-up, and swing her rear, then she's called "butch" or "tomboy." Everything has to be one way or the other. Why can't we be a little bit of both, if we so choose?

Wednesday, February 27, 1980

Denise started hinting around again last night about Sarah. Finally, I just said, "Look, Denise, I'm a lesbian. I'm sorry if that isn't okay with you. But if it isn't, that's your problem, not mine."

Her face turned pale. It was comical. Then she suddenly grabbed her coat, and left the room without saying another word.

Thursday, February 28, 1980

Now the whole dorm knows that the "Brain" is a also a dyke. I never cease to be amazed at the small-mindedness of some people. I guess I should've expected this to happen sooner or later. Sometimes I wonder why I ever decided to go to school in the South. I just can't imagine this being such a big deal at a California university. What was I thinking?

Friday, February 29, 1980

Denise is leaving again this weekend, but not before she moves into another room. One of her friend's roommates didn't return this semester, so she's moving in with her. She said to me, "It's nothing personal. I just think it's for the best. We don't have anything in common anyway."

I was most relieved to hear that.

Monday, March 3, 1980

Not only did Sarah spend the weekend here, but she's also asking to transfer to this dorm so she can share my room. That will definitely make life easier for us. I have no idea what I'm going to do about studying. But surely if we live together we won't always have to be together.

Wednesday, March 12, 1980

I guess I've been rather busy lately. What can I say? This school has definitely become more appealing. Dad wrote and asked how I was doing. I think I'll call this weekend to let him know how things are progressing here.

Wednesday, March 17, 1980

I talked to Dad last night. He was thrilled to hear about Sarah. He even talked to her on the phone, though she won't tell me what he said.

Saturday, April 19, 1980

I'm not doing too well with my journal writing. But something has to go, and I'm trying my best to make sure it isn't my G.P.A. I think Sarah has a very strong sex drive. It's really ironic. When your life gets more interesting, you no longer have time to write about it because you are too busy doing those interesting things. I'd rather have an interesting life though than a journal filled with mundane details of a boring life. I wonder if it's possible to have an interesting, yet slower-paced life. Certainly not with Sarah around. I guess that is the price I have to pay. It beats being lonely.

Thursday, May 1, 1980

Next week is finals week. I can't believe my freshman year is almost over. It went by so quickly. This semester did anyway. I'm going to miss Sarah. Her mother lives in Texas. That's a long way from California.

Monday, May 5, 1980

Dad invited Sarah and me to spend the summer with him. Mom said it was all right with her, as long as I come home for a couple weeks before I go back to school. Sarah is thinking about it. She's never been to New York. Dad has offered us both jobs as his personal assistants. He needs someone to type his new manuscript because his secretary is going to have a baby. She's going to take the summer off.

Wednesday, May 7, 1980

Dad has now officially hired Sarah and me. He needs us both twenty hours a week. He's going to pay us hourly, and we can make our own schedule. I think it will be interesting work. I'm certain that our free time will be interesting. There are so many things to do in New York.

Monday, August 25, 1980

Back to school at last. I thought about keeping a journal this summer, but never had time to do more than just think about it. Sarah and I definitely took a bite out of the "Big Apple." Dad is a riot a minute. He seems so happy now. No, he's not happy; he's exuberant! When I mentioned it to him, he said that his final fear had been banished now that I know and love him. How could I not love him? He's a wonderful person. Buddy, his partner, is great too.

Friday, August 29, 1980

Sarah and I are sharing a room again this semester. It makes life easier for us. We get along fairly well, even though our interests vary quite a bit. Sarah is trying to talk me into getting involved in sports this year. I'm not really very good in groups, so I might go with tennis. I wouldn't mind improving my game.

Dad, Buddy, and Sarah are all great tennis players, so I got lots of pointers this summer. I'm playing a lot better now. We went to a couple of tournaments in New York this summer. I enjoyed myself thoroughly. Too bad school starts so early. I wouldn't have minded attending the U.S. Open. That would have been great. Oh well, I couldn't afford the time off from school to stay long enough for that.

Anyway, I think I will join the tennis team. Basketball is a little too aggressive for me, and I like my knees too much to hurl them at the ground just to return a volleyball. Besides, there are too many other players on a volleyball team to deal with all at once. In tennis, even when you're playing doubles, there are only four people to consider.

Saturday, August 30, 1980

I've got a full load again this semester. I can't say I've been challenged yet. Dad has been encouraging me to take more literature courses. He's obviously biased, but he thinks I'll enjoy them, if I can get some good professors. So I'm taking Nineteenth Century Classics and Contemporary American Literature this semester. I'm also going to take P.E. again. I enjoy the enforced discipline of the classes. I'm taking weight training this semester.

Sarah has decided to major in P.E. It figures. She's good at anything athletic. She doesn't know if she wants to teach P.E., but she likes to stay as involved as possible in sports. I can't say that I'm interested in pursuing a career in athletics, teaching or participating.

Sunday, August 31, 1980

Sarah and I played tennis today. I'm enjoying having someone to do things with. It would be good if she cared a little bit more about academics. She's just not interested in her other classes. She's intelligent enough; she's just not interested. It seems like such a waste of brains.

Friday, September 5, 1980

Sarah and I went to the beach this weekend with a bunch of her friends. We had a three-day weekend because of Labor Day. It was fun, but there were too many people in two small hotel rooms. I discovered, however, that there are a few other lesbians on campus. Carla and Nicki, two of the women who came with us, are a couple. They were very funny. I wouldn't mind being around them more often. They seem very much like an inseparable unit, so I guess the best we could do is double date.

Wednesday, September 10, 1980

I got a pleasant surprise today. Dad sent me a brand new tent and sleeping bag. I had told him that my old bag was not made for cool weather, so he sent me one that's rated for -15 degrees. The tent he got me is made for two people. My other one is a one-person tent. I think he was hinting that I should invite Sarah next time. So I did. We're going this weekend.

Sunday, September 14, 1980

Sarah and I enjoyed camping this past weekend. I have to admit that I kind of missed the solitude of camping alone, but it was still fun. We're talking about using Thanksgiving vacation for a biking/camping trip. We thought we'd go up into the Smoky Mountains and disappear for a few days.

Tuesday, October 7, 1980

This semester is a little more hectic. I have lots of reading to do. Between that, the tennis team, and Sarah, I have a busy schedule. At least my classes are more of a challenge than they were my freshman year. I was afraid college was going to be nothing more than a repeat of high school. I'm happy to report that it's definitely not like high school, for which I am exceedingly thankful.

Wednesday, October 15, 1980

It's been difficult trying to get any research done. Sarah wants to be with me, but she doesn't want to go to the library, and she doesn't want to study. I don't know what to do. My studies are important to me. I enjoy reading and learning.

That's why I came to college.   I'm beginning to feel torn between Sarah and my studies.

Thursday, October 23, 1980

Sarah's grandmother died yesterday. She had to fly back to Texas today to attend the funeral. Sarah was sad about her grandmother, but she really didn't want to go home.   Her mother is an alcoholic, and she gets on Sarah's nerves. According to Sarah, she always whines about what a bad mother she is, hoping someone will contradict her. Sarah said that just once she'd like to say, "Yes, you are a terrible mother, and I hate you for it!"

I feel bad for Sarah.   Her father died when she was twelve. A man who robbed the liquor store where he worked shot him in the head.   After that, Sarah's mother started drinking heavily. I can't say that I blame her for being deeply hurt by it, but I really wish she could have gotten over it. She had four kids who needed a mother. Since Sarah was the oldest, she wound up raising her sister and two brothers.

Wednesday, October 29, 1980

Sarah had a rough time in Texas. Her mother made a big scene at the funeral. She came to the church, and it wasn't even her mother who died.   It was Sarah's paternal grandmother. Anyway, after the funeral, the family got together at Sarah's uncle's house. Sarah's mother came too, still drinking as fast as she could guzzle it down.

She was all right at first.   Then she started bragging about Sarah's scholarship and about how well Sarah was doing in school. Even though that was embarrassing enough, it was at least tolerable. Everyone either ignored her or humored her until she started getting angry and loud.

Suddenly she started crying again and yelling that it was too bad that her daughter had to be a "god-damned lesbian." She kept saying, "I don't know where I went wrong. I'm not a goddamned lesbian! I bet if Frank had lived, he could have helped her. I must be a terrible mother."

Needless to say, Sarah was completely humiliated. She made a quick exit. I find it hard to comprehend that her mother would say things like that.

Monday, November 17, 1980

I don't know about this camping trip we've been planning. Sarah has been talking about it to all her friends, and they want to come along. Frankly I was looking forward to some time alone with Sarah. Lately it seems like she has to have an entourage wherever she goes, unless we're in bed, of course. Besides that, she's going to have to go to basketball practice several of the days we're going to be out there.

Sunday, November 30, 1980

Whew! I'm glad that's over. No less than nine people accompanied us on our camping trip. Three of them were guys from the basketball team. I spent the whole weekend watching everyone get drunk and listening to the guys try to talk everyone into having group sex. I could not believe it, and I really didn't understand why they had been invited. Three straight college guys and a bunch of lesbians? How could anyone think that would end well? We're lucky they didn't try to rape any of us. On the other hand, they would have had six angry, athletic lesbians on the other side. Perhaps they're smarter than I thought.

Monday, December 8, 1980

Sarah doesn't know what to do for Christmas break. She doesn't want to go home because of the funeral disaster. She really doesn't want to see her mother again. I'd invite her to come home with me, but I don't know if Mom could handle having Sarah as a guest. She's quite boisterous. I guess it can't hurt to ask.

Friday, December 12, 1980

Sarah and I are flying out to California tonight. I'll be back in January!

Tuesday, January 13, 1981

Back to school. I'll be nineteen in three days. It's hard to believe that I am halfway through my sophomore year already. Time passes swiftly these days. Sarah and I had a good time in California. Peter brought his fiancée home to meet the family. Introductions were a little awkward. Peter managed to stammer, "Joanne, I'd like you to meet my sister and her, and her, uh, friend, Sarah."

It was comical though because Peter turned red as a beet. I still don't know whether he told her about me. Maybe he thinks he can keep all the family skeletons in the closet until after the wedding. Joanne may be in for a real jolt. Maybe I should rent a tux. Dad can go in drag. What a riot! Actually, Buddy is the one who should show up in drag. He's more of the queen type than Dad. Talk about memorable experiences. I wonder if I will get to dance with the bride. Ha! This gets funnier all the time.

Friday, January 16, 1981

Sarah is taking me to my favorite restaurant to celebrate my birthday. It's not really that great of a restaurant, but it is possible for us to eat in the same place anyway. There aren't many options for vegetarians around here.

Wednesday, January 28, 1981

Sarah has been complaining a lot lately that I don't socialize enough. How can I tell her that I now socialize more than I care to? She tells me that I study too much. To be honest, I really don't study much at all. Most of the books I read are for enjoyment. I just tell her I have to study so she will go off without me. Last weekend she said, "Would you really rather read that book than go out and do something with me?" To avoid telling her what I really thought I stopped reading and went with her. Sometimes I think we're total opposites.

Thursday, February 12, 1981

Sarah and her friends want to crash the Valentine's Dance. They want all the lesbians to dress up like butch/femme couples, and show up, just to see if they'd be allowed to come in. Personally, I don't want to go. I don't like dances anyway. I understand the statement Sarah and her entourage want to make, but I'm not sure that they're not just trying to raise hell for the fun of it.

If they want to go to the dance, then I think they should just go and dance with their partners. I fail to see the point in the attention seeking behavior. It's like they're asking for trouble. I'd honestly like to see what would happen if they just showed up and danced without all the hoopla. Then if they get hassled they can plan a demonstration of some sort. I think they're just looking for a fight. If you walk out on the streets with both fists up, somebody's bound to take the challenge. As far as I'm concerned you should just be yourself. If you're lucky, maybe nobody will notice or care. If they take offense and start a fight, then by all means, stand up for yourself.

It's all so confusing to me sometimes. I think it's slightly twisted that we have to "come out of the closet," and tell our family and friends that we are gay. When was the last time you heard anyone telling their parents they were heterosexual? You'd think they'd just kind of pick up on it if you live your life honestly and openly. Why the need to stage a "coming out?" It reminds me of the debutante parties of earlier generations. Why not just put up a sign? "Available: Sixteen-year-old virgin. Inquire within." This is such a perplexing world.

Sunday, February 15, 1981

A funny thing happened at the dance. A bunch of lesbian couples showed up in butch/femme attire, and the people at the door simply shook their heads and laughed. They thought it was another round of sorority hazing. At any rate, they all got to dance with their partners. I'm glad no one was hurt. I would have hated it if it had turned into a riot or something. Fortunately, the women's basketball team got back late from their game, so Sarah missed the first part of the dance. She went over later though to see what happened. I'm glad she had a game. I really didn't want to go, and I don't like to be pressured into doing things. I detest those kinds of social functions anyway.

Saturday, March 21, 1981

Sarah and I are drifting apart, and I don't know what to do about it. We're so different. Yet I don't particularly want to be alone again, and I don't want to hurt her. We're going to spend spring vacation apart. I think we both need some time alone to think about things.

Thursday, April 16, 1981

I went to New York during spring break. Dad surprised me with an airline ticket. I was just going to go camping. It's probably a good thing I didn't, though, because Sarah and a couple of her friends did exactly that.

Friday, April 17, 1981

Sarah and I had an argument today. Mostly she just yelled at me and said that I was the most boring person in the world. She said that she didn't know why she bothered hanging around me. Later she started crying, and apologized. I'm still not sure what that was all about. Something has been bothering her ever since she returned from spring break. I'm beginning to think something happened on the camping trip. I don't know what it was though, and she doesn't seem inclined to tell me.

Monday, April 20, 1981

I found out what has been bothering Sarah lately. She and one of her friends got a little cozy on the camping trip. She said that it wouldn't happen again. She also said that she still loves me. I don't know what to say. I don't know how I feel really. Part of me would be glad if she found someone else, if it meant she would leave me alone.

Monday, April 27, 1981

I'll be glad when this semester is over. I'm going to New York again to work for Dad. Sarah is going to stay with her cousin in Oklahoma. That ought to provide us with some distance. I still don't know what to do about her. One minute she yells at me; the next minute she's trying to take me to bed. I don't understand her, but I really don't want to hurt her by turning her away. I'm just kind of numb, I guess.

Thursday, May 7, 1981

Saying "goodbye" to Sarah isn't easy, even if we haven't been getting along very well. I'm looking forward to seeing Dad and Buddy though. Mom and Christine are going to fly out later for a visit. That way I don't have to go all the way to California before I return to school.

Monday, September 7, 1981

Another school year begins. I think it may be a mistake to share a room with Sarah again, but I don't know that I have any better options. I can't very well tell her I want another roommate when we're still lovers (at least in the sexual sense). I missed her this summer, but I also felt as though I'd been granted a pardon from prison. The problem now is that I've been incarcerated again. I don't know how to tell her that I want to go my own way. It hurts deeply when she lets out all her frustrations on me. I'm trying to be understanding, but it isn't easy. Yet I know it takes effort and compromise to make a relationship work. I just feel as though I'm the one doing all the compromising.

Tuesday, September 15, 1981

I think I'm going to have a double major. I've already declared an English Literature major, but I think I'm going to double with Physical Education. It won't require much extra academic work. And since Sarah's taking some of the same classes, it may help to bridge the gap between us.

Sunday, September 20, 1981

I really want to try to make things work with Sarah. I think that if I try to do more of the things she likes to do, we'll get along better. I'm probably being selfish, wanting to read so much. There are other things to do. I can join the tennis team again. I enjoy that.

Thursday, September 24, 1981

Sarah and I aren't fighting as much these days, so I guess my strategy is working. I really do enjoy sports, so it's not like it's a tremendous sacrifice to give up some reading time.

Thursday, October 15, 1981

This semester is quite hectic. I have a lot more to do in my classes. It's not hard, but it takes time. Besides, I've been doing a lot more with Sarah. She hasn't yelled at me lately, so that's good. Basketball is going to start soon. Sarah wants to try to talk the coach into letting me join, even though it's past the sign-up time. She thinks I could make first string, but I don't know about that because I'm so short. I'm not really good enough to make up for that handicap. I've been working out with her, so I wouldn't be lagging behind in practice if I join now. I'm not sure about it though.

Wednesday, October 21, 1981

I've been saved from the basketball team. The coach stuck to her cut-off date. I feel relieved. At least I'll be able to read when Sarah is at the away games. I almost feel as though I have to hide my books from her because she starts to sulk whenever I try to read.

Maybe I should break up with Sarah. I don't like to hurt people though. The only problem with that line of reasoning is that I'm hurting someone either way. If we break up, I hurt her. If we stay together, I hurt me. Why does this have to be so difficult?

At least basketball season will soon be under way. It will be fun to watch the games again. I think I like Sarah best when she is playing basketball. She has practice nearly every afternoon, so I at least have some time to myself now. I think I'll call Dad tonight. I haven't talked to him for a while. I sure could use a sympathetic ear.

Friday, November 6, 1981

Sarah and I had it out today. She found my journal open, and read the last few pages. I suppose that's one way to break up with your lover. I can't believe she read my private writings though. I had just gone into the bathroom for a moment. When I came out she was holding my journal. She was pretty angry. I think I'd better start locking my journal up or taking it with me wherever I go.

Tuesday, November 10, 1981

Sarah and I have agreed to spend some time apart. Obviously this is not going to be easy since we're roommates, but she's going to go out with her other friends two nights a week, so I can read on those evenings. I get my studying done during her practice times, so I can use those evenings for pleasure reading. We'll see how that works.

Saturday, November 14, 1981

It's pleasant to have some time to myself. I have acquired a horrendous reading list. Between my literature professors and my father, I think I have enough titles to keep me feeling overwhelmed for the next decade. It feels good to be more relaxed about reading though. I was really beginning to get paranoid about it. That seems so ridiculous to me to have to read in secret.

Saturday, November 21, 1981

I'm considering going camping over the Thanksgiving holidays. I need a break from school. I'm getting tired of it. I'm just tired, period. The only trick will be to get away from Sarah. She's been clinging to me a lot lately. She hasn't been out with her friends as much, so I haven't had much time alone. At least basketball season will last for several months.

Sunday, November 29, 1981

I spent the holidays camping without Sarah. She was invited to a friend's house for Thanksgiving break. She wasn't going to go at first, but I finally managed to talk her into it. I spent the entire holiday break arguing with myself about what to do. For my sanity's sake, this can't go on. Sarah is dragging me down, and she's dragging herself down. She needs to find someone more like herself. I think I just need to be alone. I'm afraid celibacy is looking good to me again.

While she was away, I wrote her a long letter explaining how I feel. When the time for her return was near, I left the letter on her bed and then went for a walk. I didn't want to be around when she read it. I didn't want her to start screaming at me again. I have a hard enough time with confrontations, as it is. I was afraid she'd bully me into giving in to her desires again. By the time I got back to the room she was asleep in my bed. Her bed was covered with her clothes and suitcase. Buried underneath it all was my note. Nice try, anyway, huh? She never even saw it. So I just put it away, cleared off her junk, and fell asleep in her bed. Now I don't know what to do. It took all the courage I had to write that note and leave it on her bed.

Saturday, December 11, 1981

Sarah just practically raped me. I don't know what to do about her. I don't feel right about having sex with her. I can't say that I love her any more or if I ever did. I don't have the nerve to tell her to go away, and yet I really don't want to be with her any more. I guess I'll just have to leave. I'm going to check with the dean to see if I can arrange for a single room next semester. I can't take any more of this.

Monday, December 13, 1981

I now have a single room reserved for next semester. I also have a black eye. Sarah claims that she didn't mean for the shoe to hit me, but she would have to have horrible aim if she were trying to miss me. I find it hard to believe it was an accident. She is, after all, known for her athletic prowess.

Saturday, January 16, 1982

I'm twenty now and alone again. It isn't easy, but I know it's for the best. Sarah already has a new lover--the woman she slept with during her camping trip last year. I hope she will be happy. I think I just want to be alone now. For a long,

long time. I get to read more, now that I'm living by myself. I wonder if it is always so difficult to strike a balance when you live with someone. I didn't like having to choose between being Anna Evans and Sarah's lover. I could not be both. I don't cope well with either/or situations.

Tuesday, January 19, 1982

I'm thoroughly enjoying my literature classes. The education classes can get pretty boring though, except for Dr. Stein's classes. She's a good teacher. I'm still involved in the Physical Education program, but I'm going to try to avoid the classes Sarah is likely to take. I know which teachers she dislikes, so I'm taking classes with them. They are all right, so far. I don't know if I will ever use this major, but it gives me two options as far as teaching is concerned. I've completed so much of it already it would be a shame to waste it.

Frankly, I think I would prefer to teach literature on the college level. I like the academic atmosphere of college classes, but I think I may start by teaching high school. That way I can see if I can handle standing in front of a classroom full of students before I go all the way through graduate school. I would feel less threatened by teenagers than adults, I think. Of course, there isn't always a great deal of difference between college students and high school students.

Wednesday, January 20, 1982

I want to get back into the discipline of keeping a journal. I may not have much time later in the semester though. From the looks of my classes, I'm going to have lots of reading and research papers. So my journal writing may have to be relegated to a weekly basis again, but that's better than nothing. I like the continuity it brings to my life. Plus, every once in a while I get to glance back at where I've been and compare it to where I am now.

Thursday, January 21, 1982

We're having some oddly warm weather right now, so I'm going camping this weekend. I hope I don't freeze. I heard the forecast though, and it's supposed to be in the mid-forties Friday and Saturday, with highs in the mid- to upper-sixties. I hope it doesn't get any colder than that. I don't think I'd enjoy sleeping outside in freezing temperatures, even if I had a sleeping bag rated to -50 degrees. You can't stay inside your sleeping bag all day.

Monday, January 25, 1982

I had an interesting time camping this weekend. I ran into another dedicated (crazy?) camper at the water pump. We talked about how quiet it is when you camp when most everybody else is locked inside their toasty warm houses. He came by my campsite later and we talked for hours.

His name is Jeff Prichart and he's gay, believe it or not. He's from Chicago. He transferred to Denisson this semester. He lives off campus because he can't stand the dorm scene. I concur completely with his opinion. So, anyway, we've become fast friends. He's going to come by some time this week to see me. Since this is his first semester here, he doesn't have many friends. I know how he feels. It's strange, but I feel as though I've known him for years.

Tuesday, January 26, 1982

Jeff and I went to the health food store, bought some fruit, cheese, and freshly baked bread, and had a picnic in the park. It was fun. Jeff works full-time at a bookstore, besides being a part-time student. Needless to say, he doesn't have much time for socializing. He's kind of on the quiet and shy side anyway. We make a good pair.

Thursday, January 28, 1982

Jeff came to my room before he left campus this afternoon. He had to work tonight, but wanted me to join him for another picnic. It started raining though, so we went to his apartment, which is filled with his artwork. I discovered that he is one hell of an artist. I saw more sketches of nude men than I ever cared to, but fortunately for me he does draw and paint other things. His landscapes are breathtaking. When he goes hiking, he carries his sketchpad with him, so he can capture the nicer vistas. Then he brings the sketch home, and paints his feelings for the scene into the scene itself. Instead of using the actual colors he saw, he uses colors that express his feelings about the scene.

It's really interesting to see the colors he uses. They're not ones I would think to use, but they end up looking really beautiful together. He's very talented. Or at least I think so. I'm not exactly an art critic, but his paintings are so vivid and full of life. I enjoy looking at them.

Monday, February 1, 1982

I spent most of the weekend in the library. Friday night I went over to Jeff's apartment for dinner. He's not a bad cook, and he knows how to accommodate a vegetarian diet. We had vegetable lasagna. It was delicious. It made me miss home-cooked meals. Institutional food is so terrible. Of course, if you have no taste buds, it's not so bad.

I ended up sleeping on Jeff's loveseat. I'm glad I'm so short. He doesn't have a full-size sofa. The loveseat was comfortable enough for me though. We stayed up late talking. I got too bleary-eyed to ride my bike back to campus. Jeff had a few too many beers, so he couldn't drive me home. It was great to be away from the dorm. I felt more at home in Jeff's apartment than I have ever felt at the dorm. Dormitory life is so bizarre. So far removed from anything that even remotely resembles real life.

Saturday, February 6, 1982

I'm thinking about taking a creative writing class next semester. They're supposed to be offering one for poetry. I used to write poetry in junior high and high school, but I never let anyone read any of it. I hope I don't back out before registration. The thought of turning in a piece to be graded terrifies me. I'm not that good, but then that's the purpose of taking the class — to improve my skills.

Monday, February 8, 1982

Jeffrey and I went hiking yesterday. I enjoyed myself thoroughly. There's so much to see in the mountains. I really like it here, even though most people can't even spell vegetarian. I suppose I seem a bit of an oddball to these people. Sometimes I get funny looks when I try to order Perrier. It's not easy to explain sparkling mineral water. One waiter told me that he'd never heard of anyone drinking mineral spirits before. I was rendered speechless.

Tuesday, February 9, 1982

Jeffrey borrowed a bike from his neighbor so we could ride up into the mountains. He loved it. Now he wants to try to find a good used mountain bike to buy. Mountain biking is quite addictive, especially if you're already a mountain lover. It's nice to have someone to ride with here. Mountain biking is quite popular in California. I really haven't run into too many people here who have mountain bikes. A lot of ten speed road racers, but few mountain bikes. It's such a great place to ride too.

Wednesday, February 10, 1982

Jeffrey and I are going camping next weekend. We're both taking our one-person tents, but we're going to use the same site. It's chilly right now, so I hope my sleeping bag lives up to its rating. Frankly I think Jeffrey is a little on the crazy side to suggest that we go camping in February. But then he's from Chicago. He's used to weather that's much colder than this.

Monday, February 15, 1982

That's the last time I go camping in February. It was too cold! My bag did fine, and so did I as long as I was in it. Jeffrey is crazy. He said, "Oh, come on, it will be great." I beg to differ. From now on, if it is going to be below freezing, I'm staying inside. That was way too cold for my California blood!

Wednesday, March 3, 1982

Between getting sick and having lots of papers to write, I keep forgetting about my journal, but I mustn't become a slave to it. And, it isn't as though I haven't been writing anything at all. My classes are keeping me busy in that regard.

I'm going to eat at Jeffrey's tonight. We have a great arrangement. We make out a menu together, then I buy all the ingredients, and he does most of the work. Actually he's been giving me some cooking tips. He's a much better cook than I am, although my mom taught me a lot before I left for college. Jeffrey even bakes his own whole grain breads. I really want to learn. Maybe I can get him to teach me when I'm not up to my eyeballs in reading and research.

Monday, March 8, 1982

I spent the weekend at Jeff's apartment. He was at work most of the time, so I just stayed there and studied. It was great, infinitely quieter than the dorm. Besides I didn't have to worry about running into Sarah. That happens enough during the week. I wish our rooms weren't so close. At least we don't have to share a bathroom.

Which reminds me, I haven't seen the painted plasticene woman this semester. I guess she must have graduated or dropped out. Of course, I mustn't rule out the possibility that the Gunk Monster dissolved her face totally. Now that's an intriguing thought. How would the headline read? "Death by Cosmetics?"

Wednesday, March 17, 1982

I'm going to spend spring break at Jeff's place. Dad offered to fly me to New York, but I really need to study. He was happy to hear about my new friend. He has been worried about my spending all my time alone. I think Dad's more gregarious than I am. I like spending large quantities of time by myself. I thrive on solitude.

Wednesday, March 24, 198

I'm reveling in this time off from classes. I've been in the library every day. I really don't have to worry about running into Sarah there. She seldom sees the inside of the library. I know that for a fact. It's nice to have some peace and quiet for a change. Jeff has been working extra hours while classes are out so when I'm at his place I have complete solitude. It's wonderful. I think I need all this time alone to sort out some of my thoughts and feelings.

Thursday, March 25, 1982

I guess I spoke too soon about Sarah never going to the library. Sarah and Cindy showed up there today to do some research, or so they said. Personally I think Sarah was looking for me. They certainly didn't do much research. Neither did I once they showed up. They sat two tables away and whispered loudly the whole time. Once, when Cindy went to the bathroom, Sarah came over and put her hand on my arm and asked me how my love life was. I said, "Fine."

I wasn't about to ask to her the same question, but of course she told me anyway. She said that Cindy didn't know very much, and that she wasn't very creative or romantic. I rather doubt I was either. I spent most of my time trying to keep up with her and her friends. Not much room for romance there. Although when we stayed with my dad, he was always good at creating the right ambiance. He and Buddy dine by candlelight every night. And sometimes Buddy brings home flowers. I think Sarah must have assumed that I have the same romantic streak as those two.

Anyway, when she saw Cindy coming back, she slid her hand very slowly down my arm and across the top of my hand. I don't know which one of us she was trying to annoy, Cindy or me. She managed to do both, though I tried not to show my annoyance. Cindy was a little less successful.

Wednesday, March 31, 1982

I'm trying to figure out what to do this summer. Dad's job offer is open again. He doesn't need as much help as he did the summer Sarah and I both went, but he had plenty for me to do last summer, even though his secretary was back. Mom has a job possibility for me too. My sister's school library is automating this summer, and they're looking for people to help them set up the system. The pay is not bad, and I will get to be with my family again. I do miss everyone. Sometimes I feel as though I hardly know Christine. She is so much younger than Peter and me. I guess if I can get that job for certain, I will go back to California for this vacation.

Saturday, April 3, 1982

Pre-registration is rapidly approaching. I really need to make a decision about the poetry class. I'd like to learn how to write better poetry, but I absolutely hate the thought of allowing anyone to read my poems. It would be a big risk for me emotionally. I'm not sure I'm up to it.

Sunday, April 18, 1982

I have been swamped with work. I've been spending most of my weekends in the library by day and at Jeff's by night. It's sweet of him to share his space with me. He really doesn't have much of it to share. He's thinking about moving into a two-bedroom apartment, so he'll have more room. I keep telling him that he would have more room if I weren't always around. But he insists that he likes for me to be there when he gets home. He isn't as lonely that way.

Tuesday, April 20, 1982

Jeffrey asked me to move in with him into a two-bedroom apartment. I just might do it next semester. I really detest dorm life. I think we would get along just fine. I have a lot more in common with Jeff than I did with Denise. The only thing she and I had in common was our gender.

Friday, April 23, 1982

Well, it's settled. I'm going to share an apartment with Jeffrey next semester. The difference in cost between the dorm and half an apartment isn't too great. When I talked to Mom about it, she said, "Aren't you worried about what the people around there might say? You're not in California, you know."

I said, "Yes, I know, but the scandal can't be any worse than what I live with as a lesbian. Besides, some of these people will be relieved to think that I've reformed."

When I talked to Dad, he said, "Go for it!"

So next semester we're going to get a two-bedroom apartment. Now I definitely don't have to worry about either Sarah or the Gunk Monster!

Monday, April 26, 1982

I've decided to take the library job. Jeffrey is depressed about my leaving for the summer. He's going to work two jobs, so he can save money for some more furniture. I have to admit that his apartment does look more like an art studio than a dwelling place.

Tuesday, April 27, 1982

I was hoping to get out of here without any more encounters with Sarah. No such luck. She came by my room last night to talk. She said that she wanted me back. She's willing to give me space and time for my studies and reading. She promised not to expect me to go everywhere with her. In essence, she nearly begged me to go back with her. I was tempted. I guess being alone is beginning to take its toll. I managed to tell her that I need time to think about it.

Wednesday, April 28, 1982

You-know-who came back again. I think she's feeling really desperate because the semester is almost over, and we'll be going our separate ways. I put her off again. I really don't know what to do about her. I care about her, but I can't stand the thought of going back to the way I lived before. I have to have time for myself.

Friday, April 30, 1982

I think I need to see a shrink! Sarah came to my room again late last night. She was nearly in tears, so I let her in. That was my first mistake. I was really tired though and didn't have the energy to argue with her. My second mistake was trying to be sympathetic. When I sat down next to her on the bed, she started hugging me, like she needed a shoulder to cry on. I held her for a minute to see if that would comfort her. Well, if she was really crying, she was doing one hell of a job hiding the fact. Finally she looked up at me with pleading eyes and then proceeded to kiss me. I started to resist, but it felt so good. It had been so long. I thought, "What's the harm in one kiss?"

That was my third mistake. One thing led to another, and before I knew what hit me, Sarah had her shirt off and was taking mine off too. She turned out the light and pulled me into her arms. We made love or exchanged expressions of passion, rather, for a couple hours. Then around three o'clock, she whispered that she had to go back to her room before Cindy woke up. Then I fell asleep. When I woke up later that morning, I felt strange inside. Very empty. Very used. I felt as though I had been laid, but not that I had been loved.

I'm beginning to wonder if Sarah just wants someone who can give her better sex than Cindy is capable of giving. I feel pretty low really. Why didn't I kick her out? Am I that much of a sucker that I can't stand up to her? What is wrong with me?

Saturday, May 1, 1982

Sarah tried her stuff again, but I was ready for her this time. She came to the door, but I didn't let her in. Playing the part of the innocent, she asked me what was wrong.

I said, "Number one, you already have a lover. Number two, I don't want to get back together with you. Number three, I think you're just using me."

"If I didn't care about you, Anna Evans, I sure as hell wouldn't be here."

"If you did care about me, you wouldn't be here."

"Oh, go to hell, Anna! I don't need you or anyone else!" Then she stormed off down the hall.

Sunday, May 2, 1982

I'm going to stay at Jeff's place tonight. I can't take any more of Sarah's drama. I don't know whether she's gotten the message yet, but I don't wish to take any chances. In fact, I think I'd better stay there all next week, or I won't be able to concentrate on studying for my finals.

Tuesday, May 4, 1982

I've decided not to return to the dorm until it is time to pack and leave. Of course, I'll have to stop by my room to get a change of clothing every day, but I should be able to elude Sarah for that short amount of time. I doubt that she would go to the extreme of mounting a guard outside my door. Then again, Sarah is capable of nearly anything. I wish I didn't have to hide from her, but I can't think of any alternatives.

Tuesday, August 31, 1982

Jeffrey and I are now housemates. Our apartment has two bedrooms and two baths. Dad told me to try to get an apartment with two bathrooms because we would need it for sanity's sake. He's probably right. Besides he's paying for it, so I'll take his advice about it.

Friday, September 3, 1982

I'm taking the poetry class, so far anyway. I can still drop it if I change my mind. I have to turn my first piece in next week. I have no idea what I'm going to do. I'll probably just draw a blank when I try to write something. Maybe I should turn in some old poems first. Dr. Reading said that would be acceptable for the first two or three poems.

Monday, September 6, 1982

I'm savoring the experience of not living in the dorm. I can't think of a single thing I miss about it. Jeff and I get along fine. Between work, school, and homework, we really don't see much of each other. At least our music and food tastes are similar. Some of our sports preferences vary, but he has decided that he is definitely a mountain biker. He bought his neighbor's old bike, since his neighbor never rides it. It's not in the best of shape, but as Jeff says, "It will do for now." We're going biking tomorrow because Jeff's off all day. Of course, Jeff is always "off." Ha!

Thursday, September 8, 1982

I am really perturbed. Sarah just added herself to the Sports Medicine class I'm taking. One of her other classes was canceled due to lack of interest. So much for avoiding her. Maybe I should drop the P.E. major. No. That wouldn't really solve anything. I can't run from her forever. I just need to face her and be firm. I have been enjoying my classes, and I don't want her to run my life.

Friday, September 9, 1982

I've been thinking about Sarah a lot lately. I wish she would get some help. I think the biggest part of her problem is that she's really insecure and lonely. Her father was murdered in a bungled robbery. Her mother is an alcoholic. Her siblings don't want to have much to do with her because she's lesbian. I think Sarah is just looking for someone to love her for who she is. Her entourage doesn't meet that need. They follow her because of her athletic achievements. She's simply a sports idol to them.

I can accept her as she is, but I can't be her lover. We're just not compatible. I have a hard time just being her friend because I never know what stunt she will pull next. Maybe I should talk with someone about her. I know my freshman psychology teacher does some counseling. Unfortunately he's a man. I would prefer to talk with a woman about this. I bet he could recommend someone to me. I'll have to check into it.

Wednesday, September 15, 1982

My psychology professor recommended Sharon Lithe, one of the school counselors. She's supposed to be very good at helping people with relationships. I made an appointment with her for next Thursday.

In the meantime, I have to turn in my first poem tomorrow. Help! Why did I sign up for this class? I guess I can at least rummage through some of my old poems and see what I come up with. Maybe that will inspire me to write something new. Why, oh why, did I ever place myself in such a vulnerable position? I guess it's time for me to take a few risks. I'm so very good at playing it safe. Let's see if I can muster up the courage to expose my inner self a little bit. At least Dr. Reading seems like a nice man. I hope he's not an overly harsh critic. Here goes nothing.

Nothing to Fear

"There is nothing to fear, but fear itself."

Fear
of
failure
of
success
of
exposure
of
hiding
of
darkness
of
light
of
heights
of
depths
of
people
of
aloneness
of
being hurt
of
hurting others
of
pleasure
of
pain
of
death

of
life
of
you
of
me
of
FEAR!

You call that Nothing?

Friday, September 17, 1982

One Red Rose

One Red Rose
Brings Joy
Eyes Sparkle

One Red Rose
A Token of Love

One Red Rose
Harbors Thorns
Draws Blood

One Red Rose
A Token of Love

One Red Rose
Beauty veiling Pain
Love and Hurt

One Red Rose
A Token of Love

One Red Rose
Give It Back
Close the Door
Shut out the Pain

One Red Rose
My Hand Bleeds
Alone Again
My Hand Bleeds

Sunday, September 19, 1982

Jeffrey and I are going to bike up into the mountains today. He's feeling the urge to "paint a soulful picture." He's such a pleasant person to be with. I haven't seen him much lately. I think that he may have a boyfriend. The guy is only seventeen though, and since Jeffrey is twenty-one, he could get into some serious trouble.

This potential boyfriend's name is Chuck. He'll be eighteen in two months, so Jeffrey is taking things very slowly. He doesn't want this relationship to move too quickly for a couple reasons. First, of course, is the age factor. Second is his fear of exposing his deeper self. I can certainly identify with that.

Tuesday, September 21, 1982

Jeffrey and I sort of got a young cat, or to be more truthful, the cat got us. It just showed up outside Sunday after we got back from our bike ride, so we gave it some food out on the patio. It is small and sort of scruffy looking. He is a black and white tuxedo cat with a damaged ear. He keeps coming to the door every morning and evening. I'm not sure if we're going to keep it, but we can't very well stop feeding it now that we've started. I suppose we'll have to take it to the vet and get him checked out to make sure he's all right.

Wednesday, September 22, 1982

I guess we have a cat now. The vet thinks he's about three years old, but he's on the small size. I guess he's been undernourished or is just from a smallish breed. He's adorable and very cuddly. I think he wants to come inside. Jeff wants him to be indoors for winter at least. We'll have to get some litter and a box. I like cats, but I think Jeff is in love with this little guy. We're not sure what we're going to call him yet. Jeff made a joke about calling him Van Gogh since he has a missing ear, or at least it looks like it is missing. It's really all there, just sort of shriveled up. It gives him a certain dashing air.

Thursday, September 23, 1982

I got an "A" on my first poem. Dr. Reading said that the structure was very effective, and the message rather jolting. He liked it a lot. He liked my honesty too. I haven't gotten "One Red Rose" back yet. I hope he liked that one. It is really hard for me to let someone else read my poetry. It is almost physically painful.

Friday, September 24, 1982

I got an "A+" on "One Red Rose." We had a conference in his office today about it. Dr. Reading wants to publish it in the Denisson literary magazine next month. He also wants me to enter both poems in a poetry contest. I don't think I want to do that. I haven't given him an answer yet. If he only knew how much it cost me just to let him read it.

Jeff took Van Gogh to the vet yesterday for shots. His blood work all came back clean, so we're going to bring him inside. He's definitely domesticated. The vet thinks that maybe whoever had him before moved and didn't know to keep him inside for a couple of weeks once they got to the new place. He must've lived somewhere near here, and first chance he got to go outside at the new house, he returned home. He's already neutered so we don't have to worry about that at least. Jeff also came home with a box and some litter and cat food. So now we have a cat, although he's mainly Jeff's, I think.

Monday, September 27, 1982

Rivers of My Heart

Busying myself, I fight back
the tide of desolation.
Torrents of loneliness
threaten to engulf my heart.
I stare at the window,
pondering the blur of rain on the pane.
Peering into the cloudless sky,
I realize there is no storm.
It is only the rivers of my heart,
seeping through the windows of my soul.

Tuesday, September 28, 1982

I'm really enjoying my poetry class. My other classes are fine, but not life shattering. This one is filling a deep need in me to express myself. I have a lot of respect for Dr. Reading. He's very gentle with his students. He seems to know how important it is not to rip apart a beginner's first attempts. We're going to be doing Haiku next week.

Monday, October 4, 1982

Look at the night sky.
A million points of starlight
Who's looking at me?

Tuesday, October 5, 1982

Tendrils of houseplants
explore the nooks and crannies
no one else can see.

October 7, 1982

Can't you hear him purr?
Someone needs to snuggle now.
Cat fur in my face.

Friday, October 15, 1982

Dr. Reading liked my Haiku. He said that he could really see an image in his mind when he reads them. I think he likes my work. We're supposed to do limericks soon. Dr. Reading read four or five of them today, so we could start thinking about them. The ones he read were really funny. He asked us to try not to be too bawdy. Apparently most limericks are on the risqué side.

Monday, October 18, 1982

Dad was so right about getting an apartment with two bathrooms. I've never thought about sharing a bathroom with someone who shaves every morning. That just isn't an issue in lesbian relationships. At least not in any I'm aware of, though I suppose it's possible.

Thursday, October 21, 1982

Things are starting to get serious between Jeff and Chuck. He's coming over tonight for dinner. Jeff is certain he's gay, but he doesn't think he has ever had a sexual relationship with a man. He doesn't want to push him into anything. I'm supposed to be chaperoning tonight. Frankly I think Jeff is being overly cautious. Or maybe he's just being shy.

Sunday, October 24, 1982

Dr. Reading is really eager to publish my poetry. He's the senior editor, so he knows they will publish them if he recommends them. I think I'll give him permission to publish whichever ones he likes. How daring of you, Anna!

Tuesday, October 26, 1982

I had another session with Sharon Lithe today. She's helping me to think through some of the conflicts Sarah and I had. I wish Sarah would talk to her too. I think it would help her to get her life together. But Sharon can't help Sarah unless she seeks help for herself. Sarah has to be willing to make the step I made in going to see a counselor.

Talking to Sharon helps me to see things differently. I can see now that I was contributing to the unhealthiness of our relationship by selling myself short. I hurt myself by not being me. I hurt both Sarah and myself by allowing her to walk all over me. I was encouraging her to continue in her behavior by not challenging her. That makes sense really. I can see now how it is possible to hurt someone by giving in to their desires even when they were harmful to me. I can't let Sarah run my life, but neither can I run hers.

Thursday, October 28, 1982

Limericks:

A young artist who lived with six cats
Loved to paint women with hats
      Her models were nude
      Her paintings were crude
But she never had trouble with rats

My lover has very soft breasts
My head likes to lie there for rests
    I give them a squeeze
    Whenever I please
And jealously guard them from guests

I tried hard to drift off to sleep
I even tried counting some sheep
    Embarrassed to say
    For hours I lay
Just flirting with Little Bo Peep

Oh my god, I have to make myself stop with the limericks already. Once I got started, I couldn't quit. It's like an addiction or something. It's even worse than Haiku, and I thought writing those was pretty addictive.

Friday, October 29, 1982

I turned in my first limerick today. I think I'll keep the second one I wrote to myself. I have no idea how Dr. Reading would respond to that one. He'd probably think it was funny, but I don't know what he thinks about lesbians. The only problem with not turning that one in though, is that I have to submit three limericks by the end of next week. So I either have to turn that one in, or write a new one. I'll have to give it some thought.

A cat makes an excellent pet.
I'm willing to make you a bet.
    Adopt a feline.
    His lives are but nine.
You'll find all the love you can get.

Sunday, October 31, 1982

Jeffrey and I are going trick-or-treating tonight. I'm short enough to get away with being a junior high kid. He's going to pretend to be my father. I don't know why we're doing this. It started as a dare. I'm going as a giant. Ha!

Later: We had a blast, but I'm never doing that again! We got a bunch of candy. We're going to give it to Chuck on his birthday. That is, of course, unless Jeff eats it all between now and next week. They're both so excited. I'm excited for them. We are all so excited! I think I ate too much candy, and I had only three pieces. It grossed me out terribly. I think I'm experiencing a sugar rush. I'm not used to eating all this sugar.

Friday, November 5, 1982

Happy birthday, Chuck! We're having a small party at our apartment tonight. According to Jeff, he has been a perfect gentleman. He's not planning on attacking Chuck, but he feels as though he can relax a little. I'm glad. He was getting pretty uptight.

Thursday, November 11, 1982

Well, what do you know? I've seen some of my work in print now. This month they published three of my Haiku pieces, "A Red Rose," and "Nothing to Fear." Dr. Reading asked me again about the contest. He said that first prize is $1000; second prize is $500; and third prize is $100. I don't know if I want to enter or not. The deadline is November 17th. I turned in all the limericks I wrote that one night, plus the one I wrote later about cats. Dr. Reading loved all of them, and he never said anything about them being too risqué.

Wednesday, November 17, 1982

I decided to enter the poetry contest with "One Red Rose" and "Nothing to Fear." When I told Dr. Reading about my decision, he persuaded me to submit all five of the pieces that were published in the magazine. He says that they're all good, and stand a chance of winning. He has a lot more faith in my work than I do.

Saturday, November 20, 1982

Chuck's coming over tonight, and I'm definitely not chaperoning. I'm going to the library to study until closing time. Have fun, guys! There's the doorbell now. Time to scurry off to the library.

Monday, November 22, 1982

Guess who hunted me down in the library again? I'm beginning to think that she looks for me just before every school holiday. That would make sense, since she doesn't have a loving family to visit during the holidays. She must feel very lonely at those times. I may be the closest thing to a family she's had recently. I don't know. All I know is that I can't afford to get caught up in her emotional whirlwinds again. I'll be torn to pieces if I do, and I'm doing quite well without her and her drama. If only I could convince her to go to counseling, she might get some real help. I know that I can't help her.

Tuesday, November 23, 1982

Jeff is going to teach me how to bake bread over Thanksgiving break. The bookstore is going to be closed for two days, so we'll have lots of time. I have all my research papers done or mostly done. I'm ahead in my reading, so I'm going to rest and play.

Thursday, November 25, 1982

Baking bread is fun. I love the feeling of kneading dough, the way it starts out squishy then gradually becomes more and more elastic. I love the yeasty smell too. Jeff says that kneading dough reminds him of working with clay. Baking helps him not to miss the kiln he left behind in Chicago. He's going to teach me how to make French bread next time we have a baking lesson.

Friday, December 3, 1982

I'm going to miss my poetry class. I've grown a lot through it. I've learned volumes from Dr. Reading. He's an excellent professor. My final exam is one last poem. Several more of my poems will be published in this month's literary magazine. I still can't get over the fact that I'm allowing other people to read my creations.

Monday, December 6, 1982

Dad invited Chuck, Jeff, and me to New York for Christmas. I don't think Chuck's parents will let him go, but we shall see. I hope they decide quickly though, because we need to make airline reservations soon.

Saturday, December 11, 1982

We are all going after all. Chuck is going to visit some universities in the area while we're there. That's why his parents gave him permission to go. They want him to go to medical school. He's not even slightly interested in that. He does want to go to college, though not right away. He's a really smart young man. I like him a lot. He's kind of like a little brother to me. Hmm. Better change that to "younger brother." He could hardly be smaller than I am.

Saturday, January 15, 1983

Tomorrow is my twenty-first birthday. Dad decided to combine my Christmas present, my birthday present, and my graduation present into one gift. So upon graduation, he and I are going shopping for a car. I was surprised when he told me he wanted to do that. I hadn't really thought about it, but I suppose I will need a car in the future.

For the first time in my college career, I will not have a full load. Yet, even without a full class load, I will have more than enough to keep me busy for the next six months or so. I have my internship this semester. Then I'll have to find a job for next year. I also have to figure out what to do this summer. Help!

Sunday, January 16, 1983

Chuck and Jeff made a birthday dinner for me. They baked fresh bread and made spaghetti. We also had a great salad. They're such neat friends. Mom sent me a check, since I wasn't around at Christmas to pick out my birthday present. I don't know what I want yet.

Wednesday, January 19, 1982

I'm in shock! "One Red Rose" came in second place in the poetry contest. It's even going to be published in a national literary journal. I am really surprised. I thought I might come in third at best. My Haiku pieces won honorary mentions.

Friday, January 21, 1983

I got the check today for $500. I put it in my savings account with my birthday money because I don't want to touch it. I don't really need it right now, but I might later, if I have a hard time getting a job.

Thursday, January 27, 1983

College life seems nonexistent now that I'm interning. They let me split my internship between my two majors. That's good, but it means I have more preparations to do. The school, a junior high, is close enough that I can bike, but I have to get up very early. Maybe I should have pursued a different career. I don't get along very well with mornings.

Tuesday, February 1, 1983

Interning is interesting. Dr. Stein is my advisor. She really knows kids and teaching. She's been giving me some good advice on controlling large classes, the kind you usually get as a P.E. teacher. Perhaps I should have majored in English Literature only. I'm not very thrilled about supervising large groups of teenagers. But it's got to be easier than standing in front of a classroom.

Thursday, February 10. 1983

Time is going by so quickly. Interning keeps me busy. I've been catching a ride with another student in the interning program. I decided that riding my bike at 6:30 a.m. in February is a little more than I can handle. No, it's a lot more than I can handle.

Monday, February 14, 1983

Jeff and Chuck are going to the Valentine's Dance at the student union. It's too risky to go to Chuck's high school. One of Chuck's friends tried it once, and a bunch of guys jumped him and his partner. They had to go to the hospital for emergency treatment. Nobody was ever arrested for it either.

Tuesday, February 15, 1983

Jeff and Chuck got kicked out of the dance. I can't figure that one out. Why did the lesbian couples get away with it? Maybe the establishment is more threatened when males break the rules. Of course, there were several lesbian couples that participated too, compared with just Jeff and Chuck by themselves. Safety in numbers perhaps? I'm very confused about the whole thing.

Thursday, February 17, 1983

I called my dad to tell him about the dance. He told me to be very careful and to tell the guys to be careful too. He said that there's a whole lot of "queer-bashing" going on these days. How sick! I didn't realize that some people were so militant about sexual preference.

Wednesday, March 16, 1983

I'm glad that spring break is almost here. I need a break. I think I may be getting sick. Well, it wouldn't surprise me, since I have not yet had my annual cold. I don't know how I made it this long. I guess I've been running so fast that the viruses haven't been able to keep up with me.

Saturday, March 19, 1983

How interesting. I just got up to get some orange juice, and ran into Chuck in the kitchen. I knew he and Jeff were sleeping together. Well, I assumed they were, but I didn't know he would be able to stay over. I guess he told his parents he was going to spend the night with a friend. It was rather funny. I'm just glad I was cognizant enough to put a T-shirt on before I went to the kitchen. Jeff never wakes up at night, so I don't always get dressed when I make a midnight raid on the refrigerator.

I enjoy nudity so much, you see. Well, actually you don't see. You're just a journal. You have no eyes. You have only ears, figuratively, so you can listen to my midnight ramblings. Although, since I'm writing my words, I guess you have to have eyes to read what I'm saying. This is so confusing, and more than just a little bit silly, so I think I'd better give up and go to bed.

Tuesday, March 29, 1983

Back to school and interning. I wish I could stay home and read for another week. I thoroughly enjoyed spring break. I spent most of my free time reading. It was wonderful. Perhaps I should try to get a job that would pay me to read good literature. No teaching, no students, no papers to grade. Nothing but reading. Ha! Dream on, Anna!

Sunday, April 10, 1983

Dr. Stein is going to help me find a job somewhere in this region of the country. I really don't want to go to California or New York to teach. I've grown fond of this area (the scenery anyway). It's so beautiful. I'll never tire of looking at these mountains. Their roundness reminds me of a woman's breasts. Sometimes I just want to reach out and stroke their loveliness, to cup them in my hands. There are mountains in California, of course, but they have sharper edges and angles. Not at all strokable.

Thursday, April 14, 1983

Dad and Mom both want me to stay with them this summer, so I guess I'll have to split up my vacation. California first, then New York. Everybody is going to fly here for my graduation next month. I can drive back to California in my new car and stay there until the end of June. Then I'll drive to New York. From there, Dad's going to help me to get settled wherever I get a job. Sounds like an exhausting summer to me. I'll be glad when it's over and done with, and the dust has settled again. I don't like all the upheaval.

Tuesday, May 3, 1983

Dr. Stein gave me the names of some schools to check out--two in Virginia, one in Tennessee, and one in North Carolina. I'm going to send a resume to each of them. I had one done while I was working on my valedictory address. I don't mind receiving this honor, but I'd prefer to skip the speech. I guess if I can survive this, I can survive anything, right? Well, maybe not anything.

Saturday, May 7, 1983

I did it! I am now a college graduate. It's hard to fathom. What is really odd is that even I think I did a good job on my speech. I'm rather proud of myself. I nearly panicked though, when I first stepped up to the podium and looked out at all the people. Then somehow I managed to block out their staring eyes. I just pretended that I was practicing in front of the mirror again. I was fine after that.

Sunday, May 8, 1983

Dad and I went car shopping today, and narrowed it down to two models. I think I prefer the blue hatchback. Dad was eyeing the red sporty one. Maybe I should tell him to buy that one for himself. I'm not the red sports car type. It would attract altogether too much attention.

Monday, May 9, 1983

The blue hatchback won. I love it. It's hard to believe that I have my own car. I decided to give my bike to Chuck for a graduation present. That way I don't have to haul it to California and back again. Now he and Jeff can carry on our mountain picnic tradition. We used to laugh about how much we enjoyed each other's company, but that we'd prefer to bring our one-and-only lifetime loves on those excursions. Now he and Chuck can do just that.

I hope this is forever for them. Jeff is not the kind of person to engage in multiple relationships. He's very shy and very sensitive. I'm going to miss him. It's sad to think that we have to say "goodbye" tomorrow.

Friday, July 15, 1983

Just got word from Stepford High School in Spruceton, North Carolina. I've been offered a teaching position-- Physical Education, though, not Literature. I guess I did all right on the interview last week. I'm glad I got the job. Spruceton is a beautiful town. It's nestled snugly in the Blue Ridge Mountains. There's supposed to be lots of good biking and camping spots there. It definitely looks like my kind of place. The artsy community of Asheville is only about a half hour away, so that should provide me with plenty of cultural stimulation.

Wednesday, July 20, 1983

Dad and I will be leaving next week for North Carolina. I want to find a place to live that is close to the school, so I can commute by bike. I'm going to use the money I got from the poetry contest to buy myself a new one. I'm excited about moving. I'm rather anxious about my teaching position. At least I don't have to start out teaching in front of a regular classroom. I think that teaching P.E. is a good way to ease myself into the waters of teaching. I'm just not certain how I would do standing in front of all those classes. At least when I'm outside I'm in my element.

Friday, August 5, 1983

Dad and I found a cute little house with a fireplace and a beautiful view. It has one bedroom and one bath. I love it. Dad showed me how to house hunt. He has a "system." What a joke! It worked though.

I'll start teaching in three weeks, but I have to go in before that to start preparations. I can't believe I'm actually going to teach P.E. Why didn't I hold out for an opening in literature? Ah well, I really don't want to teach high school literature. I want to teach that on the college level.

In the meantime, I want to get out on my own. I need to prove to myself that I can survive in the adult world. Dad paid for my education. He bought me a car. Now he's offering to furnish my house, but I'm going to turn him down. Everything has been so easy for me that I am going to be permanently spoiled if it continues. I know he wants to help, and I appreciate it. But now I have a job and a little house, and it is time for me to make my own way.

I will furnish my place with my own resources, as I can afford it. If that means I have to sit on the floor for a while, then that's what I'll do. I bought a waterbed already though, so I can just sit on that until I can afford other furniture. Besides, if Dad pays for my furniture, I know he'll try to get what he likes, rather than what I like. That just wouldn't do. We have very different ideas about decor.

Monday, August 8, 1983

The landlord is going to let me use one of his sofas. He had too much furniture in his house, so he wondered if I wanted to use any of it in my place. Then it can just stay with the house for the next renters after I leave. That was very thoughtful of him to offer that to me. I guess he realized that I was just getting started. If everyone who lives around here is that nice, I think I'm going to like this town. I suppose it would be too much to expect everyone to be so kind and friendly.

Wednesday, August 17, 1983

I bought an inexpensive table and chairs for the dining area. It is all wood, with a blond finish. It's very plain really. Nothing fancy. The set was marked down because there are a couple of gashes in it. You're not likely to notice them unless you know they are there. I'm going to celebrate tonight with a candlelight dinner. Who knows? Maybe I'll start my own tradition, like Dad and Buddy.

Saturday, August 27, 1983

I'm really nervous about school starting. Making plans and setting things up wasn't too bad. Julie Marshall, the other P.E. teacher, has gone out of her way to make me feel welcome there. I doubt the kids will be that considerate.

Monday, August 29, 1983

The first day of school was hectic, which is to be expected, I suppose. Taking attendance was a joke. There are so many kids in each of my classes; I'll never be able to keep all the names and faces straight.

I'm tired, so I'm going to shower and then dive into my waterbed. I should sleep soundly tonight. I hope so. I need to make up for the last few nights. I've been so nervous and excited I haven't been able to keep my eyes shut for very long.

Friday, September 9, 1983

Congratulations, Anna! You managed to survive the first two weeks of school. Everyone assures me that it gets easier from here on. I certainly hope so. If it gets any more difficult, I'll never make it.

I have my eye on several responsible students. I want to pick out a couple in each class, and assign them the task of carrying equipment and taking attendance. That should make it a little easier for me, at any rate.

Sunday, September 18, 1983

Today I assigned two students in each class to be my assistants. It's amazing how each class has one or two mature kids. The rest of them are space cadets. One student in particular has come to my attention. Her name is Alice Katz, but her nickname is "Allie." I wonder if her parents did that on purpose, or if that was just one of those inadvertent puns. At least Allie Katz is a cute name, even if it does have interesting connotations. Do her parents realize that Allie Katz stay out all night, prowling around town? Ha!

I truly hope for her sake that she doesn't catch a lot of flack. She's a sweet kid. She's always cooperative and helpful. It's funny how she makes her presence felt in very subtle ways. She's a natural leader, but a quiet one. She leads by setting herself apart from the others. No, that's not a good way of putting it. Let me try again. She's a leader because she is strong enough to stand on her own. It's apparent that she doesn't need peer approval to be who she is. She is just herself. I admire her for that. She seems older than her biological age. I guess she is like me in that sense.

Thursday, September 22, 1983

I had a pleasant encounter with Allie Katz today. I was walking out the door with an armful of equipment (one of my assistants was absent), when I met her coming in. I was going to back my way out, since my hands were otherwise engaged, but Allie saw me and said, "I've got it." So she opened the door for me and held it until I was outside. Most kids wouldn't have even realized that I needed help, much less done anything to remedy the situation.

On top of that, as I passed, she said, "If I weren't running late for my class, I'd help you carry all that stuff."

If I had been a little faster on the draw, I could've offered to write a pass for her. I keep forgetting I have that kind of authority.

Tuesday, September 27, 1983

I asked Julie Marshall if she had Alice Katz in her class last year. She said, "Allie? Yes, I did. She's a wonderful kid. You're going to love her."

Apparently Allie is not only an excellent athlete, she's a budding scholar as well. The child pulled a 4.0 last year with a hefty freshman load. It's amazing what you can find out on those office computers, especially if you have a friend on the inside. Kind of sounds like espionage, doesn't it?

Friday, September 30, 1983

Allie Katz. Her name is so cute. She fits it too. She's a very warm person. I almost feel as though she purrs when I'm talking to her. Yet she's fairly aloof with the other students. It isn't that she's a snob or that she is painfully shy. It's more like she's on another planet. Well, no, maybe it's just that she's more firmly planted on the ground, and it's the space cadets who are on another planet. She's down-to-earth, and the others are just out there somewhere orbiting.

I guess she is one of those students Dr. Stein warned me about. She said that some kids stand out from the rest. So much so, it's obvious they don't belong in their environment. They're just biding their time until they can be unleashed upon the world. I know that is the way I was. Fortunately I was allowed to graduate from high school a year early. I doubt I could have withstood another year of that. I really feel for Allie. She's just a sophomore. Three years left.

Monday, October 3, 1983

I do not really care for our faculty meetings. The one we had today lasted for two and a half hours. That's a bit much. I don't think anything was accomplished either. Except perhaps that we were all bored to death. Everyone except George Adams, that is. He's the reason the meeting lasted so long. He kept interrupting, though he never really had anything intelligent to say.

I think I'll go for a quick bike ride. Maybe it will help me unwind. I can't wait until tennis gets into full swing (what a terrible pun, Anna). I'm the girls' tennis coach. We start practice tomorrow. I had hoped to get started last week, but I didn't get organized quickly enough. I've been talking to Allie Katz about signing up for it. She said that she hasn't played much, but I bet it wouldn't take her long to pick it up. She's a natural athlete. I think she could do anything she wanted with very little effort.

Wednesday, October 5, 1983

Allie came to tennis practice today. I can tell that she hasn't played much, but it won't be long before she's one of the best on the team. What's really great about this kid is that she's not just a "jocque." The intelligence in her eyes leaps out at me. It's good to see a well-rounded teen.

There are two seasoned players on the tennis team. One is a junior, the other a senior. Their groundstrokes are clean and precise. I can tell they have been working hard at perfecting their game. Besides Allie, there are two other players with potential. Unfortunately there are also a couple of girls on the team who must have joined for social purposes. Or perhaps they wished to please their parents. Not the greatest reasons to join, I must say. Who knows? Maybe they will surprise themselves and fall in love with the sport for its own sake.

Friday, October 7, 1983

Allie is in incredible shape. Her muscles are nicely toned and well defined. She really has a good body. I enjoy watching the way she moves, even when she's not doing sports. She walks with such poise — athletic poise, that is, not charm school grace. She's a very solid and real person. She seems to have a lot of depth too. I thoroughly enjoy talking with her. She has beautiful blue eyes. Listen to yourself, Anna. You sound like a lovesick puppy. Stop it!

Saturday, October 8, 1983

The leaves are rapidly changing colors. I wish I had more time and energy to admire them. I truly love autumn in the mountains. When I bike to higher elevations, I catch panoramic views of their changing hues. How poetic, Anna.

Wednesday, October 19, 1983

My schedule has gotten full since the tennis team started playing matches. I don't have time to do much of anything these days. I admit that it feels good to be busy. I think I was spending too many evenings and weekends brooding over the vicissitudes of life.

Friday, October 21, 1983

It's Friday evening. Now what? I think I'll read this weekend. I haven't had a good reading marathon in a long time. But first, I want to go for a bike ride. I need to keep my legs strong for tennis. Some of my students are already in top form. They keep me on my toes, especially Allie. She's got incredible endurance. Definitely a natural athlete.

Monday, October 24, 1983

This has been a pleasant weekend. I reread Tolkien's *The Hobbit* and *The Lord of the Rings*. I needed to travel to a land far, far away, where they don't take attendance or organize herds of teenage girls. I thoroughly enjoyed revisiting Middle-Earth. I really wish that Tolkien had developed Galadriel more. She is such an enticing creature. I can picture her in my mind — tall, long limbed, and beautiful. Very powerful, yet gentle and caring. In her eyes are the fiery sparks of intelligence and passion. She embodies wisdom and grace. I wonder if she would like to go out with me. Her husband might object, but maybe not. We can always write him out of our book. It is fantasy, after all.

Friday, October 28, 1983

I think I'm beginning to settle into a routine at school. I don't feel quite so frazzled at the end of the day. Exhausted, yes; frazzled, no. I could use a good soak in the tub. I think I'll put on some tea to brew and some soft, relaxing music. That should calm me down a bit. Too bad I don't have anyone to give me a back rub. That is one of the few things I miss about Sarah. She knew a lot about massaging tired muscles.

Friday, November 4, 1983

I'm enjoying my candlelight dinners. They make me feel quite cozy. I like treating myself like this. Every once in a while, I buy flowers for the table. I wouldn't mind planting some wild flowers around the house this spring. That way I could have my own garden to pick from.

Monday, November 7, 1983

I catch myself watching Allie more and more. There's something very special about her. Sometimes I sense her presence, even before I see her. I don't know what it is about that girl, but I am definitely attracted to her. If she were a year older, I would ask her out. She's really beautiful. Well, I guess I should go find a book to read. I can't let myself think about her. She's just an adolescent. A mature one, no doubt, but an adolescent nonetheless.

Friday, November 11, 1983

I can't stop thinking about Allie. I guess I really need a lover. I can bury myself in my books for only so long. Then my need for companionship and intimacy hunts me down. Unfortunately, the only person I am attracted to is sixteen years old. That puts a tremendous kink in things. I'm only five years older than she is, and she really is a mature seventeen-year old. Of course, the law wouldn't look at it that way. Nor would her parents, I'm sure.

Thursday, November 17, 1983

God, I sound like a broken record. I really need a lover. Masturbation doesn't seem to help much. Solo flights may release the sexual tension, but they do nothing for the emotions. I need intimacy with another human being. Besides all I can see is Allie's face with those deep blue eyes, her bright smile, and that long, wavy brown hair. Her nose is really cute too, especially when she crinkles it up and makes that grimace when the sun gets in her eyes.

Monday, November 28, 1983

I think I'd better go out of town for Christmas break. Staying home alone through Thanksgiving break was not a good idea. I definitely needed the physical rest, but this brooding is not good. In fact, it's downright depressing.

We got our school pictures back today. I want to ask Allie for one of hers, but I don't know how to go about it. She was absent today though, so I didn't even see her.

Tuesday, November 29, 1983

I surprised myself today. I actually asked Allie for one of her school pictures. When she came to tennis practice this afternoon, she had them on top of her books. So I asked her how they turned out. She just shrugged and said, "Okay, I guess. I don't really like getting my picture taken."

I asked to see them. They are wonderful, of course. How could they not be? Look at the subject. A photographer's dream. So I said, "Those are really good. If you have any left, you ought to let me have one. That way I can always remember my star tennis player."

"Well, if you have any scissors on you, you can take one now. Otherwise I'll bring you one tomorrow."

"It isn't a good idea for P.E. teachers to run around with sharp instruments, so I guess I'll have to settle for waiting until tomorrow."

She gave me a funny look and said, "Okay. I'll bring one tomorrow, if you're really serious."

"I'm always serious."

"No you're not. I see you smiling and laughing a lot."

"I see. I didn't realize I was under such close scrutiny."

Looking embarrassed, Allie said, "Well, I see you every day in class and at practice. It would be hard to miss."

Monday, December 19, 1983

I've decided to go to California for the holidays. I really need to get away from here. It's a long flight, but I went to New York last year. I suppose I really should have settled down a little closer to home. Of course, with my father in New York and my mother in California, I wouldn't have been able to establish myself near both of them at the same time. So I seem to have settled for living near neither of them. Smart move, Anna.

Monday, January 2, 1984

My Christmas trip was a little hectic, but it was good to see everybody. Peter was there too, with his wife, Joanne. I hadn't seen him since he and Joanne moved to Minneapolis. He couldn't come to my graduation because of his job. It's just as well though. That made it easier for me to skip his wedding last July. I couldn't afford the plane fare then, and I didn't really want to drive that distance. The trips back and forth to California were bad enough.

Saturday, January 7, 1984

Mmm. I feel very cozy right now. I just threw another log on the fire so it's getting nice and toasty in here, which is quite a contrast to what it's like outside. It's really cold tonight. The wind is whipping around the house rather violently. It keeps banging at the windows as though it would like to come in and share my fire. I don't think I care for its company tonight. I'm having quite a pleasant evening alone, warming my hands around a mug of tea, staring into the firelight. It's very peaceful.

I've been perusing cookbooks, in search of new recipes. Jeff sent me a new vegetarian cookbook for Christmas. He said that they had just gotten it in, and he thought I would like it. I miss his sense of humor and his kind manner. I like living on my own though. I like the solitude. Yes, I would very much like to have a lover, but there don't appear to be any prospects at the moment.

Perhaps I can hang around until Allie turns eighteen. There is of course just one problem with that idea. I'm not even certain that she's a lesbian. She may not even know yet what she is. Not everyone does at that age. I know she's different. I know she's not a socialite. She doesn't date guys, and she's really cute.

I've been carrying her picture in my wallet. I take it out and look at it sometimes. Sigh. How stupid I am to get a crush on one of my students. Going away for Christmas helped a little, but now that I'm back, and I see her nearly every day of the week, it's getting to me again.

Friday, January 13, 1984

I think it's time for another reading marathon. It feels good to be able to do that whenever I want. How about *War and Peace*? I read an abridged version in high school, but I have never tackled the whole thing. Go for it, Anna!

Wednesday, January 18, 1984

Now I know more than I ever wanted to know about freemasonry. It actually took me more than the weekend to finish the whole book. I kept falling asleep. There's something very relaxing about a crackling fire and soothing herbal tea. I'm certain it had nothing to do with the tedious passages on freemasonry.

Dad mailed me a copy of *Anna Karenina* for Christmas. I have never read it, though Dad told me the whole story years ago. It's one of his favorite books. I suppose I should read it next. He'll probably quiz me on it next time I see him. Forever the literature professor!

Friday, January 20, 1984

We had to cancel the intramural tennis tournament this weekend because of icy roads. I wish we had indoor tennis facilities. I hate putting tennis on hold until spring. Winter has been really bitter so far. It's a little colder here than in Tennessee. The wind bites into you. I'm glad I have a solid little house. I've already had to start driving to work. It's just been too windy and cold to bike.

Monday, January 23, 1984

They closed the schools today because of the treacherous driving conditions. I'm glad for the extra day of rest, but it means I won't see Allie today. I was really looking forward to seeing her at the tournament. Ah well, next weekend perhaps. Now if the weather would just cooperate. This is a fairly moderate climate, but it has its moments. Very unpredictable.

Tuesday, January 24, 1984

It's supposed to heat up enough today to melt the snow. In the meantime, there's no school again. I think I'll take my bike out and see the snow-covered scenery before it all disappears. The wind seems to have died down somewhat.

Wednesday, January 25, 1984

Our tournament has been rescheduled for this weekend. Nearly all of the snow has melted, so it looks good. But then, so does Allie. It was great to see her at school today. I don't think I care much for snow days.

Sunday, January 29, 1984

The tournament was excellent. Allie and Theresa did really well. Clarisse captured the girls' title, as expected. I also discovered some good players who aren't signed up for the team. I think I'd better get busy and do some recruiting. Of course the socialites were there too, concentrating on looking cute in their tennis togs. I wish they would get serious. If I hear one more complaint about broken fingernails, I may scream.

Friday, February 10, 1984

I've been a little melancholy lately. I don't know what's wrong, but I feel as though I'm always on the verge of tears. Maybe I should see a psychologist. Last night I went to the movies, and cried most of the way through it. It wasn't even a sad movie. I'm just feeling depressed and lonely. I think I'm going to start my period soon. That never helps matters any. Sometimes I feel so small and fragile I don't know if I can make it through the day.

Sunday, February 12, 1984

I think I'm suffering from a bad case of the Valentine's blues. We're having a dance at the school Friday night.   I wonder if Allie is going. Probably not.   She isn't dating anyone that I know of, and I cannot imagine her going stag. She doesn't seem to participate in any of the school social functions. Unfortunately I have to chaperone, so I have to go. At least if she went I could talk with her.

Tuesday, February 14, 1984

Allie is not going to the dance. I felt like an idiot asking her, but I had to find out. Alas, I'm doomed to watching the mating dances of the young and brainless. I wish I could ask Allie to go with me, but I don't think that would go over well with the school board. School officials frown upon teachers dating students, especially in a homosexual context. Legal officials like it even less.

I guess I'll just sit around now and think depressing thoughts. If I really want to get depressed I could think about what would happen if I asked Allie to go to the dance with me. She might call the police and have me arrested. She might call the school and have me fired. Then again, she might just laugh in my face. I think I could deal with the other possibilities better than I could deal with that one.

Friday, February 17, 1984

Finally, the Valentine's Dance is history. I stood around trying not to look as bored as I was, but I suspect that I failed miserably. For the first hour I prayed that someone would spike the punch. Should that miracle have occurred, I would've proceeded to get thoroughly smashed. No such luck. I don't know why I wanted to get drunk. I just thought it would be better than dying of boredom. I don't really drink much though, so I probably would've succeeded only in making myself sick.

I really don't know what is wrong with me. I'm acting like a lovesick puppy. I'm fine when I'm at school, especially when Allie's around. Otherwise I just feel depressed.

Tuesday, February 21, 1984

I wonder what Sarah is doing these days. I managed to avoid her during the last week of school. Now I have no idea where she went after graduation. I guess I'll never see her again. I hope she gets her life straightened out. She's basically a decent human being. She's just very insecure. Not like me, of course. I have no fears or insecurities whatsoever.

THUMP!

Pardon me. I just fell on the floor laughing at that one.

Thursday, February 23, 1984

I'm glad we have a preseason tournament coming up. That means I get to see Allie even more than usual. That ought to cheer me up for a few days. I really enjoy talking to her. She is such a fascinating person. She's says things that I don't expect someone her age to say. That's not to say that I wouldn't have been able to guess how old she is if I had met her beyond the parameters of school. She looks very much like a teenager. There's just something special about her that makes her seem older.

Monday, February 27, 1984

Allie didn't do as well in this tournament. She was off her game a little bit. She appeared to be rather distracted. Theresa, on the other hand, played beautifully. She even beat Clarisse. Unfortunately everyone else played as though they had their rackets in the wrong hands and their shoes on the wrong feet.

Sunday, March 4, 1984

It's snowing today. I'm glad it's Saturday. At least they can't cancel school. I think I'll try to plow my way through the snow on my bike. I like riding in the snow. It's so quiet. It's a little strange, however, when your tires hit a patch of ice. All you can do is to keep peddling, and hope that you gain some traction before you fall over. I tried to put my foot down once, but that didn't help, since my shoe couldn't get a grip either. I fell down rather gracelessly in the middle of the road.   Fortunately for me it was on a road without a great deal of traffic.   I don't think anybody saw my clown-like routine. At least if they did, they didn't laugh loud enough for me to hear.

Tuesday, March 6, 1984

We're going to have a teacher workday today.   The roads are better, but there are some spots where it's still very icy, so they don't want to run the buses. I can hardly blame them. I almost wiped out again when I was biking yesterday. I managed to keep my bike and myself vertical this time. I wonder why they don't have more snowplows. It's not like snow is a rarity here in the winter. It just doesn't come down as fast or as often as it does in New York.

Sunday, March 11, 1984

I think it must be time for another read-a-thon. I don't want to read anything too depressing. That eliminates a lot of authors completely. I think I'll ride over to the library and check out something totally different. I'm in a weird mood right now. I need to get engrossed in someone else's world for a while. I'm getting annoyed with mine. It's so blasé.

Wednesday, March 14, 1984

I definitely found something different to read. I checked out *The Autobiography of Alice B. Toklas,* by Gertrude Stein. It is intriguing, to say the least. It's a shame Stein doesn't include any of her personal romance with Alice. That would have made it more interesting. It was just what I needed to shake my mental lethargy. Stein is a humorous writer. It is well worth the time it takes to get accustomed to her writing style.

Thursday, March 29, 1984

It's good to be back in my quiet little house again. I went to New York for Spring Break. Dad called and said that he'd send a ticket if I would consent to come and help him for a week. His secretary's kids have been sick, so he's swamped with work. I figured I could use some of Buddy's cheerfulness, so I accepted. He was right about being swamped. I worked at least ten hours every day. I got him caught up finally. His secretary is back now, so he should be all right. I like proofreading for him because I get a chance to see what his books look like before they're published.

I thoroughly enjoyed being with Dad and Buddy. They kept trying to get me to go on a blind date with a friend of Dad's. Actually she's one of his students, a Literature major of course. I finally consented to have her over for dinner, if Dad and Buddy dined with us. They agreed to the double-date stipulation, so we all got to witness the disaster.

Paula, my date, was very nice, but she was terribly uncomfortable. I don't know whether it was the blind date situation itself, or the fact that she was dining with her professor and his lover. Whatever the reason, it wasn't much fun. We all felt sorry for her, but we never quite managed to overcome the awkwardness of the situation.

I thanked Dad and Buddy for trying to be helpful, but I told them that I'd prefer to stay single forever than to force a relationship. Love is something you stumble over, or falls on top of you, or chases you into unfamiliar territory. It isn't something you phone out for and have delivered to your door. It's more like a phantom train. You don't see it coming, but you know when it runs over you and leaves you bleeding on the tracks.

Tuesday, April 10, 1984

I'm really depressed. I just can't stop thinking about Allie. I felt so weird in New York when I ate with Paula. I kind of felt as though I were betraying Allie by eating with this woman by candlelight, even though Dad and Buddy were right there. Or perhaps it was because they were there. Had it been just the two of us I would not have lit candles. Of course, it could be that I felt as though I were betraying myself by having an intimate dinner with someone I have no feelings for. I don't know. It's all so crazy, but I think that this feeling I have for Allie is for real. It's more than infatuation. I have tried not to allow myself to feel these things, but they won't go away. I really want to see Allie. I really want to be with her. I want to love her and have her return my love. Oh damn it, Anna! You have really screwed things up this time.

Thursday, April 12, 1984

I wouldn't mind talking to a psychologist about this, but I don't think it would help much. No one can alter Allie's age. No one can alter the laws and prejudices of this society. I'm just stuck. The only thing I know to do is to move far away from here. Then in two years, if I still feel the same way about Allie, I can come back and see if she will have me. If, on the other hand, I've gotten over her, then I can get on with my life.

Sunday, April 15, 1984

I've begun the process of job-hunting again. I called Dr. Stein and put her on the trail of something in another state. We'll see what she comes up with. She sounded a little puzzled when I told her that everything had gone well this first year. I tried to reassure her that I'm fine, but for personal reasons I needed to transfer. I think she sensed the gravity of my feelings. She won't pry either. She's very sensitive. Maybe after this is all over, I will go and talk with her. She might understand. I know she would at least sympathize.

Wednesday, April 18, 1984

Damn it! Am I destined for despair? I guess I'm going to have to steer clear of the locker room from now on. After tennis practice today, I went into the locker room to turn out the lights and lock the doors. It was very quiet, so I assumed the girls had all gone home.

As usual, I heard a showerhead dripping, so I found it and turned it off. On my way out, however, I caught a glimpse of Allie toweling off in another stall. She had her face in the towel, so she didn't see me. I saw her though. All of her. My heart jumped into my throat and stuck there. That girl is beautiful! She's simply flawless in every way. Every line and curve is perfect. I can't stop thinking about her. I can't get that picture out of my mind. For that matter, I don't want to get it out of my mind.

Wednesday, April 25, 1984

I called Dr. Stein today. She's still working on finding me a new position. She is waiting for an update on openings. Only a few responses to her inquiries have been returned so far. I suppose I need to think about what I should do if I can't find another teaching position. One option comes readily to mind, but I'm trying not to think about it too much.

Sunday, April 29, 1984

Dr. Stein called. I have three opportunities open to me. One is in Kentucky; two are in Virginia. She's going to mail me the details. I'm anxious to resolve this issue. I don't want to leave here, but I know I can't stay. I just want to find a job and move to another town so I can get on with my life.

Thursday, May 3, 1984

I'm feeling very weary. I think these strong emotions are draining all my energy. I just want to sleep all the time. What I would really like to do is to go to sleep and never wake up again. That would simplify things immensely. Then I wouldn't have to worry about this any more. There would be no more decisions to make, no more pain to feel. I hate to admit how much that idea appeals to me right now.

Monday, May 7, 1984

I just talked to Dad on the phone. To be more precise, I cried to Dad on the phone. I didn't do a whole lot of talking. He just kept saying, "It's okay, baby. Don't let it get you down." I think he's worried about me. Hell, I'm worried about me! I thought very seriously last night about swallowing a bottle full of aspirin. Much to my chagrin, I didn't have a full bottle. I didn't know whether nineteen would be enough or not. I decided not to chance making myself sick without the certainty of stopping the ache in my heart.

Tuesday, May 8, 1984

Mom called tonight. I think Dad must've called her because she sounded as though she were trying not to sound alarmed. It didn't work, as usual. I told her that I would survive. She wants me to come home as soon as school is out. I can't though. I have a lease that runs through August. I'll have to stay until then or pay even though I'm not staying here. I know I could break the lease in the event of an emergency, but I don't want to do that. I would feel as though I had failed in my agreement with my landlord. It's bad enough that I'm going to have to change schools after only one year.

Besides, if I go running home now, it will be that much easier to run home every time things get difficult. I have to stand on my own two feet. If I go to California or New York for the summer, my parents will try to persuade me to settle down near them. Then I wouldn't have to face the world by myself. I simply cannot continue to dive for the womb whenever life gets scary. I tried that enough when I was younger. Now I am an adult. I need to solve this problem on my own no matter how uncomfortable it may get. I have to make my own decisions and find my own jobs using the contacts I have established. I must go on with my life as it is.

Thursday, May 10, 1984

I got the information packet from Dr. Stein today. As soon as I looked through it, I went out and mailed a copy of my resume to all three schools. I'm going to tell Jay Wallace tomorrow that I won't be back next year.   The more time I give him to find a replacement, the better.   I really hate to inconvenience the school because of my love life.   What a mess I have made of my life and career.

Friday, May 11, 1984

Jay was disappointed when I told him I was leaving.   I made it clear that my leaving had nothing to do with the school itself, but that I needed to leave for personal reasons. He was really concerned and supportive.   He offered to help in any way he could.   I just hope my next school has such a competent and sensitive principal.

Saturday, May 12, 1984

I think word has gotten around school that I am not going to be here next year.   I'm fairly certain that Allie has heard about it.   She looked at me rather strangely yesterday.   I almost felt as though she were angry with me.   Perhaps I should have told her personally about leaving.

Tuesday, May 15, 1984

Allie is definitely displeased about something.   I don't know what is happening in her personal life right now, but whatever it is, it isn't positive.   I wish I could put my arms around her and comfort her.   Sometimes she seems like such a child, and other times she seems very mature.   Growing up is never a straightforward thing.

Thursday, May 17, 1984

I have an interview Monday at the school in Kentucky.   I think I'll drive over Saturday and stay in a hotel for a couple nights. I need to escape for a few days anyway. The extra time there will afford me the chance to explore the town.

Tuesday, May 22, 1984

The interview went well, I think, but then you never can tell exactly. I haven't heard anything from the schools in Virginia yet. Kentucky is pretty, though less mountainous. There are lots and lots of hills. I think I could stand to work there for a year or two. I'd rather stay here, but I think it would be easier on my heart if I didn't see Allie every day. It has been getting increasingly more difficult to stick to "safe" topics when I'm talking to her.

Thursday, May 24, 1984

I got a call from Martha Gavins, the principal of Burkefield High. I have the position in Kentucky if I want it. I don't particularly want it, but I'm going to take it. I have to get out of here. I can't stand this depression any longer. I feel a little better already, just knowing I have an escape route. Of course, I have no idea what I'm escaping to. What will I do if I fall in love with a student there? I guess if it happens again I will just have to quit teaching high school, and go back to college. If I get my master's degree, I can start teaching college while I work on my doctorate. Then if I fall in love with a student, she should not be a minor at least. Though I would probably need to avoid freshmen, er, freshwomen. On second thought, I would probably do better with fresh women. Gosh, Anna, you are really losing it! At least I'm beginning to regain my sense of humor. Maybe things will work out after all.

Friday, May 25, 1984

I told Allie today that I got a teaching position in Kentucky, and that I'd be going there next year. Tears welled up in her eyes, and she nearly started crying. I felt horrible. I just wanted to tell her myself, instead of letting her hear it through the Stepford grapevine. When she regained her composure, she asked me why I was leaving. I would have liked to have told her everything. That I have fallen in love with her. That I'm afraid of myself and of her. That every time I look at her, I am overwhelmed with the desire to feel her lips on mine. That when I close my eyes, I see her naked body as she was that day in the locker room. That if I can't tell her how I feel, I'd rather not be around her at all, because it hurts so much to keep it bottled up inside. That I cry nearly every night because I long to feel her arms around me. That I'm afraid if I told her all these things she would laugh at me.

Instead I just told her that it would be better if I left this area. I almost starting crying too, but I didn't, amazingly enough. She looked so sad. It hurt to know that I was the cause of her sadness, but it has to be better this way. If I stay here, there's no way I will be able to hide my feelings for her. It has to be better to hurt her a little now, than to hurt her a lot later. She doesn't need to get embroiled in this emotional mess of mine. She'll get over losing her favorite teacher soon enough. A lot faster than I will get over losing her, no doubt.

Sunday, June 10, 1984

Now that school's out I hardly know what to do with myself. I have always put my journal aside during the summer months. Now that I'm not rushing off somewhere to live in another world for three months, I can't imagine what I will do with the free time. Until now, my summers have been full and hectic. Too bad Dad didn't need any help this year. I know I could have gone there anyway, but I do need to work on getting everything settled for the move to Kentucky.

Tuesday, June 12, 1984

I just received my first newspaper from Kentucky. I need to get busy and start house hunting. I'm going to try out Dad's system. Let's see if it works for me. Dad offered to pay the last two months rent on my lease so I could go to New York, if I so desired. I declined. I've really got a lot to do before I move, and I need to do it on my own. Except for this little matter of the heart, I've done all right with my life.

Thursday, June 14, 1984

I've eliminated all but three apartments on my list. The others were either rented or they wanted a couple. A couple of what, I wonder? I'm going to drive to Kentucky so I can check out the last ones. They all sound promising, so here goes nothing.

Friday, June 22, 1984

Not only have I found a decent place to live, but also I've gotten everything set up already. I didn't even have to use "the system," because I eliminated all but one apartment. I already paid the deposit, so it's mine. I can move in any time after August 17th.

Monday, June 25, 1984

I saw Allie today. She was on her bike. I don't think she saw me though. She was flying downhill, while I was puffing and panting up a dirt trail, just off the road. I wonder if she rides around there often. I knew she liked to bike, but I've never encountered her before on any of the roads where I ride. I guess I've been riding in the wrong places all this time. It would be nice if I could run into her again somewhere so I could say goodbye, but I guess that might be a little awkward.

Thursday, June 28, 1984

I've been burying myself in sorting through things, clearing out stuff I've accumulated this past year that I really don't need to take to Kentucky with me. Mostly paperwork, old bills and junk mail, but some school stuff too. I'm doing my best not to think about Allie, but the future looks and feels so bleak to me. I'm really going to miss her smiling face when I go to school every day. It just won't be the same, but I guess that's the point of this move. I need to make a break with my life here, even though I was enjoying this school and my classes.

Wednesday, July 11, 1984

I need to go to the mall to pick up some empty boxes. There's a liquor store near there that stacks their boxes out back. If I start packing my books now, I can organize them so they won't be so chaotic when I unpack them. The thought of going to the mall is nauseating though. There is just too much traffic and too many people. Ah well, better to get it over with, I suppose.

I had a rough time last night. I kept dreaming about Allie. Then I would wake up in tears. Why did I have to fall in love with a sixteen-year-old? When I moved here, I had great hopes of finding a quiet cove where I could settle down and lead a hermitlike existence. Well, I found a quiet enough house to live in, but I seem to have filled my hermitage with the emotional upheaval that comes with unrequited love. Of course, I can hardly expect Allie to acknowledge or return my love when she isn't even aware of it. Or at least I hope she isn't aware of it. I have tried very hard to keep it to myself.

Monday, July 16, 1984

Packing is good therapy. It helps me to feel that I have a measure of control over my life. I am taking steps to change my life by moving. Packing is the first step towards moving on to a new life. Besides it gives me something to think about besides Allie. I can't pack very many things though because I'll need some of my belongings between now and moving day. I'm mostly just packing my books. I need some more packing tape so I'm going to have to go to the mall again. Damn! I really dislike that place. There's no good place to lock my bike, and parking is usually impossible. I should probably get a couple more boxes too, so I guess I'll have to take my car.

Thursday, July 19, 1984

For once in my life, procrastination paid off. I put off going to the mall until today. After spending half the summer hoping to catch another glimpse of Allie on the biking trails, I ran into her at the mall of all places. I nearly fainted. It took me a couple minutes to convince myself it was really Allie. I'm so good at seeing her when she isn't there. I figured that it was just wishful thinking again.

I came to my senses just in time to catch up to her. Her face lit up when she recognized me. My heart jumped into my throat. I thought I wasn't going to be able to say anything at first. It was all right though because she started talking excitedly. By the time she paused for a breath, I had collected my wits. I managed to invite her to have lunch with me. That may not have been a wise thing to do, but it was such a shock to see her. I didn't want to lose my chance to tell her goodbye.

She consented to have lunch with me, but I couldn't think of a good place to take her. I suggested McDonald's because it was nearby. I didn't want to invite her back here. I figured that would have been an awkward situation. McDonald's turned out to be awkward anyway, but we managed to get beyond that. It was rather humorous really. Somehow it came out that neither of us like fast food, so we left and went to the Garden Place instead. All I can say is that Allie must've been trying to be polite at McDonald's because she told me there that she wasn't hungry. Then at the Garden Place, she helped me put away my favorite entree. Because it is meant to be a dinner for two, I always have to take most of it home. Not this time. Allie has a healthy teenage appetite!

We talked a lot between bites. We laughed a lot too, though it was mostly nervous laughter. She was as nervous as I was. She invited me to go mountain biking with her tomorrow, but I didn't give her a definite answer. I have had so many fantasies involving her, that now I'm almost afraid to go biking with her. I don't know if I'm afraid it will ruin all the fantasies I've had about her, which are always perfect of course, or that I will be unable to conceal my feelings for Allie. Doing so could not only ruin my fantasies, it could also pretty well screw up my life.

My mind keeps playing a videotape of my most depressing fantasies—I come on to Allie, she calls the police, etc. Or she just laughs in my face then rides away on her bike. I don't think I could handle anything like that right now. So I told Allie I had an appointment, but that I would call her later and let her know about a rain check. I don't really have a formal appointment, but I do have to go back and get the packing supplies at the mall. Running into Allie made me forget everything else.

Friday, July 20, 1984

Okay. I went to the mall as soon as it opened. I got everything I needed. Now what? It's only 11:00 a.m. I can't call Allie yet. It's not even noon. Oh, hell! Call her anyway. I've got to see her again, but not today. I don't think I can deal with it today. Maybe I can just daydream about what I'd like to do with her. Better yet, I'll write about it.

The scene opens with a long bike ride to my favorite picnic spot up in the mountains. After we stop huffing and puffing, I say to Allie, "It sure is hot today! This is one of those times when I wish people had never invented clothes. It's too hot to wear any. Would you mind it terribly if I shed a layer or two?" Of course she won't mind and will even decide to join me. So I pull off my shoes and socks just to tease her and to see if she's interested in seeing more. She is obviously disappointed.

"Gee, I thought you were going to be more daring than that."

Pretending to ignore her remark, I mention the lake on the other side of the trees and suggest that we wade in it to cool off.

Allie says, "Wade in it? Let's go swimming! Of course I don't have my swimsuit with me, so I guess I'll have to go skinny-dipping. How about it? Are you game?"

"Race you to it!" I yell, as I take off running.

At the lake, Allie boldly strips off her shirt and waits to see if I follow suit. Taking the bait, I quickly undress and dive into the lake before she is fully unclothed. She dives in and swims towards me with the strong, smooth strokes of an athlete.

When she reaches me, I compliment her on the strength and gracefulness of her body. She complains that she didn't get a chance to see my body because she was busy getting undressed.

"Oh. I suppose that can be remedied."

I swim back towards the shore. Allie, of course, follows. On shore I pull a towel from my backpack and start drying off slowly. Coming up behind me, Allie reaches around to take the towel from my hands, turning me towards her in the process. Looking deeply into my eyes, she strips away all my fears about her. I sway forward into her arms as she bends her head to kiss me. The towel falls to the ground unnoticed as our lips meet in a passionate kiss. In that moment time becomes frozen. There is nothing to hear, nothing to see, nothing to feel, nothing except the desire of our bodies.

After we exhaust ourselves in our lovemaking, we fall asleep in the warm afternoon sun. Upon awakening, we find that we are still engaged in the contented embrace of lovers. We cuddle for several minutes, caressing and admiring the beauty of each other's body. Drawn into the passion of the moment, we begin again to explore the depths of our sexuality, until the urgency of new love is quieted in temporary satisfaction.

As the sun begins to sink, we realize it is time to return to the world below. But before we leave, we make a vow to come back here as often as possible, sealing the promise with a long kiss. Racing back down the mountain on our bikes, we realize that not only did we forget to eat lunch, but we also forgot to get dressed.

Ha! I couldn't resist that last sentence. I had to lighten up before I created a puddle. It's amazing how aroused I get just thinking about Allie. Wow! I'd better call her. It's nearly noon now. I hope she's home.

Later: Well, she was home, and we have a date to go biking tomorrow. I am going to bring a picnic lunch. I think I'll see if she wants to go to the tennis tournament that's going on in Charlotte this week. The tennis coach at Benson-Leigh High School gave me two complimentary passes. They've been sitting around here for a month because I couldn't think of anyone who would want to use them. I wasn't planning to go because I didn't want to drive there by myself every day. Of course, her parents may not let her go.

In the meantime, I'd better release a little bit of this sexual heat before I go up in flames. I think I'll ride my bike for a while and then take a chilly shower. Whatever is left by then should dissipate after a solo flight.

Saturday, July 21, 1984

My afternoon with Allie was lovely. It felt good to be with her. She's a delight to my soul. She accepted my invitation to the tennis tournament, but only tentatively. She's supposed to call me tonight to let me know what her parents say. Ah, there's the phone now.

Later: Her parents gave her permission to go all week. She explained that it was her tennis coach who invited her, so they didn't mind if she went off to Charlotte every day for a week. I offered to talk to them, but Allie said it was okay because they remembered me from P.T.A. and from the tennis matches they attended. This is truly a strange situation. Now I know how Jeffrey must've felt with Chuck. Only it's worse since I used to be her teacher. I guess I'd better fill my gas tank for tomorrow and find those tickets. I think I may have buried them under my moving supplies. I would hate to have to cancel our plans because I lost the tickets.

Monday, July 30, 1984

I am exhausted! I had to get up early every morning last week, drive to Allie's house to pick her up, and then drive two hours to the tournament. Allie and I spent all day, eight days in a row, at that blasted stadium. It was great fun, but extremely tiring. By the time I got home at night and fell into bed, it was midnight or later.

I thoroughly enjoyed her company though. Allie can be very mature, and yet she can be so childlike too. Not childish, mind you, childlike. All week she ate, drank, and slept tennis. She was like a little kid on Christmas day. She radiated happiness. I knew she liked the game, but WOW! She seemed to be in her element. I'm glad I invited her. She was elated when Martina won. Martina is Allie's favorite tennis player. She's my favorite too these days, though I still like Chris Evert a lot too.

I want to get Allie a copy of *Tennis My Way*. I think she could glean a lot from Martina's method. Her body type is similar, and she's already developing a powerful one-handed backhand. She definitely has the explosive power necessary to play that kind of game. She's a little timid at the net, but she's starting to come in more. I wish I were going to be here next year to coach her.

Ah well, I know I can't stay here, feeling about her the way I do, especially not now. I know I'd eventually give myself away, if I stayed here. I really love that girl. She's truly a special person. She has a lot of depth, intellectually and emotionally. If she were just one lousy year older, it wouldn't be an issue. But she's not, and that fact isn't going to change, at least not any time soon. In the meantime, I need to disappear and wait. At least now I am certain that she wants to be my friend. I don't think it's just a teacher-student relationship either. She's not exactly a peer, yet, but it's beginning to move in that direction. Sometimes it's easy to forget that she's only sixteen.

Tuesday, July 31, 1984

Pull yourself together, Anna! If you can't restrain yourself, you're going to have to leave early. After all, you still don't know that she's a lesbian. You're probably reading more into her words and body language than is actually there. You were her teacher. She may just idolize you. Even if she has a crush on you, you don't know if she wants to act on it. She may not even be aware of her feelings. It's very likely that she has no idea she's sending out such loud and noticeable signals, so stop kidding yourself. You're going to get hurt, and if you're not careful you're going to hurt Allie too. Just back off, Anna Evans!

Wednesday, August 1, 1984

Allie and I walked and talked for hours today. She told me about a couple of relationships she had that got very intense and sexual. First she told me about some guy named Jimmy. She met him when she went with her parents on vacation. From the sounds of it, he really took advantage of her innocence and budding sexual curiosity. That really burns me up. I wish I could have protected her from that. Yet I know she has to deal with her sexuality in her own way. I can't protect her from herself. He didn't rape her, even if he did coax her a bit. I'm willing to bet that he didn't even appreciate what she was sharing with him.

She also told me about an encounter between herself and her best friend Sherri. I'm not positive, but I think that took place before the Jimmy affair. Unfortunately Sherri denied her feelings, so nothing ever came of it. Instead of discovering the joys of lesbian sexuality, she experienced rejection. It's a shame Allie didn't have anyone to talk to about her feelings. I was lucky enough to have someone in my family who was openly lesbian. My talks with Aunt Donna saved me a lot of grief, I'm sure.

Right now I think Allie's confused about her sexuality. From the way she talked, it's apparent that she strongly preferred her encounter with Sherri to the ones with Jimmy.

Too bad Sherri shied away from the whole thing. I got the feeling she was hinting around that it's all right to approach her, but I'm not certain. She may have simply been asking for my help. I really don't know what to do. There is a lot of sexual tension between us. Something is bound to happen sooner or later. If only I can hold out for two more weeks. Then I'll be gone.

Thursday, August 2, 1984

Okay, Anna, was that a Freudian slip or what? Allie and I were going to play tennis today, only I forgot my racket. So we had to come back here to get it. We didn't leave the house again until I took her home after supper. I was just going to run into the house, grab my racket, and run back out again. Instead Allie asked for a tour of the house. I'm glad I had cleaned up my packing mess somewhat.

I felt strange showing her my bedroom, but it would've seemed odd had I omitted it. After all there isn't much to this little house. The omission of the bedroom would have been obvious. Allie really liked my waterbed. She had never been on one, so she asked me if she could lie down on it. I said, "Sure," and then promptly went into the bathroom to splash my face with very cold water. It helped some. When I came out she had gone back into the living room and was looking at my books. Apparently she is an avid reader too. It certainly shows. She's quite sophisticated in some ways. It's as though she has read about many things in life, but hasn't participated in them yet.

I fixed supper for us. She didn't seem to mind it being meatless. She has been very careful to eat vegetarian foods when she's with me. I keep telling her that I don't care if other people eat meat. It isn't as though it's a religious conviction with me. I just prefer it for myself. I was raised vegetarian, so I've never eaten meat nor wanted to do so. I don't think she cares one way or the other.

Allie liked dining by candlelight. I felt as though I should have had a bottle of wine to accompany our meal. Dad and Buddy always do, but I rarely drink it unless I'm with them. I'm more of a Perrier person. Allie got to try sparkling water for the first time. She wrinkled up her cute little nose and said, "Ooh, neat."

Sunday, August 5, 1984

If I didn't feel so paranoid, I'd probably feel wonderful right now. I kissed Allie today. Or she kissed me. I don't know who started it really. Not that it matters, I guess. I hardly knew what was happening until we were in the middle of it. Talk about magic. That was the most powerful kiss I've ever felt. It was soft and sweet and tender. Allie seems to have learned the fine art of kissing quite young.

I really don't know what I'm going to do. I love that girl, but we can't go any further. She's too young. I don't want to get her into something she's not ready for. She seemed willing enough to kiss me. It was obvious too that she didn't want to stop. Of course, I didn't want to stop either, but I was afraid not to stop. I've got to get out of here. This just isn't going to work. She's so young.

I guess it's a good thing I have to go to Kentucky tomorrow. I have an appointment with the principal, and then I have to get the key to my new apartment. It isn't ready yet, but the landlord told me I could pick up a key since the previous tenants are already gone. That way I don't have to track him down when I'm ready to move. I really don't want to go though. I want to be with Allie. One thought that plagues me is that I was sixteen when Tammy and I got together. I know I was ready for that relationship. It's the age gap that's bothering me. Tammy and I were both teenagers.

We had a peer relationship. I used to be Allie's teacher, for goodness sake. I can't cross that line. Hell, I guess I already crossed that line. Oh my god. I am so confused. Maybe the drive to Kentucky will clear my head.

Monday, August 6, 1984

This has been a long day. I got up at six a.m. to drive to Kentucky. I did everything I had to do there then came home again. I had considered staying in a hotel, but decided I'd prefer to sleep in my own bed and save the money. It was a long drive though. It isn't that late. I think I'll call Allie. I missed her so badly today. I cried half the way home. I hurt so much because I want to be with her, yet I know she needs time to grow up. She needs a chance to be a teenager. I can't rush her into an adult relationship. She's not ready for that kind of commitment.

Tuesday, August 7, 1984

Allie came over today. We spent the whole day cuddling. It was wonderful, but it really hurt too to know that this love can't be fulfilled now. I must wait for her. I feel very fragile, like I'm going to burst into tears any moment. I would give anything to be able to love her openly and completely. I don't even care that I could get into trouble, though I do care if she does. I don't want to do anything she would regret. This love is too powerful for a sixteen-year old. She can't deal with volatile stuff like this. I can hardly deal with it myself. How can I expect her to handle it? I'm so happy and so miserable all at once.

Wednesday, August 8, 1984

Today was a particularly difficult day emotionally. Maybe I should have left early for Kentucky. The sexual tension between Allie and me is very high. Somehow I need to try to back off a little. She's young and eager for sexual experience, but we really need to hold off until she's an adult.

Oh god, it was so painful when Allie begged me to make love to her. I can still see the look in her eyes when she asked me if I would like to touch her breasts. I wanted to tell her that I have wanted desperately to touch her breasts ever since that day in the locker room when I first saw her naked body. Her breasts are so beautiful. They are so round and full. Her nipples are small, and such a delicate shade of pink. The image of her body is permanently etched in my brain. What am I doing to do? Like an idiot, I started crying when she invited me to touch her. I tried to explain why I couldn't or shouldn't. I tried to make her see that she has a whole life ahead of her and that she needed a chance to be sixteen. But my words seemed meaningless in the presence of our desire. Maybe this is what it means to be sixteen.

I told her that I had to leave because I love her and don't want to hurt her. That, I think, hurt her worse than if I had told her I wasn't interested. Apparently I haven't been imagining the depth of her feelings for me. This is definitely more than a crush, but what can we do about it? I have to leave. I have already resigned my job here, and I've signed a contract in Kentucky. I don't have much choice. And she really does need to be a teenager. She doesn't need me around all the time. She's too young for the intensity of a relationship with me.

I love her so very much. This is such a ridiculous situation. I am such a fool. Where do we go from here? A short honeymoon, and then I move to Kentucky? No. I'm just going to have to leave for Kentucky. Then when she's older I will return, and if she still wants to be with me, well, then we shall see what happens. I have to deal with this very moment in time. All I can do right now is stop us from making a mistake we might both regret. The future will have to wait.

Monday, August 13, 1984

I can't believe this part of my life is going to end soon. I wish Allie could go with me, or I could stay. What a fool I was to think I could run from something this powerful. Our love is bigger than both of us; it is stronger and more lasting than laws or mores.

Thursday, August 16, 1984

For every falling star I see
I wish that you could live with me
And share the stars, the moon, the sun
Until, at last, our lives are done

Friday, August 17, 1984

Don't let tomorrow come. I cannot believe that I have to move away from Allie. I love her so much it hurts. What is done is done. I must go. All the wheels have been set in motion. There is no turning back. Goodbye, my cozy house. You will always hold the secret of our love. No matter what happens after this, you will be the haven where our desire was first revealed.

Goodbye, Allie. I love you. I really do. I'm doing this for your sake. You still need a chance to be sixteen. This is the only way I know to give it to you, or at least to stop interfering with it. I feel awful, but I've got to stop writing. I can't see very well through the tears anyway. I've got to walk out of this house tomorrow and drive three hundred miles to my new job, new apartment, and new life.

Monday, August 20, 1984

I feel horrible. I cried all the way to Kentucky. Well I did stop briefly to pump gas. I had to dam up the flow long enough to do that. I must have looked atrocious. But I don't really care. I don't care about anything except Allie. I miss her so badly I can hardly stand it. I think I'll call her tonight. I've already written her two letters. I think I'll mail them both tomorrow, so she'll know I'm thinking about her all the time.

How am I ever going to survive this year? Since it isn't that far to drive, I could go back for an occasional visit. Hell, I could go back every weekend, but that would not give her the time she needs to be an adolescent. I'd be monopolizing every hour of her weekends.

No, Anna, you have to be realistic. You have to stick it out here. The reason you left was to give her a chance to be a teenager without being in an intense relationship. She's just not ready for it. I had time to grow up. I had time alone to think things out. I've gone to college, and lived on my own. I'm ready to settle down with Allie, but I can't rush her growth. She hasn't been on her own. She hasn't even graduated from high school, for goodness sake.

I'll visit later. I need to give her time to get used to my absence. If I show up too soon, it will just make things more difficult. She needs to make her life there with her family and her school friends. Somehow I must make a life here.

Thursday, August 23, 1984

Preparing for this school year is a lot easier, even though I'm at a different school. I think it's because I'm no longer trying to do everything perfectly. Experience has taught me that my plans have to be flexible, because they will get messed up, no matter what I do.   I have to admit though, that I'm more than a little nervous about the kids coming next week. There will be hundreds of new faces and names to learn.

They don't have a tennis team here, but they have girl's volleyball and basketball.   Sally Gingress is the volleyball coach.   She has offered to help me coach basketball.   She seems like a really nice person, but I can't figure her out.   She's wearing a ring on her left hand, but she goes by "Miss Gingress." I don't know whether she's single and wears a ring to ward off the wolves, or if she's coupled, but not married.   I guess I'll find out eventually.

Saturday, August 25, 1984

I just talked to Allie on the phone.   She sounded miserable.   I feel so bad for her.   But this separation would have been even harder for us both if we had gotten sexually involved before I left.   We probably shouldn't have gotten involved as much as we did.   I am not sorry about that though.   How can I be sorry for the most wonderful moments in my life?   For the most beautiful and perfect kisses I've ever shared with anyone.   I really love her.   I can tell she loves me too, though I know that her love will have to mature.   She loves me and wants me.   That's all she can see right now. She's not wise enough yet to see what kind of trouble we could get into because of our relationship.

One good thing about being in another state is that I can relax a little.   I don't get tense every time I hear a siren now.   Seriously though, if Allie were of legal age, I wouldn't care about our age difference.   But she definitely has some growing up to do, so I guess I have to cool my heels for a couple of years.

dearest allie,
life is bittersweet for me;
you are the sweet;
the arrangements
are the bitter herbs,
the healing medicine
for our future.

Wednesday, September 12, 1984

I'm not interested in keeping a journal right now. Every time I sit down to write, I'm reminded of my misery. I just need to keep busy right now. If I stop long enough to think, I think about how much I miss Allie. Then I hurt. Then I cry. I'm tired of crying. It's time to lay this pen down for a while, and with it, this gnawing ache in my heart.

Thursday, September 27, 1984

Tomorrow I'm supposed to be going back to North Carolina to see Allie, but my car has started making a strange noise. I'm afraid it's getting ready to do something weird. I guess I'd better postpone my trip until I can have someone look at it.

Monday, October 1, 1984

I took my car to a mechanic to have it checked out. Of course, it would not make the weird sound it was making last week. It figures. I had them change the oil anyway, since it needed it. I can't believe I canceled my trip because of a phantom noise.

Thursday, October 4, 1984

I have a temperature of 102. I guess that means I get to stay home from school tomorrow and torment myself with feverish thoughts of Allie. I miss her so much. Well, I guess I'd better call the school so they can line up a substitute. I hate to miss a day of work so soon, but I know I shouldn't go there and expose everyone else to whatever I have.

Monday, October 8, 1984

Basketball practice starts this week. With games to attend every weekend, I won't have an opportunity to visit Allie for a while. I guess it will be Thanksgiving or Christmas before I can get there. What really perturbs me is that my car has not made that noise since I took it in to be checked. I guess that trip wasn't meant to be.

Sunday, November 4, 1984

With practice every day after school, I'm starting to dream about basketball. Sarah keeps jumping into my dreams too. Sometimes she's on the team I'm coaching. She's herself, but she's a high school student. As usual, she is trying to get back together with me. I keep telling her that if I get involved with two high school students, then I'm bound to get caught. It's weird when I wake up, because I expect to see Sarah lurking about somewhere.

Saturday, November 17, 1984

It's kind of exciting to be starting basketball season. Yet one side of me doesn't care. That side just wants to chuck everything so I can go home to Allie. What is really annoying is that our team will be participating in a tournament during the Thanksgiving holidays. That means I can't go to North Carolina then like I had hoped.

Monday, December 10, 1984

The basketball team is playing well. Apparently my predecessor knew her stuff. Sally Gingress has been a gold mine as an assistant. She has really helped to provide some continuity for the girls. She was the assistant last year so she knows the former coach's philosophy. I'm trying to work with the girls in a manner that is consistent with their earlier training.

I finally found out more about Sally's situation. She has never been married, but she has a three-year-old daughter. She wears a ring because she doesn't want to be bothered right now. She plans to remove the ring after her daughter goes off to kindergarten. For the time being, she just wants to make herself available to her child. She doesn't have time for a romantic relationship.

Sally has been filling the assistant basketball coach's role because of the extra money. She's trying to make herself as indispensable to the school as possible, so they'll keep her in spite of the fact that her babysitter calls her at work frequently. Plus, she has had to miss school a lot to take care of her daughter when she's been ill.

Saturday, December 15, 1984

I must be overwrought. I saw a girl in the stands tonight that looked like Allie from afar. My heart skipped a beat when I saw her. I kept straining to get a better look at her. In the process, I missed a couple of crucial plays. Fortunately Sally noticed my distraction, so she took over until I could regain my concentration. After the game, Sally asked if I were okay. She said that she thought I'd seen a ghost or something.

I said, "I guess I did in a way. I thought I saw someone I knew from the school where I taught last year, but I was mistaken." I thanked her profusely for jumping in with the signals and plans. She saved my neck and the game.

Monday, December 17, 1984

Time is passing so slowly. I want to see Allie. I can't stand this much longer. My motel reservations have been made; my bags are packed. The car is fine, so far. No strange noises. Four more days.

Tuesday, December 25, 1984

Being with Allie is the best Christmas gift I have ever received. She has to spend most of today with her family though, so I have some time to think. It's been good to be back, even if I am holed up in a cheap motel. I can't afford anything else. Not for two weeks, at any rate. It's worth every penny to see my Allie. Unfortunately I don't really have any money left to buy her much of a present. I was able to find Martina's tennis book, so I finally got around to buying that for her. It's not very romantic, but I'm trying to remedy that situation in person.

Monday, January 7, 1985

Back to school. Back to missing Allie. Back to tears. I really enjoyed seeing Allie again, but it makes this second separation that much harder. At least basketball season will be over by the time we get to spring break. I'm planning to go back then to see Allie. I can't wait until summer. I miss her too much to go that long without seeing her again.

Thursday, January 17, 1985

I've been sick all week, but I haven't been able to stop and rest. Time marches on, and so does basketball season. I didn't even do anything special for my birthday. Why bother? I got cards from Mom, Dad, and Allie. Each of my parents sent me a birthday check, but I'm just going to save the money for my trip in March. Even cheap motels can deplete your resources, if they're meager enough. Of course, I'd probably have an easier time saving money if it weren't for the huge phone bills. But I'd rather have a high phone bill than go without hearing Allie's voice.

Dad also sent me his latest novel. I will have to wait to read it though. Right now I'm incapable of concentrating on anything that doesn't rebound or dribble.

Friday, January 25, 1985

Basketball, basketball, and more basketball. I'm glad I'm busy, but I'm getting exceedingly tired of basketball. I guess I'm not a very dedicated P.E. teacher, although I haven't read any decent literature lately either. About all I can read these days are short stories. I haven't even started Dad's book yet. It will probably be a bestseller before I get around to dusting off the cover. At any rate, I'm too busy to brood about my loneliness, so that's good.

Mom sent me a box full of health food items I can't get here. There is no health food store in this town. That was one minor detail I neglected to check before I moved here. If I had noticed that last summer, I would've stocked up before I moved. I purchased a few things during my Christmas trip, but I didn't have enough funds with me to restock my pantry.

Mom also included a late birthday present from Christine. She's taking Art this year in school, so she made me a wall hanging. It's interesting. I don't know what it is exactly, because it's kind of abstract. But it gives my eyes something different to look at. That was sweet of her to make me something.

Sometimes I feel really bad though because she is growing up, and I hardly ever see her any more. It's hard to believe she's the same age as Allie. I can't imagine Christine being involved with an older woman or man either for that matter. I sincerely doubt that she's a lesbian, but then, I never would've guessed that Tammy was either. Tammy taught me that lesbianism doesn't restrict itself to society's stereotypes.

Thursday, February 14, 1985

Happy Valentines Day, Allie, my love! I remember last year all too well. That was before I knew you cared for me. Had I known then, I would have asked you to that stupid dance. You could have at least gone to keep me company. Now I know you love me, and we still can't be together.

Saturday, February 23, 1985

I'm sick again. This is so frustrating. I don't have time to be sick! What is wrong with my body? Why does it keep betraying me? I'm beginning to think that even my body knows I don't belong here. It's almost as though it is in self-destruct mode. I need to find some way to survive this school year.

Thursday, March 21, 1985

Life is beginning to slow down now that basketball season is over. I guess it's a horrible thing to say, but I'm glad the basketball team didn't do well enough this year to get into the spring tournament. I would have had to spend spring break with the basketball team, and therefore miss my trip home. I would have resented every minute of it. How's that for a bad attitude? The girls on the team had a great season, but I just don't think I could've taken any more of it. I definitely don't want to have to wait any longer to see Allie. God I miss that girl! I don't know how I thought I was strong enough to walk away from her for two whole years. Though perhaps things would have been different if we hadn't started seeing each other last summer. I could have tried to convince myself that it was a one-sided infatuation.

Monday, March 25, 1985

I'll be leaving to visit Allie Friday afternoon. I'm not looking forward to staying in that grubby little motel, but it's better than nothing. The things we do for love. At least there is a place where I can afford to stay for a week.

Sunday, April 14, 1985

I'm feeling much better these days. I've just gotten over another cold. I'm beginning to think I have mono or something. I've been trying to get plenty of rest. I've started taking an herbal remedy for nervous tension and sleeplessness. It's non-addictive. It knocks me out so that I don't dream about Allie or basketball either for that matter.

I need to stay healthy for the rest of the year. I want to start doing some serious biking, and I'm really out of shape. I want to be able to keep up with Allie this summer. That's a pretty tall order, since she has boundless energy. It was great to see her during spring break anyway.

Friday, April 26, 1985

Happy Birthday, Allie! I miss you terribly.   I look forward to the day when we can be together. I love you, Allie. I truly love you.

Tuesday, April 30, 1985

I've come a long way in two weeks time. I nearly died the first time I took my bike out. Talk about muscle burn. I'm biking every other day, and I've seen much improvement in a short time, especially in my cardiovascular condition.

Wednesday, May 14, 1985

I just got back from a long bike ride. I finally made it all the way up this giant hill that's been plaguing me for weeks. It's about 5 miles into my ride, and every time I've made it only halfway up or so. Then I have to stop and walk it the rest of the way. But I did it this time. It was exhilarating to be able to top the hill then fly down the other side.

I feel really good about myself. I really wanted to get up that hill at least once. Now that I've done it, I know that I can do it again. I must say that I'm pretty well exhausted for now, but I feel very good. Downright giddy, I must confess. Must be the endorphins.

Tuesday, May 28, 1985

I've gotten everything packed and ready to go, including my waterbed. I've been sleeping in my sleeping bag inside my tent in the middle of my living room. Am I ready to get out of this place? Yes! I have reservations for a week at my favorite (Ha!) motel. It's not all that bad. I'm just feeling feisty right now. I really need to find a house quickly though, because I can't afford to pay that much for very long.

Wednesday, June 5, 1985

I'm going home to my baby tomorrow. I feel good. Tired, but good. Sometimes I thought I would not survive this school year. I don't know how I made it through. So much of this year is cloaked in fog. I feel as though I sleepwalked through most of it. I guess that's how I made it through. Well, at least it's over now, and I'm going home to my Allie.

Friday, June 14, 1985

I found a little cottage to rent for the summer. I'm exceedingly glad to be out of that motel room. I had to stay there only three days. I used Dad's "system" to find a place this time. It worked like a charm.

Speaking of Dad, I finally got a chance to read his last book. I've had it for a mere five months. It's nice to have time for pleasure reading again. It's also nice not to have to walk around feeling empty inside. I love being able to see Allie everyday. We went swimming yesterday at her house, while her parents were at work. I thoroughly enjoyed watching her swim. She looks great. I, on the other hand, am really out of shape. The last few weeks of biking helped, but it didn't do much for my upper body. Maybe if I swim a lot this summer I can regain my overall conditioning.

Tuesday, June 18, 1985

I think I'm finally unpacked. Of course, I'll have to move again in a couple of months since I've rented this place just for the summer. I really don't know what to do about next year.

I know that I cannot return to Kentucky. On the other hand, I know I can't work at Stepford because it would be too easy to make a mistake there. I'm too relaxed in my relationship with Allie. I don't want to have to re-establish professional distance between us. I'd be sure to let my guard down at the wrong time. That kind of game requires too much emotional effort. I know that changing jobs again won't look good on my resume. Perhaps I should just go into another field until Allie graduates. Then we can be together. Unless of course she decides she wants to be free when she goes off to college. That's a possibility I mustn't rule out. She's still so young. She may not want to be tied down during those years of maturation and exploration.

Sunday, June 23, 1985

On the days when Allie's mother is home, Allie comes over here so we can be together. When she's at work, I go over there. This hide-and-seek game is a little wearisome, but it's infinitely better than not seeing Allie at all. I really hate it that we have to be so secretive about our relationship.

Wednesday, June 26, 1985

I've been talking with Allie about going to college. She's being very lackadaisical about the whole thing. She's got such a good mind. She's still pulling a 4.0, so I see no reason why she wouldn't have her pick of schools. I checked out a book from the library this evening. It is a resource guide for choosing a college. I want to go through it with Allie soon. Sometimes she is so shortsighted. She doesn't realize how many schools there are to choose from, or how difficult the choice can be. We could always adapt Dad's "system" for house hunting to college hunting, but I don't think that would be a very good idea.

I'm also reading a book of lesbian coming out stories. Dad was talking about me to a woman in a gay bookstore. She recommended it, so he bought it and sent it to me. If it's a good one, and Allie is interested, I'll let her borrow it. I don't want to push her into anything, but I don't think she comprehends the ramifications of our relationship. All she sees right now is what is expedient. She loves me and wants to be with me. Nothing else matters.

She has no idea what it means to be a lesbian. We're so closeted now it's highly unlikely that anyone would figure out that she's different from any other bright teenage girl. She talks about wanting everyone to know, but she has no clue what repercussions she'd experience if her fellow students knew about her. I don't know if she has even admitted to herself that she is lesbian.

It's also a possibility that it's too much for her to deal with right now. I had someone to talk to when I was fourteen, someone who knew who she was and what she wanted out of life. Apparently, I'm the only one filling that role in Allie's life, and I'm hardly objective. It's difficult enough to reach conclusions about your own sexuality without having to take into account what everyone else is going to think about it. I'm really sorry Allie has to drag this out with her family. If we were peers, things might be different. She could tell her family now, and they could either like it or not like it. As things are, we have to deal with the added problem of my being older than she is, and the fact that I'm her former teacher. What a mess. So far at least, we've managed to keep our relationship limited to cuddling and kissing. It's hard, but I'm still not sure that she knows what she wants.

Saturday, June 29, 1985

Allie and I have been having some long talks lately about school and the future. Allie borrowed the book about lesbians, but I have no idea whether she's read any of it yet. She hasn't commented on it. Sometimes I wonder what is going on inside her head. She talks a lot about most things, but she's pretty shy when it comes to talking about her sexuality.

Monday, July 1, 1985

Allie finished the books I loaned her. She asked to borrow JoAnn Loulan's *Lesbian Sex* book. I'm afraid to let her borrow that one since it's so sexually intense. It's hard enough as it is to keep things under control between us. I told her that I would let her borrow it later, but that I'd rather hang on to it for the moment.

I realize that she probably wouldn't be asking for it if she weren't ready for it. I just don't think I'm ready for her to read it. I'm afraid that we would not be able to contain the fire that it is bound to ignite in her. It's hard enough for me to hold myself back, but at least I've had some practice at channeling my sexual energy into other areas of my life.

I let her borrow another book of coming out stories instead. Let her think about the concept of lesbianism a little more before we get into a full-blown passionate affair. We need to keep her education on a more theoretical basis for now. Once she's eighteen, I can always do a little private tutoring to help her catch up, if need be.

Wednesday, July 3, 1985

I need to get serious about job-hunting. I'm glad I was on a twelve-month contract this past year. I needed the summer break just to catch up with myself. I never would have survived without a steady paycheck coming in. I'm looking into teaching in one of the surrounding counties. That way I wouldn't be connected with Allie's school, yet I would still be close to her. Leaving her again is not an option. I know I couldn't take another year like last year. I know Allie doesn't even want to think about us being separated again, so I need to get busy.

Sunday, July 7, 1985

Allie has been really sweet lately. She usually is sweet though. I guess what I mean is that she is being even more thoughtful and helpful than she usually is. That's saying a lot, because she gives to others without thinking about it. It seems to be the way she responds to people naturally. Anyway, I've been getting uptight lately about finding a job. She has noticed the tension in me, so she has been giving me the most glorious back rubs. I don't know where she learned to do that so well, but she's good.

She's also wanted to cook vegetarian dishes for me. She actually cooked a complete gourmet dinner last night. I usually eat pretty simply, but she wanted to try something different. She looked through my cookbooks, picked out a meal, and then did the whole thing herself from beginning to end. I might add that she did it flawlessly. I don't think she knows the meaning of the word *difficult*. Poor Jeffrey had to put up with a lot of burnt or undercooked food when I was trying out new recipes.

Monday, July 15, 1985

I don't know what's going on inside Allie's head, but something must be stirring in there. Perhaps it was the book I loaned her recently. She suggested today that I might prefer an older girlfriend. I'm not sure if she was trying to tell me that she's not ready for this relationship. I told her that I didn't need or want anyone else, but that I would understand if she decided she needed someone her own age. I want her to know that she is free to change her mind about us. I don't want to tie her down, if she wants to go elsewhere. I really love her and would suffer a lot if she left me, but I don't want to squelch her in any way. I guess we really need to talk about that book. She may want to tell her parents about herself but is afraid to because of me. I don't want to hurt her or her relationship with them.

Friday, July 19, 1985

   Allie told me that her family vacation is coming up soon. I'm really going to miss her. I've come to take for granted our being together several hours every day. I guess I've settled into a comfortable rhythm. I'd prefer to have her here all the time, but I know that isn't possible yet.

   I sent my resume to three different counties. I have no idea if there are any openings, but we'll see. If I don't have something lined up by mid-August, then I will start looking for a job in another field. I hope something turns up in education though. At least I have some experience in that.

Wednesday, July 24, 1985

   Well, not only is Allie foregoing the beach trip with her parents, but also I'm going to be staying with her while they're gone. Her parents told her to have one of her friends stay with her at night so she wouldn't get scared. I felt bad at first that Allie was going to miss out on this special time with her family until she reminded me about Jimmy and her memories of that summer.

   One of these days, I need to go to the beach with her, and provide her with a new set of memories. Maybe we should go to a different beach altogether. Whatever it takes. She loves the ocean so much. I'd hate to see her memories of Jimmy destroy that love.

Sunday, August 4, 1985

Allie and I had fun playing house while Allie's parents were gone. I hope she enjoyed it as much as I did. It was difficult to restrain from making love to her when we went to bed at night. I tried very hard to fill every minute of every day with activities, so we'd be exhausted and ready to fall asleep at night.

It was lovely to hold her at night though. I love her so much. I wish we didn't have to live in two different places, but she still needs time to be a teenager. She's matured a lot. That much is obvious. At least we aren't living in two separate states any more.

Wednesday, August 7, 1985

There are two possible openings. One is in P.E.; the other is in Literature. I've contacted both schools. I hope I hear something soon. I'll be getting my last paycheck at the end of the month. Fortunately I got a good deal on this cottage, so I've saved a lot of money this summer. It was easy to do without the horrendous phone bills.

Sunday, August 11, 1985

Allie was so cute today. She asked me what lesbians do in order to be together, since they don't get married. When I pulled out a book on alternative lifestyles, she started laughing and said, "I just knew you were going to give me a book to read." It was very funny.

I hope she learns something from the book. We talked about it for a long time. I think she must have liked our week together. I don't know what to tell her about lesbian relationships. There are no established patterns, the way there are with heterosexual couples, at least not ones that are acknowledged and actively supported by our society at large.

Monday, August 12, 1985

I told Allie about the teaching positions open in this area. She was ecstatic to say the least. If I get either one of those positions, then I can live in Spruceton and commute to work. I can't stay in the cottage though, because the owners need it in September. But I can find another place around here, so I can be near Allie.

I think Allie was afraid I was going to go back to Kentucky, but I've already turned in my resignation. I guess I hadn't told her that yet. I'm really not very communicative about daily things. When I'm with Allie, I just want to think about her. I just want to be with her. I have plenty of time after she goes home at night to deal with other matters. I guess I should let her in on my musings, so she isn't left wondering.

Wednesday, August 14, 1985

What an ass you are, Anna! Yesterday I got annoyed with Allie and her careless attitude towards college. I don't know why I reacted so strongly. I don't want her to miss out on the opportunities of life, but I can't push her into doing something she doesn't want to do. Perhaps she doesn't want to go to college right away. I think it would be better if she did, but I can't make her decisions for her. I guess I need to back off, but sometimes I think she just needs a nudge in the right direction. So now that I have nudged, I need to let her make the next step. It's her life.

Thursday, August 22, 1985

I got the P.E. position at Mitchell. I may regret having to drive that far, but at least I can live near Allie. Now I just need to resolve the housing issue. I think I'll go buy a newspaper and start calling numbers right away. I don't have much time to get settled. I'm getting really fed up with moving.

Saturday, August 24, 1985

Well, I have located a place to live and can move in the day after tomorrow. Then I have to start back to work Monday. Nothing like cramming everything together. I think I must have a masochistic streak when it comes to relocating. Between college and my first two years of teaching, I'm sure I've moved a half dozen times since I left California.

Saturday, August 31, 1985

My new house is wonderful. It's a little more expensive than the cottage, but it's also a lot bigger. I'm exhausted from school and moving, so I'm going to bed. Goodnight.

Wednesday, September 4, 1985

I'm beginning to get settled a little bit. Most of my stuff is unpacked, thanks to Allie. She's been in charge of the kitchen and library, while I've been working on the bathroom, bedroom, and living room.

Saturday, September 7, 1985

Allie is poring over the college catalogs these days. Good for her. I'm glad she talked to the school counselor. I know Marsha Sarens. She'll give Allie a kick in the pants for me. Allie is in good hands with her. Wait a minute! What am I saying? She's in good hands with me. You know, I really need to stop thinking what I'm thinking right now. I guess I need a new mantra. "She's not eighteen. She's not eighteen. She's not eighteen." Keep your hands and your thoughts to yourself, Anna. Oh help!

Sunday, September 8, 1985

Talk about a ghost out of the past. Sarah called me late last night. She's coming to visit next weekend. I don't know what she is up to, but I hope I can survive her visit. I must confess that I'm not looking forward to it, though I am curious about what she's been doing since graduation.

Monday, September 16, 1985

Sarah left this morning. I don't know what her purpose in coming was, but she managed to embarrass the hell out of me several times. When she first met Allie, she made some smart-ass remark about my robbing the cradle. I felt like stuffing her car into her mouth but managed to restrain myself. Instead I punched her on the arm. That was the way we used to signal each other to shut up. She got the message, but apparently she couldn't heed it for very long. All weekend she made innuendoes about our lovemaking practices in college. She never said enough for Allie to figure it out, just enough to make me thoroughly uncomfortable.

Allie was waiting for me today when I pulled up in the driveway. It was wonderful to see her. However, we didn't get to spend a whole lot of time together because I had to go back to school for a meeting.

Tuesday, September 17, 1985

You'd think I'd learn to shut up when I'm about to start my period. I jumped on Allie's case tonight when she said something negative about Sarah. Don't ask me why I was defending Sarah. I guess I still feel protective towards her. She's had such a rough life.

While she was here, Sarah caught me up on the events of the last two years of her life. As is usual for Sarah, life has been pretty traumatic. To begin with, her mother killed herself about six months ago. She took a whole bottle of tranquilizers. Sarah's youngest sister found her and called the paramedics, but she was already gone. Sarah has been carrying around a load of guilt about that because she never spoke to her mother after her grandmother's funeral. Her mother's suicide note didn't help any either. She said something about failing her children, and not being able to do anything to "cure her sick daughter," i.e., Sarah, the lesbian. Of course, she didn't mention Sarah by name, but the implication was clear.

Then a couple months later, Sarah was fired from her first teaching position for "immoral behavior." In other words, for being a lesbian. One of her fellow teachers saw her coming out of a gay bar. According to Sarah, that was all there was to it. No dykes allowed. Case closed.

On top of all that, she found out that her last lover has venereal disease. The strangest thing about this part is that this former lover is male. I can't imagine what Sarah was doing in that relationship. She has always been a very outspoken lesbian. At any rate, he thinks he was exposed after they had separated, but he's a little fuzzy on the dates, so he decided he'd better warn her, just in case.

I don't know about Sarah. I really feel sorry for her, but I don't want her in my life. I feel somewhat guilty about that, but I've already learned that I can't help her. When I asked her if she had anyone to talk to about all these things, she said, "Not really. That's why I tracked you down."

I suggested she see a psychologist, but I don't think she will. She's too independent or stubborn really. She needs help, but I can't help her. It's more than I can handle. After all, I didn't major in psychology.

Anyway, I was feeling tired and bitchy after spending so much time with Sarah, and I took it out on Allie. I'm really angry with myself for doing that. I tried to apologize, but she left in such a hurry I don't think she heard me. Frankly I don't blame her for walking out on me. I was a real jerk.

I think I'll send her some flowers. I'm pretty certain her mom works tomorrow, so Allie should get them before her parents get home. I have to do something to let her know I'm sorry.

Wednesday, September 18, 1985

Things seem to be patched up now. I didn't tell Allie everything about Sarah because I didn't really feel at liberty to do so. But I did apologize thoroughly. I explained about my fatigue and my relief at having Sarah out of the house. I just wanted to be alone with Allie.

I don't want Sarah in the middle of my relationship with Allie. She's so good at manipulating people. Even during the short time Sarah was here, she managed to plant seeds of doubt in Allie's mind. I guess I'm in for a round of reliving the past for Allie, so she'll know how Sarah fits, or rather doesn't fit into my life. I wish I could simply forget that I ever met Sarah, and yet I sincerely care about her. I think I prefer caring about her from a distance though. She makes my life too complicated when she gets in close range.

Friday, September 20, 1985

I think Allie is sorry that she asked about Sarah. I don't think it was easy for her to hear about my past relationship with her. But she asked, so I told her the truth, the bare essentials at least. I especially emphasized that the relationship has been over for a long time.

Saturday, September 28, 1985

I'm already wearying of this long commute in the mornings. I don't mind the afternoon drive as much, since it gives me time to unwind. It's difficult, however, when we have faculty meetings. They seem to last forever. We have P.T.A. Open House next week. That means I will either need to stay at school all day or make an extra trip that night. I can't decide which would be worse.

Saturday, October 5, 1985

Spending time with Allie is such a joy. I miss our long summer days together, but this year's arrangement is infinitely better than last year's. At least I get to see her for a couple of hours every day. Well, almost every day. Sometimes I have responsibilities at work or she has family obligations that interfere with our time together.

Monday, October 7, 1985

Allie is maturing at a rapid pace these days. I enjoy the teenager in her a lot, but I also enjoy the young woman in her. She is so beautiful. I wish I were an artist. It would be wonderful to be able to sculpt or paint her. She is a living work of art.

Friday, October 11, 1985

There's a nip in the air now. I love the feeling of autumn. The chilly breezes whisper to me, "Anna, just wait until you see what the trees are going to be wearing next week. You're going to love it." My heart is one step from bursting as I watch the leaves change from green to orange, red, and yellow. Autumn is a kaleidoscope of colors that changes with every turning of the sun. I think that I shall never tire of watching the seasons change. What a wardrobe has Mother Nature!

splashes of color,
kaleidoscope trees,
chilly winds blowing,
leaves chasing leaves.
beautiful patterns,
multiple hues,
sweet-tasting potions,
our Mother brews.

Monday, October 21, 1985

Allie's tennis game is improving rapidly. She's on the tennis team again this year. I wish I were the one coaching her every afternoon, but I prefer the time we spend together alone. At least her tennis practice is over by the time I get home. I'm afraid I would be jealous if any of our time were taken by that. Yet I don't want to interfere with her extracurricular activities. She's need to be free to be a teenager.

Wednesday, October 23, 1985

The autumn leaves are at their peak this week. I'm amazed at the blazing colors that ignite the trees. I marvel at

Nature's audacity. I would never have the nerve to make such a spectacle of myself. Mother Nature does it so well though.

Autumn is a gay
and festive time.
If you don't believe me,
just ask the trees.
They put on their
most colorful frocks,
and dance in the wind
for days on end.

Sunday, October 27, 1985

Allie and I carved a jack o'lantern today. It looks funny. It's sitting on the porch now, scaring away any bad spirits that dare to venture up the driveway. Of course, this house is nestled so far back in the woods it is unlikely that anyone will come trick-or-treating. I just wanted to do something fun with Allie.

Saturday, November 2, 1985

A few of my students have been talking about attending my alma mater. I'm thinking about taking them for a visit during the College Days Preview in February. Allie is invited too, if she is interested. Of course, I need to find out if the administration will allow such a trip, since it would require us to go out of the state for an entire weekend.

Monday, November 11, 1985

I've made all the arrangements for the College Days trip. There are three or four students who are interested. If they all decide to go, I'm going to have to rent a larger vehicle. I bet I could borrow the school activity van, if it isn't otherwise engaged that weekend.

Thursday, November 14, 1985

Jeffrey just called. God, I can't believe this! Chuck was struck by a car yesterday while he was riding his bike. He died on the way to the hospital. Poor Jeffrey. I feel so awful. Chuck was so young. I really can't believe it. I think I'm too numb to cry right now. This can't be happening. Not to Chuck. Not to Jeff. What is he going to do? Jeff could hardly stop crying on the phone.

The funeral is in two days. I guess I'd better call the school. I really need to be with Jeff right now. His family doesn't know about Chuck. They don't even know Jeff's gay, so he can't lean on them. I would hate it if my parents didn't know about me. He must feel awfully alienated from them during this time of loss.

Sunday, November 17, 1985

Chuck's funeral was so sad. Jeff looked horrible. I don't think he has slept much since the accident. I invited him to come and stay with me for as long as he wanted to. He told me that he couldn't afford it, so he's just going to work as much as possible. Poor guy. I don't know what I would do if anything happened to Allie.

Wednesday, November 20, 1985

I've been trying to contact Jeff for a couple of days, but haven't been able to reach him. I'm really worried about him. I'm afraid he'll neglect his body totally and work himself into an early grave. He looked so heart broken at Chuck's funeral.

Saturday, November 23, 1985

I finally got to talk with Jeffrey. He has been working long hours then going to the library to study until midnight. He sounds exhausted. I don't blame him for doing what he's doing, but I'm afraid he's going to make himself sick. I feel so helpless when I talk to him. I wish I knew what to do to help him. It's so hard for me to do anything when I'm a couple hundred miles away. Maybe I should make a visit some weekend soon. I hate to leave Allie, but I know Jeff could stand to have some company. The only problem is that he doesn't really have any free time.

Monday, November 25, 1985

Allie has to go out of town for Thanksgiving. Her family is going to her grandparents' house in Virginia. I'm going to miss her. I think I'll read *Anna Karenina* while she's gone. I never have gotten around to reading it, though I tried several times. Talking to Dad on the phone last night reminded me of it again. Let's see if I can buckle down and complete it this time. It will give me something to think about besides how much I miss Allie and how much I hurt for Jeff.

Monday, December 2, 1985

I can't shake the haunting image of Anna Karenina. I can understand why she finally despaired of life. I have to admit that I seriously considered suicide when I was so depressed about my love for Allie. I'm glad I didn't act on that impulse. Look at all the good things I would have missed had I gotten impatient with life.

I'm not sure that there was any possibility of happiness for Tolstoy's Anna. Women in those days had fewer options than they do now. Society is a little more tolerant in some social circles; though economics still keep many women bound to men they do not love.

Now I understand Dad's attraction to *Anna Karenina*. I know he suffered a lot, making the decision to leave Mom. I would not have wanted to be in that position. Though I suppose, in my own way, I was in the same type of situation. I had to decide whether I should verbalize my feelings towards Allie, in spite of society's injunction against adult/teen relationships, especially homosexual ones. That was not an easy decision to make. I know I chose the right thing for Allie and myself.

Thursday, December 5, 1985

I'll be glad when Allie turns eighteen. We'll have to wait until after graduation before we can even start thinking about having her move in with me, but at least we will be able to breathe a little easier. I won't be so afraid of touching her. I don't know yet what I'm going to do next year. I want to be with Allie, but I don't know where she's going to attend college.

Friday, December 6, 1985

Allie looks very cuddly when she's all bundled up in her winter clothes. I don't think she has any idea how beautiful she is. She doesn't have a glamorous beauty. Hers is a very solid and earthy beauty. When she smiles, she has two big dimples, one in each cheek. She has a very wholesome look about her. She's very sturdy-looking too, although she isn't that big. She's 5'4". Of course I'm only 5'2", so she has to look down at me. I think she likes that, and I don't mind. Sarah is 5'9", so I got used to craning my neck when I was with her. With Allie it's not such a strain. With Allie though, nothing is strain.

Tuesday, December 10, 1985

Jeffrey is coming to visit this weekend. I'm glad he and Allie are finally going to meet. I suppose I fairly gush whenever I talk or write to him. I've tried to be careful since Chuck's accident. I almost feel guilty for being so happy.

Friday, December 13, 1985

Jeff and I had a good time, as much as was possible, anyway. We spent a lot of time remembering all the good times with Chuck. That led to a lot of crying. My heart aches for Jeffrey. He and Chuck were meant for each other. Now Jeff has to go on without him. I don't know if I would be able to do that. Allie is so much a part of my life. I don't know if I could stand to continue without her. I suppose I would find a way somehow, but it would be a tremendous task. I love her so much.

Allie didn't get to spend much time with Jeff and me. She had family obligations that weekend. I guess it may have been for the best that Jeff and I had a lot of time alone. He probably wouldn't have felt comfortable expressing his grief around a third party. I think Jeff is going to make it through this, though I know he still has a lot of healing to do. I was beginning to think he was going to destroy himself by overworking. He looks and sounds much stronger now.

Tuesday, December 17, 1985

School will be out soon for the holidays. I bet my car will enjoy the break as much as I will. I'm certainly racking up the miles. It's a good car though. I haven't had any trouble with it, except that time it was making that strange clunking sound. The only thing I can figure out is that I must have had something in the back that was rattling. When I cleaned out the excess junk before I took it in, I must have fixed the problem. I'm very sorry I missed a visit to see Allie, but perhaps she needed more time alone then.

I'm torn in two about her sometimes. On the one hand, I want to spend every free moment with her, just because I love to be with her. On the other hand, I want to back off, and give her time and space to do adolescent things. Yet aside from sports, she seems no more interested in high school activities than I was. Perhaps we should discuss these matters. The only way to find out what she wants is to ask her. I'm not very good at reading minds.

Thursday, December 19, 1985

Allie's best friend Sherri is pregnant. That's going to be rough on her, being pregnant in high school. I hate to see it when young women get labeled as "bad girls," just because their birth control methods were lacking. It isn't as though Sherri is the only senior having sex. She's just the only one who got pregnant and opted not to get married or have an abortion.

Friday, December 20, 1985

I'm making supper for Allie tonight. Her parents are going out on to some office holiday party, leaving Allie to her own devices. Sometimes I wonder if they suspect anything. They are intelligent people. I can't imagine that they have no clue as to what Allie is all about. They seem to have a good relationship with her. They seem to have a good relationship with each other, as well. I'm glad of that. It bodes well for our relationship. I have learned that Allie doesn't like to fight any more than I do. That doesn't mean we don't get into it sometimes, but at least we don't try to start fights the way Sarah used to do with me.

I am so miserable when there is conflict between us. I just want to run and hide. I guess I hope that it will go away if I do that, but it never does. I have to drag myself out of my hole and crawl back to the situation so I can help find a resolution to the conflict. It definitely isn't easy, but it's worth it. I want a good relationship with Allie. I took too much abuse from Sarah. I don't ever want that kind of relationship again.

Friday, December 27, 1985

Allie and I have been keeping late hours lately. Her parents have to work longer hours this time of year. I feel bad for them, but I certainly enjoy having Allie with me. Our time together tends to be so peaceful and refreshing. I really love my little Allie Katz.

Monday, January 6, 1986

I love it. It's snowing. We just started back to school, and now we have another day off. As long as we don't rack up too many of these snow days, I don't mind the time off. I like being able to crawl back into bed after I get the school closings for the day.

I think I hear Allie's bike crunching through the snow, up the driveway. Looks like I get to spend a cozy day in front of the fireplace with my Allie. Mmm. I think I'll start the water for some herbal tea. I may need to warm my baby if the effort of riding up this hill hasn't already done that.

Wednesday, January 8, 1986

Back to school today. I enjoyed my two days with Allie. I never get enough of her. I cherish the thought that one day soon we'll be together openly. I hope her parents can handle it. To hear Allie speak, they seem to be very open-minded people. But I've learned in recent years that "open-minded" doesn't mean quite the same thing in Appalachia as it does in California or New York.

Wednesday, January 15, 1986

I've finally pinned down who is going on the College Days trip. I will be taking only two girls from Mitchell. Allie is going too. I will be taking my car, which is more comfortable than the van, but I wouldn't have objected to giving the poor thing a rest.

Wednesday, January 22, 1986

Allie just left. She was so precious. She didn't want to leave tonight. I think she feels as strongly as I do about living together. I yearn for the day when our goodnight kiss can be delivered in our own bed instead of at the front door. Every time she leaves, she takes a little part of me with her. I never feel quite complete when she is away from me. There is enough of me left to cope, and to make the most of my time, but it's only a matter of biding my time until her return. I can't imagine how Jeffrey can continue getting up every morning to a world without Chuck. That can't be easy.

Saturday, February 1, 1986

I've been talking to Dad a lot recently. A good friend of his died last month. He had AIDS. A couple of his other friends have it too, so he's really depressed. He has called me almost every night for the past week just to talk about it. Dad has also been worried about Jeff's situation. He doesn't like him living all alone in the Bible belt, so he invited him to New York City to work for him. His secretary is having another baby. She's going to quit working full time to spend more time with her growing family.

I don't know whether Jeff will accept the position. I know he was planning to go to graduate school after he finished this year. Of course, he worked the whole time he was doing his undergraduate work, so surely he could go to graduate school part-time, while he works for Dad. I know Dad doesn't mind being flexible with the hours. I hope they can work out some arrangement. I think it would be good for both of them.

Thursday, February 13, 1986

I'm planning a special dinner for Allie on Valentine's Day. I want to do something special for my love. Every day with Allie is enjoyable, but I really want to show her how much I love her. I don't want to take her for granted. I know I will love her forever. I can't imagine not loving her.

Friday, February 14, 1986

Our special dinner was wonderful. I'm glad Allie appreciates my romantic streak. We had a good laugh about Valentine's Day two years ago when I was teaching at Stepford. She remembered that I had asked her about going to that stupid dance I had to chaperone. She told me that she wondered then about me. I guess I wasn't the essence of subtlety. Apparently she was very disappointed when she heard that I had chaperoned the dance. She wished then that she had gone so she could've talked with me all evening. I believe she had a crush on me then, though I doubt she realized it or would have admitted it to herself at the time. And to think that I stood there all night by myself.

I told her tonight that I want to skywrite "I love my Allie Katz." She got a kick out of that. I guess I'm kind of sappy when it comes to stuff like that. But the point is that I love her, and I am not ashamed of it. I'm proud of our love. It is beautiful and, for us, it is perfectly natural.

Tuesday, February 18, 1986

We're leaving for the College Days trip in two days. It will be nice to spend lots of time with Allie even if we won't be completely alone. I think I got spoiled during the Christmas holidays. I just can't get enough of that girl. For that matter, I don't want to get enough of her.

Sunday, February 23, 1986

I suppose I should have known better than to express my feelings towards Allie while we were on the college trip. I was just so glad to have a few moments alone with her. Tina and Laura were acting like leeches though. It felt so good to shake them momentarily. I can't believe Tina walked in on us.

I fully expect to be fired soon. I really don't know what I'm going to do. I guess I'll have to get a job in another field. I'm too depressed at the moment to think about it any more. I was foolish. I definitely should have been more careful. At least Allie doesn't go to my school, so the scandal shouldn't reach her for a while. Perhaps I should go ahead and quit now before it has a chance to do so. If I'm no longer around, it won't create such juicy gossip.

Monday, February 24, 1986

I feel as though I'm waiting for the other shoe to drop. I keep thinking that people are talking about me behind my back. I'm getting really paranoid. Well, I suppose I was already paranoid. Let's just say I'm feeling more paranoid than ever, and I won't ever get any less paranoid if things like this keep happening. I wonder if Dad would like an extra housemate or two. I don't think I want to live here any more. Then again, there's always San Francisco. Not that I really want to go back to California. I may someday, but not yet.

Tuesday, February 25, 1986

I haven't heard anything yet about the College Days incident. I'm so tense and edgy though. I can hardly stand to be around myself. I really think I should get out of this profession. At the very least, I should not teach high school any more. I think I should go back to school so I can teach college literature. That's what I really want to do. I wouldn't be as much of a sitting duck there. I'm really tired of P.E. anyway. My first love is literature, not sports.

Wednesday, February 26, 1986

No news. Perhaps Tina's going to keep her mouth closed. Right, Anna, you do live in a dream world sometimes. Tina is too much of a gossip to keep quiet about such a juicy tidbit. I guess I never should have attempted such a trip. I should have known better than to trust myself to behave circumspectly with Allie when other people are around.

Thursday, February 27, 1986

Still no word. The suspense is killing me. Perhaps if I survive this week, I will still have a job. At least I was finally able to rise above my paranoia enough to figure out a plan that might save my neck. While I was at Denisson, I ran into my cousin Trish, who is attending there this year. She informed me that she had some good news, but she was late for class so we arranged to meet later that day at my temporary room on campus. This happened earlier on the same day that Tina walked in on Allie and me.

So while the girls were all at lunch, I met with Trish to catch up on family news. She told me that she and her boyfriend, Eddy, had decided to get married this summer. Of course I was happy for her, so we exchanged all the pleasant hugs of congratulations then went our separate ways.

Last night I decided to call Trish to see if she would be willing to swear that the person I was embracing when Tina came into the room was her and not Allie. After all, I could hardly be faulted for congratulating my cousin on her engagement. Trish readily agreed to the plan. She also agreed to testify in court, if necessary. I figured she would. She feels strongly about gay rights because her mother and my aunt Donna are the ones who raised Trish after her father abandoned the family. She knows a lot about the fears lesbians have living in this homophobic society.

Tina really can't prove anything to the contrary, since Allie's back was to the door when she entered. She never saw the face of the woman I had my arms around because she spun around and left the room again. Trish's build, though not nearly as athletic, is similar to Allie's, and her hair is only slightly lighter than Allie's. I think it's going to be okay now, though it makes me tremendously angry that I should have to lie about my relationship with Allie!

Friday, February 28, 1986

It has been three hours now since I got out of Sam Richardson's office, and I'm still shaking. Apparently the only reason Tina didn't talk to him earlier is because he's been out of his office most of the week. That was fortuitous for me anyway. At least I was able to pull myself together before I had to face the firing squad.

I managed to tell my story with a degree of credibility, I think. Sam bought it, at any rate, though I think he would've accepted nearly any explanation just to get himself out of an awkward situation. I think having Trish's support helped me feel a little more confident about my story. I really need to watch my step from now on. This cannot happen again. I don't want to find myself in the same position as Sarah.

Monday, March 3, 1986

I ran into Sam today in the hall. I asked him if I should have a conference with Tina to explain the misunderstanding. He told me that he had already taken care of it. He said that he simply informed Tina that the woman she saw me embracing was a relative of mine, so there was nothing to be concerned about. I don't know if Tina believed it, or if she cares. Besides I don't know how many people she told before she managed to unload her story to the principal. This is such a nightmare.

Wednesday, March 5, 1986

I'm definitely getting more paranoid. Every time anyone laughs, I think they're laughing at me. I don't want to teach again next year. This is preposterous. I think it is time to move on to other things.

Monday, March 10, 1986

Things seem to be fine on the surface at school, but I can't be certain about the rumor level. I've gotten some strange looks lately. It hurts me deeply to think that my relationship with Allie might be turned into the gossip topic of the month. That there are people in this world who would love to sully a beautiful love relationship with filthy comments based on bigotry and hatred is beyond painful to me. Have they no life of their own? Have they no love of their own? How would they feel if the tables were turned on them? How would they feel if the person they loved most in the world was someone our society had stamped as forbidden territory?

Too many people are so quick to put restrictions and boundaries on love. Isn't there too little love in the world already? Why must they try to squelch those of us who love deeply someone of the same gender? Why must my love for Allie be viewed as anathema to those who do not understand, or have not experienced it for themselves? Why must their fear of otherness turn them towards hatred?

I realize that our age difference is an issue as well because Allie is still a minor, although she is over the age of consent. Of course this would matter nearly as much if I were a man. This is so ridiculous. If a woman is capable of getting pregnant and giving birth to another human being by the time she's eleven or twelve, then why can't a seventeen-year-old fall in love? Why should it matter if the reciprocator is five years older? I love Allie with all my being. I would never intentionally do anything that would hurt her. Oh God, this world doesn't make sense.

No wonder Anna Karenina despaired of her lot in life. She felt that she had no recourse, no choice, but to remain tied to someone she did not love, while loving someone she was forbidden by her society to love. It's Romeo and Juliet all over again. But unlike them all, I'm going to continue living and loving the woman of my choosing. If our society is ever going to learn to accept love in all its many dimensions, it will be because they see living examples of how beautiful, sane, and normal it can be. They'll never see that if we all kill ourselves in despair. That would just reinforce the notion that we don't deserve to live and be happy.

Monday, March 17, 1986

Allie's excitement about her upcoming birthday is contagious. I want to do something memorable, but I don't know what. I'm sure she'll have to spend most of that day with her parents, so we'll probably have to wait until the weekend to celebrate. I would like to buy matching rings, but it's still too soon for that. She needs to graduate first then explain everything to her parents.

Thursday, March 20, 1986

I think I'm coming down with a cold. I hope it goes away fast. I still can't afford to take any time off. I cannot let it get around that I'm not at school. Nothing has ever gotten back to me about the College Days incident. But then, those who would talk behind my back are unlikely to say anything to my face. I feel like I need to stay at school and in control. I'll just have to sweat this one out.

Sunday, March 30, 1986

I can finally think. There was so much pressure in my head I could hardly stand it. I made it through the week though, and my head is clearing up slowly. I've been sleeping around the clock since Friday afternoon. Allie has been taking care of me. She made me some soup to eat. She has also been filling up the humidifier, and keeping the fire going. She's good to me. She's so helpful and caring. I feel as though I'm in good hands with her here.

Monday, March 31, 1986

I've been looking at the paperwork I did last week. Some of it doesn't make any sense. I wonder what kind of nonsense I wrote on student passes. At least I was able to stay in school.

Tuesday, April 8, 1986

I've decided to buy Allie a dozen roses for her birthday. I think I'll just give them to her here, so I don't have to take a chance on them being delivered at an inconvenient time. I'm going to fix her favorite dish and get out all her favorite music. I hope I can light a fire to make things cozy. If it gets too warm I might have to open the windows. The things we do for a little romance.

Sunday, April 20, 1986

It's been awfully warm lately. I may not be able to light a fire for Allie's birthday after all. At least not in the fireplace. What I'd really like to do is light a fire in her body. I'd better quit talking like that. Just because she's going to eighteen soon doesn't necessarily mean she's ready for us to become sexually involved. It's a little more complicated than that. I love her so much. I long for the day when I can express myself freely with her.

Saturday, April 26, 1986

Happy Birthday, Allie! She is now eighteen, the magic number that instantly turns a child into an adult. Ha!

Sometimes I thought this day would never arrive. Unfortunately she won't be over today. Her mother isn't going to work this afternoon, and her father's going to come home early so they can celebrate. I'll be glad when we can share special days together. I just hope her parents will be able to handle our relationship. I want her to be able to be open with them.

Sunday, April 27, 1986

So much for my special dinner for Allie. The food was fine, but apparently my company wasn't. Allie thought that she could move in with me now that she's eighteen. She hadn't thought about all the problems that would cause in our respective schools. She'd have to deal with the rumors at her school. Both school boards would probably have me investigated. All that nonsense from the Denisson trip could come up again. Then, of course, there are Allie's parents, who might not be cordial about all of this, in spite of what Allie thinks. If things blew up during the school year, it would be a real mess. I'm afraid I burst a very large bubble for her. I feel awful, but I don't know what else I could've done. I think she was ready to pack her bags and leave tomorrow. That just wouldn't be a good idea, no matter how badly both of us want it. I guess I spoiled her birthday.

Monday, April 28, 1986

I think Allie is leaning towards attending Denisson. I think I'll go with her if she doesn't mind. I want to get out of the Physical Education department and back into literature. I have more confidence now. I think I could handle teaching college lit.

Wednesday, April 30, 1986

Allie mentioned the *Lesbian Sex* book again yesterday, so I went ahead and let her borrow it. I suppose it's all right now that she's an adult. It's a great book. I just don't know how she'll take it. There's some pretty wild stuff in there for an eighteen-year-old. Hell, there's some stuff in there that blew my mind when I first read it. We'll see what happens with Allie. Perhaps it will stimulate some good conversations.

Thursday, May 1, 1986

Allie has applied to Denisson, and so have I. I'm going to work on a Master's in English literature. But first I'm going to teach summer school, so I can save some extra money for school. I hate the thought of driving all that way for another six weeks, but I really need the extra money.

Saturday, May 3, 1986

Yes, well, the *Lesbian Sex* book certainly did some stimulating, but it didn't have anything to do with conversations about sex. Unless of course you count body language. Allie was very, um, how should I say this? She was very aroused when she came over today. She wanted to talk to me about the book, only she didn't talk. Or I guess I should say that she didn't use words to express herself.

I guess I could say that she had her way with me. She started to say something, but instead she leaned over and unleashed her sexual energy, probably for the first time in her life. I could tell she wasn't quite sure what do, or how to touch me, so I took over for a while and made love to her.

I think it blew her mind a little bit. She didn't know what to expect. Just before she soared, she looked at me with questioning in her eyes. I said, "It's okay, Allie. Let go of your control, and let it flow. You're safe with me. I love you, baby." That's all the assurance she needed. She let go all right. Wow! She is incredibly beautiful. I have always enjoyed watching my lover's face in the midst of orgasms, but Allie's was more beautiful than I could have imagined. And her breasts, how luscious! They definitely responded happily to my caresses and kisses. I thought I was going to soar too, just from watching her.

After she experienced what was her first orgasm ever, she looked at me very seriously, and asked me to show her how she could make me feel like that. So I did; and she did. It was all so powerful it took my breath away. I can't even begin to describe how wonderful it felt to be in her arms.

I suppose I should feel guilty, but I don't. I love Allie, and although she's five years younger than me, she's more mature emotionally than Sarah was in her early twenties. She's more caring, more sensitive, and more responsible. Age is such an arbitrary thing. All that waiting just because she wasn't eighteen yet. In this state what we did would be against the law if she were sixteen, eighteen, or twenty-one, but at least Allie was able to make this choice as a legal adult. She was ready to get involved sexually or what happened today wouldn't have happened.

Wednesday, May 7, 1986

My, my, but Allie is insatiable. I'm not complaining though, mind you. I've been waiting a long time for this. Our relationship has deepened as our passion has been given free reign. I love feeling her body writhe when I make love to her. I love the way she reaches up and grips my shoulder just before she comes. She is such a beautiful woman. Mmm. I love her. She is truly a work of art. Sometimes when I touch her, I close my eyes and pretend that I am a sculptor sculpting her form. I slowly move my hands all over her body, massaging her taut muscles, following the dips and rises of her figure. God I love her!

Saturday, May 10, 1986

It's almost physically painful when Allie leaves at night. We've spent so much time making love lately that it feels like we've been brutally severed when she walks out the door to go back to her parents' house. I can't call it her house any more. Somehow I feel as though this is her true home now. She belongs here with me. I miss her when she's gone.

It's difficult sometimes to remember that she's still in high school. I wonder if she feels alienated from the rest of her school friends and acquaintances. How does she feel when the girls start talking about their boyfriends? Would she like to tell them about us? Is she ashamed of us? I guess I should ask her how she's handling all this when she not here. It must seem awfully strange to her.

Sunday, May 11, 1986

In her typical fashion, Allie shrugged off my questions about how feels when she's at school. She said that she didn't care what people thought, so what would be the point in telling anybody? She has always felt alienated from the high school crowd anyway, so our relationship apparently doesn't change anything in that respect. I'm glad of that. I wouldn't want her to feel like an oddball. I can definitely relate to her feelings of disassociation from the high school crowd.

I will be glad though once she's out of school. Then I won't feel as paranoid. I know she's legally an adult, but I still can't help but think that it wouldn't be good if people found out about us being involved. Hell, what am I saying? I guess it will never be good if people find out. At least not if they're the wrong people. I've heard enough stories from Dad about

gay baiting and gay bashing to render me permanently
paranoid. Though perhaps it isn't paranoia, if people truly are
out to get you.

I get worried sometimes about some of the people
around here. They're not exactly progressive thinkers. Not
that anywhere else would be any better. There will always be
bigotry in this world as long as there are people who don't
love and understand themselves and thus can't accept the
variety of lifestyles and personalities inherent in the human
race. Ah well, don't depress yourself, Anna.

Monday, May 12, 1986

Dad sent me a copy of his new manuscript. He wants
my editorial feedback on it. This should be interesting. He
told me to take my time, because he's not planning to work on
it any more until this summer. I've already gone through the
first three chapters. I enjoy doing this kind of work.

Wednesday, May 21, 1986

School's almost over. I've been neglecting my journal
writing to work on Dad's book. I'm thoroughly enjoying
myself. I hope he will find my questions and suggestions
helpful. He's a good writer. I wonder if it runs in the family.
I rather liked helping him polish his book. Perhaps one day I
will find myself polishing my own. I think I would like that.

Monday, May 26, 1986

Allie is getting very anxious about the end of school.
Not only is she worrying about graduation, but she's also
worried about telling her parents about us. I don't envy her. I
think it was easier for me since my Aunt Donna paved the
way. I suppose my mother had already thoroughly worked

through any issues she might have had when my Dad left her and my aunt came out. Of course I didn't know about Dad at that time, but Mom certainly did.

Tuesday, June 3, 1986

Allie and I talked at some length today about her parents. I offered to be there when she tells them, but she opted to face them alone. I think that is both wise and brave. I'm really proud of her. I gave her a book that my dad sent me recently. It tells how other gay teenagers have come out to their parents. I hope it will help her. It would be beneficial if her parents read it as well.

11:00 p.m. — Allie just called. She talked to her parents tonight, and they seem to be all right about her being lesbian. They don't know yet who I am though. She's going to drop that bomb on them tomorrow. One crisis at a time, I suppose.

I will definitely need to be on the alert tomorrow. If I hear any sirens, I'll just duck out the back with my bike and disappear. I really don't think I would like jail very much. I wouldn't be able to be with Allie. This is all so nerve-racking. I'm just glad school is out now. Summer school doesn't start until next week. So much for a week of rest and relaxation. I get a week of insomnia and nervous tension.

Wednesday, June 4, 1986

All is well at the Katz residence. Allie's parents have invited me to dinner tomorrow night. I'm really nervous, but I'm glad we're getting all this over with now, before the summer term starts. Of course, I have considered the possibility that Allie's parents are setting me up. That's such a comforting thought.

Friday, June 6, 1986

I enjoyed having dinner with Allie's family, though I felt like I was being examined under a microscope. At least they were gentle with their inquisitiveness. I wonder if that is what men go through when they ask a woman to marry them. I almost got the feeling they were trying to assure themselves that there wasn't any insanity in my family. It bordered on the comical really.

I finally found out about Allie's nickname tonight. Her parents started calling her "Allie" when she was a baby, not realizing the connotations. By the time it dawned on them, it was an ingrained habit. Their family told them not to worry about it because most kids outgrow early childhood nicknames. Allie never did. She liked her name and stuck with it. I'm glad she did. It fits her.

Allie told me that she has been teased about it, but no more than anyone else with an interesting name. She just figures it makes her a little bit more unforgettable. After all, how many Allie Katz are there running around this town? You are so punny, Anna.

Saturday, June 7, 1986

Allie moved in today. Too bad we can't have a honeymoon. Instead she has to get settled while I prepare for summer school. Her dad was very helpful. He borrowed his neighbor's pick-up truck and hauled Allie's belongings over here. She doesn't have all that many belongings yet. I'll give her a couple years. They're sure to multiply. I know mine did. I can hardly believe that our life together is about to begin. I hope we're not rushing things. I guess this is the only thing to do for now. If she decides it is too much domestication, then I won't chain her to me. She's in the shower right now. It feels strange to have her here this late at night. I guess I'm not used to sharing my space with anyone. It's been a couple years since I've had a housemate.

Friday, June 13, 1986

We found a summer job for Allie. She'll be working at the Polar Bear. Not exactly high class, but I think she'll learn a lot from the experience. I know she will do well. She always does. I guess she is kind of like an alley cat. She's tougher than she looks, she always lands on her feet, and she purrs when she's pleased with herself. I love my little Allie Katz. Little, ha! She's bigger than I am.

Monday, June 16, 1986

I've started back to school, and Allie went to work for the first time. She hasn't gotten home yet, so I don't know how things went for her. I'd better start working on supper. It's nice to have someone to share my table every evening. It's even nicer to have Allie to share my bed every night.

Saturday, June 21, 1986

Ahhhh. It felt positively delicious to sleep in this morning. It's wonderful to wake up to Allie's sleepy little face in the mornings. She's adorable. It felt good to have some cuddle time before she had to get up to go to work. Our schedules are such that we will not share any of our days off. At least not until I'm finished with summer school. But at least every free moment we have together is truly ours. We have only one home now.

Wednesday, July 2, 1986

Allie's parents came over for dinner a couple nights ago. We had a good time. I really like those two. They're decent people. I guess that shouldn't surprise me though, when I look at Allie. I enjoy seeing her interact with them. It's obvious that they respect one another.

Saturday, July 5, 1986

Allie's friend Sherri came over with her little boy. He's a newborn, so he looks more prune-like than anything else. Babies are so funny. I don't understand how they can look so funny and yet be so cute. Allie wants to buy Sherri a rocking chair. She and Teddy loved mine. We're going to go shopping soon to look for one.

Tuesday, July 8, 1986

Allie and I found a lovely rocker for Sherri. I paid for part of it so Allie wouldn't completely wipe out her paycheck. She really wants to help Sherri. I suggested that she offer our babysitting services once a week. Sherri's too young to be completely tied down to a baby. She kind of reminds me of a wild horse. She has a never-ending supply of energy and a distinct stubborn streak that makes her strong enough to endure anything.

Wednesday, July 9, 1986

Allie is funny. She calls the Polar Bear "P.B." It took me a moment to figure it out the first time she called it that. I barely managed to refrain from laughing when she said that today. I've never heard anyone abbreviate it before. She does that with a lot of things.

Monday, July 14, 1986

Summer school is nearly over. Needless to say, I am delighted. Have you ever noticed that people write and say very contradictory things? For instance, I just wrote "needless to say," then proceeded to say that which was needless to say. How about the phrase, "not to mention?" That is always immediately followed by the mention of the very thing that you weren't going to mention. Well, there's no doubt about it now. Anna, you have been working too much! You're starting to babble.

Saturday, July 19, 1986

I enjoy watching Allie with Sherri and Teddy. She is beginning to relax around the baby. She's such a caring and compassionate person. She gets along with people so well. I watched her watching Sherri nurse Teddy. She looked beautiful. I wonder if she will decide that she wants to have a baby. I hope not. I don't think I'm interested in long-term childcare.

Sunday, July 20, 1986

Today is our anniversary. Allie slipped out very secretively this morning. I feigned sleep until she left then I decorated the house with banners. I'm so glad Allie got the day off from work. I'm still waiting for her return. I have a bit of a surprise for her. I want to read her the fantasy I had about her two years ago and see if she would like to act it out sometime. Uh, oh. I think I hear her now. I need to find my place in my old journal. I'm excited.

Tuesday, July 22, 1986

I think Allie enjoyed our anniversary as much as I did. She liked my fantasy so much; we never made the trip to the lake. We were both so aroused by reading about it; we couldn't wait to make love. So we stayed at home and made love all morning. We're probably a lot safer at home anyway. I'm so much braver in my fantasies than I am in reality. I would never do half the things I have dreamed of doing.

Friday, July 25, 1986

Dad called today to thank me for my contributions to his book. He really liked my ideas and comments. He told me to look for a card from him in the mail because it would contain a check for my services. He also let me know that Jeff is doing really well. Dad and Buddy have been trying to fix him up, though they've been as unsuccessful with him as they were with me. At least Jeff is doing all right. I know Dad and Buddy will look out for him. If there is such a thing as a "papa hen," that would be a good way to describe either of those two.

Sunday, July 27, 1986

I got the check from Dad today. Somehow I think he must be accustomed to paying inflated New York prices. He sent me $500. I put it in savings for school. In his card he asked me if I would consider doing that kind of work again sometime. I think this must be his way of telling me that he wants to help me pay for graduate school.

Thursday, July 31, 1986

I think Allie's getting tired of "P.B." The kids that hang around there really annoy her. I understand completely. I think I'll slip by there today, just to say "hello." I need a ride anyway. It's been much too hot to ride lately. I don't like to ride when it's really hot and humid. I tend to turn into a puddle of sweat on days like that.

Tuesday, August 5, 1986

I got a letter from Mom. She's worried about my little sister Christine. She's dating some creepy guy. He must really be creepy for Mom to complain. She's very tolerant of diversity. She's also a good judge of character. I hope Christine will get away from him. It's so easy to be led astray at that age. Seventeen doesn't know the meaning of moderation or restraint. Everything tends to be all or nothing. At least she will be going to college soon.

Sunday, August 10, 1986

Allie and I had a pleasant surprise the other day. We found out that Sherri has a girlfriend. I had a feeling exciting things were happening in her life. Her girlfriend's name is Carol. She's a little bit older than Sherri. Tougher too.

On the surface, Carol is one of those people who can entertain a crowd for hours, the life of the party. I think there's another story behind her laughter though. She reminds me of Sarah in that way. I get the feeling that she has a lot of anger deep down inside her. I just hope she can deal with it without dragging Sherri down to hell and back again. That kid has had a hard enough time already.

Thursday, August 14, 1986

We've had a steady stream of company lately. Of course, it's the same stream nearly every night, and I'm getting a bit tired of it. I want Allie's friends to come over, but not every night. I miss having Allie all to myself. Maybe I'm too reclusive. I hope this doesn't become an issue between us. I enjoy Sherri and Carol's company, but I think I'd enjoy it more in smaller doses.

Saturday, August 16, 1986

I think things are moving fast between Carol and Sherri. I hope not too fast. Allie wants them to move to Tennessee with us. I wouldn't mind that, as long as we don't all try to live together. I could not handle that at all. I'm too much of a hermit to live with that many people. I doubt if Allie would care for it either. She seems to enjoy a lot of quiet time too. She might like it for a little while, but I think the novelty of it would wear off quickly.

Sunday, August 17, 1986

I spent the day house hunting. I did most of the legwork via newspapers and phone calls, so the final choice was easy enough. I didn't really need to resort to Dad's "system." I made the mistake of mentioning the "system" to Allie a long time ago, but apparently never explained it. I wonder if she'll be disappointed when she learns that it is really pure silliness, and not a "system" at all.

First, you make all the phone calls, eliminating the unacceptable possibilities. Then if you have several equally appealing options, you just close your eyes and point. Wherever your finger lands, that's the place you choose. It's really just a joke, but Allie thinks it is some sort of magical system. I'm not sure how she got that impression. I guess it's just another result of my hesitancy to explain the little details of life. Anyway, I chose the duplex that had both sides vacant. That way, if Carol and Sherri accompany us, they can move in next door. They can live near us, without living with us. I'm not interested in living in a commune.

Monday, August 18, 1986

Allie and I had an adventurous driving lesson today. She's going to drive my car when we move because I'm going to drive the pick-up truck Carol's father is loaning us. Allie has never driven a standard before, so she has to learn immediately. This process is always such fun.

Monday, September 1, 1986

I finally unearthed my journal. I thought for a moment it had slipped into the fourth dimension, along with all the ballpoint pens I've lost through the years. Moving is such an ordeal! Classes start tomorrow. I'm excited. I'm even more excited now that Carol and Sherri have signed the lease for the other half of the duplex. They are leaving tomorrow to go home and pack. Allie and I will finally be alone. I guess I'm selfish when it comes to being alone with Allie. I don't mind people around some of the time, but I don't want them around all the time.

Thursday, September 4, 1986

It's good to be back in school. I didn't realize how much I missed it until I went to my first class. I'm going to use Allie's class time for my study time. Then when she gets home, she can work on her homework while I fix supper. On the nights I have class, she's going to fix supper, and then study while I'm in class. It sounds like a good plan. Let's see if we can stick to it.

Sunday, September 7, 1986

I'm thoroughly enjoying my classes. I love the discipline of academics. It's positively delicious to be able to savor my classes without having to deal with dorm life. This is so much better than college. I'm especially enjoying the writing assignments. It's seems so long since I've had the motivation to sit down and write. I'd like to expand my journal writing. Do some creative writing for a change, though my journal writing helps me to clear some space in my head for creative work.

When I first begin to write, the words come slowly, like drops of water from an annoying faucet. But before I realize it, the drops have turned into a flowing stream, carrying with it my thoughts and feeling. When I'm finished writing, I often discover that the stream has flowed into a lake, where I can sit and look at my own reflection and the reflection of the world all around me. Even though it is only a reflection I see, I find that it helps me to understand my world and myself a little better.

Wednesday, September 10, 1986

Carol, Sherri, and Teddy have settled into their new home. They look quite cozy and domestic. I hope Teddy can settle into a more stable routine now. All this moving must be upsetting for him. Allie and I were supposed to help them move, but they called and said that they were finished and ready to go. I'm glad though because it gave us some time alone before our neighbors came back.

Sunday, September 14, 1986

I like living at home and attending classes only at night. It's definitely better than dorm life. I'm glad Allie doesn't have to go through that. It's a pleasant feeling too, knowing that Sherri and Teddy live next door. It gives me a warm feeling, a sense of home and family. I never had that when I was in college. Plus now that Sherri and Carol live next door, they no longer feel the need to come over every night. That gives Allie and me more time together.

Saturday, September 20, 1986

Dad mailed me part of another manuscript. This one is nonfiction. He wants to write about real life experiences of lesbians and gays in America. He not only wants my feedback on what he has thus far, he also wants to include me in it, without using my name. It's a pretty tall order, and I don't know if I want to expose myself that much, even anonymously. If anyone else had asked me to do that, I would have turned it down immediately. However, I know Dad is an accomplished author with a large gay readership. If I could say anything that would help other people come to grips with their own sexual feelings, then I want to help. I don't know when I would have time to tackle it though. It will probably have to wait until summer.

Jeff enclosed a letter in Dad's package. He thanked me for helping him through the most difficult times after Chuck's death. He joked about Dad and Buddy's dating service. He likes double dating with them, but more for their company than for the dates themselves. He's really enjoying living in New York. I'm glad they are keeping him busy. He'll find someone when he's ready for it. In the meantime, he's making some good friends and having fun. He needs that right now.

Saturday, October 4, 1986

I've gotten thoroughly engrossed in Dad's project. I may speak to Carol and Sherri and see if they are interested in telling their stories. Allie already knows what I'm doing, but she's not sure what to think about it. I think she may be too involved with her classes right now to participate. Dad isn't rushing me, so maybe she can think about it over Christmas break.

Tuesday, October 7, 1986

Perhaps I was wrong about Carol after all. She, Sherri, and Teddy seem to be doing all right. I have sensed a little tension now and then, but nothing serious.

Allie is doing well in her classes and so am I. I'm enjoying the writing assignments. I'm glad now that I kept this journal all these years. I would've gotten rusty. You don't have to write a lot when you teach P.E. I like the idea of writing, more and more. Perhaps Dr. Anna Evans will be an author too. Just like her father.

Saturday, October 11, 1986

Dad called tonight. I gave him permission to use my story in his book. After all, I do have an unusual story to tell. How many women fall in love with one of their high school students? A female student, no less. Of course, some people may think I'm crazy, but that's only because they don't know Allie. She's a unique person.

Saturday, October 18, 1986

I got a letter from Peter today. His wife left him, and he's terribly upset about it. Apparently he totally immersed himself in his work and forgot that he had a wife at home who would like to see him occasionally. He arrived home one day last week to find her closet empty. I feel bad for both of them. They're rather mismatched. She's interested in a husband and children. He's interested in his career. I don't know why he ever got married to begin with. Marriage requires too much effort for someone like him. Well, I guess now he'll have to decide whether he wants a long-term intimate relationship or an all-consuming career.

Wednesday, October 29, 1986

I'm nearly finished with my section of Dad's book. I proofread the part he'd already written. It was in good shape, so that was quick work. It's a good thing too, because my paper deadlines are rapidly approaching. I need to get busy with school for a change.

Wednesday, November 5, 1986

I finished my story. I like it. It's really rough right now, but it's workable. It's only about thirty pages long. Sherri wants to contribute to Dad's anthology. Carol, on the other hand, doesn't want to have anything to do with it. She doesn't mind if Sherri talks about her anonymously, but her past is nobody's business. She was very emphatic about that. I have a feeling there is something lurking at the bottom of her well. I have to respect her decision though, since I nearly passed on the project myself.

Allie said that she doesn't need to write because she will be covered in my story and Sherri's too. Sherri and I both laughed at that one. Sherri said, "Yeah, but you need to tell your side of the story too. You shouldn't trust us with it." Allie finally agreed to work on her story but not until later. She's got too much schoolwork right now. I can understand that. I had a hard time keeping up with my schoolwork while I was working on it.

Saturday, November 8, 1986

Mom called tonight to warn me that Sarah's on my trail again. She gave her my phone number, but she suggested that it might not be a good idea to visit right now because I'm so busy with school. Nice try, Mom, but Sarah will view that warning as irresistible bait.

Thursday, November 13, 1986

Basketball season is coming. I think I'm starting to get the fever again. I haven't been very interested in basketball since the year I coached the girls' team. I think I must have gotten an overdose then, but it has worked its way out of my bloodstream. Now I'm excited. Maybe it's just the emotional connection with the past. I have fond memories of college basketball.

Monday, November 17, 1986

Sarah called finally. I'm glad she did. I was getting tired of jumping every time the phone rang. She's coming to town for Thanksgiving break since I'll be on vacation. I really wish she would leave me alone.

Thursday, November 20, 1986

I wish Thanksgiving would hurry up. The suspense is killing me. I just want Sarah to visit then leave again, so I can get on with my life. I feel as though I cease to breathe whenever she's around. I'm so afraid of what she'll say and do next. Maybe she'll change her mind at the last minute.

Right, Anna. Who do you think you're kidding? Damn! Why does she keep hounding me? What does she want from me? I do not want to be her lover. I don't want to be her friend even. I can't trust her.

Wednesday, November 26, 1986

Tomorrow is Thanksgiving Day. I'm so glad Allie suggested inviting Sherri, Teddy, and Carol to eat with us too. Perhaps with so many people present Sarah's poison will be diluted. When there are only two other people in the room, she can play them off each other too easily. When several people are present, her maneuvers are less effective.

Friday, November 28, 1986

Allie's plan seems to have worked mostly. I think Sarah decided to work on Sherri and Carol instead. I feel bad for them, but Allie and I have had enough problems with Sarah already. The only catch is that I'm the one responsible for bringing her on the scene. Well, I'm just going to have to be honest with her. I've got to tell her that as long as she insists on trying to disrupt my relationship with Allie, then she's not welcome here. I've stood up to her before; I can do it again. I do hate confrontations though.

Monday, December 1, 1986

Trouble is brewing next door, and I feel partially responsible for it. If I hadn't let Sarah walk all over me, she wouldn't have met Sherri and Carol. On the other hand, Sherri is obviously encouraging the contact with Sarah, which is making Carol jealous. I can't say that I blame Carol either. The flirting between Sarah and Sherri is rather blatant.

Thursday, December 4, 1986

Carol and Sherri have split up. I'm not surprised though, and it may be for the best in the long run. As for the immediate future, Sherri is in a tight spot financially. I'm going to offer to pay her bills for a month so she can find a job and a babysitter. This is all so depressing. I'm just glad Dad is sending me another check for the work I did on his book recently.

Saturday, December 6, 1986

My worst nightmare has come upon me. Sarah moved in with Sherri yesterday. I wonder how long that arrangement will last. I can't figure out what Sarah wants. Of course, I have to admit that I don't know what Sherri is after either. Maybe she doesn't know herself. Maybe this relationship won't last long. Sarah hasn't exactly broken records for relationship longevity. Hopefully she'll get tired of bothering Sherri and move on again.

Sunday, December 7, 1986

Last night, Allie and I had the worst argument we have ever had. She accused me of wanting to get back together with Sarah. Nothing could be farther from the truth, but Sarah is so good at the divide-and-conquer game. I don't know how to make Allie see that I want only her. I know I could get back with Sarah, but I'm no masochist. I'm happy with Allie. I adore the woman. Why on earth would I want to go back to a dysfunctional relationship with Sarah? If Allie doesn't believe me though, there is nothing I can do. She will have to learn to trust me. I can't force it. I've tried to show her every day how much I care for her. I tell her how I feel about her. I show her how I feel. What else can I do?

Friday, December 12, 1986

I think Allie and I need to charge for our counseling services, but since I'm partially responsible for this soap opera, I suppose I shouldn't complain. The dynamics in this situation are so confusing. If each person would be honest with all the others, we might get somewhere. There are so many psychological games being played. It's difficult to sort them all out. I don't think any of them are being truly honest with themselves. How then can they begin to be honest with others?

Monday, December 15, 1986

This semester is over for me. Allie still has finals this week. I have only papers, and I turned my last one in today. Now I can rest for a while. I certainly need it. Dad and Buddy are thinking about coming down right after New Year's Day. They are anxious to meet Allie. She and I talked about going to New York for a visit, but we decided to stay close to home for our first Christmas together. I'm glad we did. I think we will have fun. I'm starting to get very excited about Christmas. I want to make it a special one for Allie.

Tuesday, December 16, 1986

I hope Sherri knows what she's doing. I told her that I would pay her bills for a month or so, until she could get her life together. I really don't want to see her stuck in the position of depending on Sarah. She's less reliable than Carol. Sherri said that she would think about my offer. I doubt she will take me up on it. She's rather dazzled by Sarah right now. At least she knows she has another option. Hopefully that will ease her sense of dependence on Sarah.

Thursday, December 18, 1986

Allie has been talking to me a lot about her feelings. I think she is growing up fast. Of course, if you live next door to a war zone, it's difficult to ignore important life issues. At any rate, Allie's been searching inside herself, discovering feelings she never realized she had. Some of these feelings she finds distasteful. Others are good, though I don't think she realizes it yet. She's been asking me insightful questions about my actions and emotions, probing me almost as deeply as she's probing herself. It isn't altogether comfortable, but I like the change in her.

Friday, December 19, 1986

I've decided to let Allie read my journals. She has been asking me so many questions lately that I honestly don't know how to answer them adequately. If she reads my journals, she may be able to understand my thoughts and feelings a little better. I think that in many ways I'm still a bit of an enigma to her. I feel really good about doing this, which surprises me. I never dreamed of allowing anyone to read my journals, but I think it will help our relationship to achieve a better balance. If Allie can learn that I am human, flawed as any other, maybe things will be easier for me. I won't feel quite so much like I'm up on a pedestal.

Sunday, December 21, 1986

Things have really quieted down next door. I haven't heard any yelling for a couple weeks now. I think Carol moved back to her sister's house. I hate to admit it, but I'm glad. I have a hard time dealing with violent people. Not that Sarah's a much better neighbor, especially since she's the one who gave me the only black eye I've ever had. But at least I know what to expect from her, and this time, she's not my lover. She'd better not ever hit Sherri or Teddy because I will call the police on her.

Monday, December 22, 1986

It's a relief to have some time off from my classes. It's fun to be back in school, but it has been an adjustment getting back into the habit of studying again. Of course, it was very difficult to study with the ruckus next door. We found out from Sherri that Carol is indeed gone for good. Amazingly enough, Sarah has left me alone. She's been busy substitute teaching in the secondary schools. Don't ask me how she got into teaching again. Maybe her old school didn't put anything down in writing. I have no idea. I'm glad she was able to get on as a substitute as a way to get started again.

Wednesday, December 24, 1986

This is my last entry in this journal. When I am finished, I am going to wrap all my journals so I can give them to Allie for Christmas. I'll start a new journal later, but I think I'll end this one with a dedication:

To My Dearest Allie,

I love you, baby, and I want to live with you forever. I want to share with you all my dreams and wishes, all my days and nights. To you, my love, I want to be an open book. Ask me any time, and I will allow you to catch up on subsequent journals. It has never been easy for me to share my thoughts and feelings with others, but somehow you have reached into my heart and unlocked that rusty door. I am yours forever. Merry Christmas, Allie! Love, Your Anna

EPILOGUE: ALLIE'S RESPONSE

Friday, January 23, 1987

Dear Anna,

Thank you for sharing your journals with me. I'm not quite sure I know what to think about everything I've learned about you. I feel as though I've been introduced to another Anna. This second Anna is very different from the one who lives with me. The Anna who writes is more fragile and more frightened. She talks a lot more about her feelings. I hope you don't mind that I've fallen in love with this Anna too. I also hope that the Anna who writes will share herself with me more often in the future. Your journals have answered a lot of my questions, but they've also generated more. I'm glad we have the rest of our lives to figure out the answers together. Thanks for being patient with me, Anna.

Love, Allie

About the Author

Beth Mitchum is living in Central Florida again. She lived in the Seattle area from 1993 to 2010. When she moved there, she was able to say, for the first time in her life, that she felt at home. Although she lived in multiple places all around the Seattle area, her favorite nesting spot was on the Kitsap Peninsula, where she was able to enjoy waterfront living and bald eagle watching for most of the time she lived there. Before moving to Seattle, she spent eight years in the Asheville, North Carolina area, a place of great beauty and folk art culture. The thing she misses most about living there is the great community of lesbians. You could walk into Malaprop's (a most excellent bookstore) in downtown Asheville and be guaranteed to run into several lesbians, many of whom she already knew. Before moving to North Carolina in 1985, she lived in Lakeland, Florida, where she attended college, landed her first great job, and found the first of many really cool living spaces. Beth grew up in Winter Park, Florida, a European-style city in the heart of Central Florida.

Follow Beth's work at BethMitchum.com and SlicesOfMyLife.net. Her books are available at Amazon.com, CreateSpace.com, BarnesandNoble.com, and bethmitchum.com, where you can order autographed and personalized copies from the online bookseller, bookshopwithoutborders@gmail.com. You can also write to the author at the above email address.

Titles by Beth Mitchum

bethwor(l)ds: 20 years of poetry
Slices of My Life: So Far
Slices of My Life: Still Standing (forthcoming)
Driftwood
Driftwood: The Music (companion music CD for the novel, *Driftwood*)
Higher Love
In My Dreams
Naked on the Beach (forthcoming)
If Wishes were Horses (forthcoming, working title)
The Diary of Allie Katz

The Goddess Series:

Artemisian Artist
Gaia's Guardian
Demeter's Daughter (forthcoming)
Hestia's Healer (forthcoming)

Also look for the forthcoming poetry series UltraVioletLove Presents:

Sappho's Corner, Volume 1
The Poetry of Jae Dee (working title)

Made in the USA
Charleston, SC
04 August 2011